Once in a While

In
Northern
Ireland

By
Betty Hueston

This novel is a work of fiction. Names and characters are the product of the author's imagination. Any resemblance to actual persons, living or dead is entirely coincidental.

First Published in 2012 by
Holmleigh Publishing
48 Townhill Road
Portglenone
BT44 8AD

ISBN 978-0-9572483-0-4

About the Author

Betty Hueston lives with her husband Alex on the outskirts of Portglenone, and is well known for her interest and affection for the area, having compiled two collections of stories and poems by and about the people who live, or have lived in the village and surrounding district, aptly named **'Echoes of Portglenone'** followed by **'More Echoes of Portglenone.**

Other publications by the author include numerous stories, poems and articles published in Newspapers, Anthologies and Magazines, plus two collections of her own work, **'Down Memory Lane'** and **'Memories are Made of This'** also two compilations with another writer, **'Country Tales'** and **'Humble Happiness.'**

Writing the lyrics for a song, **'Please Cancel the Taxi'** recorded by the well-known Country singer, Billy McFarland is another of the author's successes. She is no stranger to the media either, having read her work on radio and given several interviews concerning her writing.

'Once in a While' is the author's debut novel, but a sequel is already under way.

Acknowledgements

Thanks to my husband Alex, for his helpful comments and knowledge of farming life, which were invaluable as I created an environment for my characters.

Thanks also to my son Alistair, who said, "Go for it!" when I first mentioned the possibility of writing a novel.

Thanks to my grandchildren, Billy, Chloe and Ellie, who always take an interest in 'granny's stories' and not forgetting their Mammy – my daughter-in-law, Donna, who quietly lets us ramble on.

Thanks to Mrs Anne McCusker for proof reading and Mr Pat McErlean for his comments and advice.

Thanks to all the friends who have purchased my previous publications – their support and feedback is much appreciated.

Heartfelt gratitude to my late mother, Lizzie, who often told me, "Never say can't before you have tried."

CONTENTS

THE PROPOSAL 1965

"What about you and me hanging our coats on the same nail?"

"I beg your pardon!"

"Martha me dear, you have no need to beg for you're oul enough to steal."

It was the day that Sammy McCracken proposed to Martha Sloan. A somewhat unusual sort of proposal, but, a proposal none the less, and it was the biggest surprise the folk in the nearby village had received in a long time. Everyone thought Sammy was a confirmed bachelor. Just goes to show – you never can tell what goes on in a man's mind. Many would have argued that there was very little in Sammy's mind apart from a packet of Gallagher's Blues and a pint of stout. Martha was different – Martha was the sort of woman who kept her cards close to her chest. A down-to-earth, no nonsense sort of woman who was liked and respected by everyone who assumed she wasn't marriage material – she'd left it too long - she was too set in her ways. However, Tam Lorimer, owner of the only taxi in the area, wasn't so sure, but could never be persuaded to explain why he doubted their opinion.

Sammy pondered over the day's events as he rested his elbows on the bar in Murphy's public house, a cigarette in one hand and a glass of shandy in the other (he said he needed to keep a clear head – he had a lot of thinking to do). Maybe he should have done the thinking first, but his father was a very persuasive man. It was all his fault and his idea Sammy decided. But, to be fair to Martha, she was still a very attractive woman for her age – a man could do worse. Maybe his father had the right idea after all. But what if Martha refused - he'd never live it down, the shame and the gossip would be unbearable. She couldn't have been too anxious, he decided, or she wouldn't have needed time to think about it. What was wrong with the woman? Did she not realize what a good catch he was? He was a hard working man – up with the lark (after his father had shouted for nearly an hour). He never took a day off and he owned the farm adjacent to hers – well, not exactly owned, not yet, not until the old man went to the great harvest in the sky, but in the meantime it might as well be his, for everything was signed and sealed and there were no siblings or close family to contest the will. In the meantime, life would go on as it had done for the last number of years, except that his father wasn't as able as he used to be, hence his idea – Sammy needed a wife to organize him – get him up in the morning and make sure he started the day with a good Ulster fry inside him, and what better choice than Martha? A good, church-going woman who knew all about farming, and they could make the two farms into one. He could picture it all, it would be great, and if Sammy got a move on there might even be a few sons to carry on the name. But Martha wasn't getting any younger, so there was no time to lose.

Sammy drained the last drop from his glass.

"Same again," he said.

"Right you are now," Hughie replied, sliding off the stool he frequently sat on when business was slack or when he was having a chinwag with some of the locals. Hughie Ferris had worked in Murphy's bar for 'many a long year' as he informed anyone who inquired about his employment and only the very elderly could remember a time when he wasn't there. Hughie was as much a part of Murphy's as the old red tiled floor or the long oak counter where it seemed everyone in the district had carved their name. Hughie considered himself something of an expert on human nature. Hughie knew when a man was doing a bit of serious thinking. Sammy raised the glass to his mouth and after a few long sips and a muffled burp he declared that thinking was thirsty work. Hughie agreed, but didn't ask any questions – he didn't need to – he knew what was on Sammy's mind – he'd heard the gossip. It had been sheer chance that Matt Hamilton's young boy had ridden past on his bicycle just as Martha had declared, 'Marry you!'

The young lad had hurried home to tell his Ma, as he thought that it must be the most exciting thing that had ever happened. His Ma rushed to the front door. "C'mere quick till you hear this," she called to Bobby Birch as he free-wheeled down the street in his usual way – sitting on the parcel carrier of his old upstairs model bicycle - both his legs stretched out in front of him and the customary smile on his thin, pale face.

And so the news travelled like lightning – in back doors and front doors - through open windows and over hedges. To the butcher's – the grocer's – the newsagent and of course, Murphy's bar – the repository of all knowledge and sanctuary for the confused. Within minutes, it was common knowledge that Sammy McCracken had proposed to Martha Sloan. Some were pleased and hoped they would be happy; others pulled their lips into a tight O, raised their eyebrows and nodded their heads as if to say, "That's a bit sudden." The majority assumed that young Hamilton had misunderstood what he had heard, and, knowing his mother, the story could only have improved with the telling.

While Sammy was pondering over his rash proposal, Martha was doing some pondering of her own. Why now? Why so unexpectedly? There had been nothing to indicate that Sammy had been thinking along those lines. She had known him all her life. They were neighbours – always had been. The same bumpy, potholed lane that veered off left and right reached both their homes. Their fathers had shared farm equipment, cut the peats in the same moss, helped each other as folk did in those days and Martha had always tagged along. Sammy had been like a big brother –picking her up and drying her tears when she fell over, and when she was having one of her 'terrible twos tantrums' he would pull funny faces and within seconds she would be smiling again. In later years he taught her how to master the complexities of long division when Miss Hardy, teacher and terror of the primary school, had been unable to convey the necessity of such knowledge to the nervous child she had been back then. Now he wanted to marry her! Somehow it didn't seem right – didn't seem normal - they knew each other too well.

Martha sighed. If only she could turn back the clock – live again those happy untroubled days of childhood – no responsibility or fear of the future or the heartache and loneliness it might bring. Those seemingly endless sunny days when they had run barefoot through the lush green County Antrim countryside without a care in the world. She remembered them all. Twin sisters Mary and Jean, who were well behaved and liked to play Hide and Seek through the orchard, and Victoria who always went home early, usually in a huff about something. Davy was the dare devil of the troupe - always way ahead of the rest regardless of the dangers or the warnings from Sammy, the capable, reliable one who, at all times, watched out for any hazards such as stray barbed wire or broken bottles.

Then there was Bobby who only went to school when he couldn't find anything more interesting to do. Behaviour that puzzled the others, but when they inquired about how he got away with mitching so often his reply was always the same. "It's no problem. Me Ma disn't care where I go. She'd rather sit at the fire way a bottle o' stout and me Da left long ago. He said he couldn't put up way me Ma's drinking and that I was out o' control."

Then there was Willie, the newcomer. She would never forget Willie. How happy they had been back then, with their dreams and their plans. But nothing lasts forever - it's just the way life is, she decided. One minute you think you are in control – have it all figured out, then without warning, something unexpected happens and the whole situation changes and there's not a thing you can do to alter it. Just like today when she had her mind firmly fixed on the chores that she must attend to and suddenly, Sammy

10

McCracken asks her to marry him. She gave herself a mental shake and turned her thoughts to earlier in the day.

She had been struggling to fix the hinge on the gate that led to the field where Ned, the old grey donkey, was grazing. Apart from the chickens he was all that was left now since she sold the dairy herd. But old Ned wasn't for sale. Old Ned listened when she wanted to share her thoughts. Old Ned was there when she wanted to sit quietly in the shade of the big oak tree. Old Ned's gentle presence was comforting and reassuring when so many other things in her life had changed so dramatically. She was still reeling from her father's sudden death, so soon after the long illness that had eventually taken her mother. Martha's days were long and uneventful now. The land had been let to Sammy and his father. The spare bedroom had been rented to the young girl who was taking a Gap Year from her studies at University. Martha had been persuaded by Tam Lorimer to take the lodger.
"She's a young girl travelling alone – she needs somewhere safe to stay and she won't stop for long, she's only passing through."
When Martha hesitated, Tam continued, "It would be a bit of company for you."
Tam had been right. It was nice to have someone to make breakfast for again, and someone to chat to in the evenings. During the day she didn't see much of her as she was usually off somewhere on Martha's old bicycle. Lorna had a great interest in the countryside and the history of the area and the local people. Martha assumed it was all research for whatever she was studying at University and had commented to Sammy that she thought the young girl would be well suited to journalism. But Sammy thought she was a nosey wee so an' so, although he had to admit that she was a nice wee buddy and very likeable.

"Here, let me do that."

Sammy had jumped off the tractor, adjusted his cap over his thatch of thick auburn hair and taken the screwdriver out of Martha's hand.

"That's no job for a lady," he said, trying to look serious.

"Some lady," Martha retorted, looking down at her rough hands.

She hadn't been born to be a lady. There had been no career choices for her – not like the delectable Victoria Burnside. No, Martha had been born to be a farmer's daughter and that was her lot. She remembered the one occasion when she dared to speak about the other things she would have liked to have done.

"You're exactly where God meant you to be," her father had told her. "If you weren't meant to be here, then He would have sent you somewhere else."

Henry wasn't a church goer, but appeared to have a great understanding of God's intentions when he found it convenient. That had been the end of the conversation. Nobody argued with Henry Sloan. Henry Sloan knew his own mind and, once made up, was never known to change. Educating a girl was a waste of time and money was one of his firm beliefs, resulting in Martha finishing her school days at the local primary. Her mother tried to persuade him to change his mind and let her further her education, but Ruby was a weak woman, both in body and temperament, so her opinion carried little weight against the mighty force that was Henry Sloan.

"That should keep it secure for now," Sammy said, straightening up and pushing the screwdriver into the back pocket of his dungarees, "but it needs longer screws. I'll get some and sort it out for you tomorrow."

"Thanks, Sammy, that would be great. I never realized how many wee jobs keep cropping up. Da must have kept an eye out for all these problems, but I never noticed."

"Well, don't you go worrying your head about things like that; sure you know you can call on me any time."

"I know, Sammy, you're a great friend. I don't know what I would do without you."

She pushed her hands deep into the pockets of her old faded coat and shrugged her shoulders. She had looked so pitiful, and suddenly Sammy felt this overwhelming sense of compassion for her. She needed someone to protect her, someone to look after her, and with his father's earlier suggestion still buzzing round in his mind, he made the bizarre suggestion about the two coats before he even took the time to think about the possible outcome.

Martha ran her fingers through her short curly perm – a habit she had when either worried or uncertain. Her normally pale cheeks were flushed a dark crimson. Whether from surprise, excitement, shock or anger, Sammy couldn't be sure so he continued. "So Martha, what do you think?"

"What are you on about, you great big lumbering fool?"

Sammy didn't speak; instead he smiled, closed his right eye in a slow *'you know what I mean'* sort of wink. They say 'a wink is as good as a nod to a blind horse' but as Martha was neither blind nor dumb, a wink wasn't the answer to her question.

"I'm waiting," she said, straightening her shoulders and looking him square in the eye.

"All right then. Will you marry me?"

"Marry you!"

"Hello Sammy, Hello Martha," young Andy Hamilton shouted as he hurtled past on his father's big black bicycle.

"Take her easy," Sammy called after the retreating figure. "Reckless young devil," he added, turning back to Martha.

"I thought you were going down to the wee meadow today," she said, in an attempt to change the conversation.

"It's still too wet, and stop evading the question. Just picture it – your wee fawn duffle coat and my big black woollen coat hanging together on the back of the kitchen door, keeping each other warm."

"If I didn't know you, Sammy McCracken, I'd think you were serious," Martha replied.

13

"But I am serious," he said, "I've never been more serious in my life."

Martha had never been known to be lost for words when words were needed or expected, but this was a whole new game that she had never played before. She'd never considered him marriage material or even boyfriend material for that matter. He was just Sammy, friend, neighbour, someone she could depend on in a crisis. Now he was proposing that they become man and wife. It was all too much to take in.

She didn't want to offend by giving him an instant refusal, although that had been her first reaction. The whole situation was just too unthinkable after all the years of friendship. It would almost be like incest. But that was a ridiculous thought, she immediately chided herself. What was wrong with her, thinking such silly thoughts? He was a good man – he would take care of her. But that wasn't a basis for marriage. Or was it? Maybe it made good sense; maybe friendship *was* the best basis for a lasting commitment. Or maybe the whole idea was laughable. She wasn't sure what she thought or how she felt, so she resorted to the old familiar banter that had always existed between them. She told him she would think about it and to go away and give her head peace, and by the way, that was *her* screwdriver he had put in his pocket. The fact that Sammy could see just the glimpse of a smile forming at the corner of her mouth took the sting out of her comment. But even without the smile Sammy wouldn't have been offended, for it was something she had told him on numerous occasions over the years when he would have been teasing her or just 'getting on her nerves' as she often described it. Yes, they had always been friends - good friends. She cared about him – couldn't picture her life without him – even loved him. But where was the spark – the fire – the all consuming passion she knew she was capable of?

"Well Sammy, how's the world treating you?" Tam Lorimer hopped onto the empty stool beside Sammy. Tam was teetotal, but did a roaring trade in Murphy's bar. The sight of his round chubby figure was always a reminder to somebody that it was time to go home. As a rule, by then there was no hope of them being able to walk the distance or manoeuvre the bicycle they had propped against the wall earlier in the evening. But Tam was always ready to shove the piece of pedal power into the boot of his old black Rover and deposit it and its owner back to the comfort and safety of home and, usually, the wrath of the woman with the curlers and the rolling pin.

"I've been hearing things about you," Tam continued when Sammy didn't respond immediately to his question.

"The jungle drums have been busy I suppose," Sammy replied, taking another sip from the glass then placing it carefully on the little cork mat that bore the advertisement for Guinness.

"They certainly have," Tam said. "In fact, you have even upstaged the new arrival."

"What new arrival?" Sammy asked. But it was obvious from his tone of voice that he was merely asking the question that

was expected, rather than inquiring with any particular interest.

"The young woman who's lodging with Martha."

"Oh aye, her," Sammy replied, but it was obvious that his mind was on more important matters as he twirled the glass in a circular motion to increase the froth on the top.

"The usual?" Hughie inquired, with the glass of brown lemonade already poured.

"Of course," Tam replied, "and the same again for Sammy."

The two men drank in silence, a companionable silence where each understood the other. Then Tam asked the question that had been uppermost in his mind since he'd heard the gossip. "Ever thought about going back to England?"

Sammy shook his head, stared into his glass and said, "I burnt my bridges there a long time ago."

"Hi Tam, would you take us home?" someone called from the dimness of the snug.

"Are you in a hurry?" Tam asked.

"Not atal," was the slurred reply.

"All right then, I'll give you a shout in a minute or two," Tam promised.

Tam knew Sammy needed to talk to someone – someone who would listen and not blab. Tam was good at keeping secrets. Tam had collected a lot of secrets over the years, some volunteered, some overheard, but none repeated. He remembered the day that his wife had heard some snippet of juicy gossip and was sure Tam could confirm it, or at least give some hint as to whether there was any grain of truth in the rumours.

"You must know something," she insisted. "You're the only hackney man in the village."

Still Tam said nothing.

"You shouldn't be a Protestant," she shouted, "you should have been a priest; you would make a very good priest – you would be perfect for listening to the confessions."

"Do you think so?" Tam laughed. "I suppose it would always be something to consider if ever the taxi work dries up."

THE WEEKEND

Martha had been dreading the weekend. The thought of being completely alone again was depressing. She had got used to having her young lodger around, but as Tam Lorimer had said, Lorna was only passing through. Nevertheless, the house seemed unusually big, lonely, and quiet. Martha paced around the kitchen not sure how she was going to pass the remainder of the evening. For the last few weeks, she had spent the latter part of the days listening to Lorna enthusing about the beautiful scenery she had discovered on her rides through the countryside and the interesting folk she had been chatting to in the village. Then Martha would amuse Lorna with tales of the various eccentricities of some of the local people. She was fascinated when she heard about how Joe Haggerty, the cobbler, was able to talk and smoke a Park Drive while holding several nails between his lips as he stood at his ancient bench mending boots and shoes of all styles and sizes, and although he never put a name tag on any of them, he always knew who they belonged to.

"But how could he?" Lorna had asked.

"According to Bobby Birch he knew them by their smell," Martha told her laughingly, and went on to describe Bobby's unusual style of riding a bike. On hearing this Lorna was certain that he had been the man who had come to her rescue the evening she had got a flat tyre.

"He had one of those little repair kits in his coat pocket," Lorna explained, "and he found the puncture in the tube by moving it around in a puddle of rain water. I thought he was very clever."

"There's no flies on big Bobby," Martha said.

"He was very chatty," Lorna remarked. "He seems to be very fond of you and Sammy. He said you would make a great couple. He hoped you would both be very happy."

"That was kind of him," Martha replied. Then, in a bid to get away from the subject of Sammy, she said, "I wonder did you encounter Nancy Shaw on any of your trips into the village? Small, slim woman – greying hair caught back in a bun and calls everyone 'pet'."

"Oh yes," Lorna clapped her hands in amusement. "That must have been the lady I met in the Post Office today. She said 'Well, pet, what do you think of our wee part of the world?' and she said 'Cheerio pet' when she was leaving."

"That's Nancy all right. From the bin man to the doctor, the minister or the priest, they're all the same to Nancy."

Martha went on to tell Lorna that Nancy was the midwife who had assisted Doctor McGoldrick in bringing her into the world. "He was the *young* doctor then, but that was a long time ago," she added, "and before you decide to ask *how* long, we'll talk about something else - how about another wee cup of tea and a Rich Tea biscuit?"

Martha smiled at the recollections, but pleasant and amusing as they were, they weren't enough to keep her from thinking about Sammy. Sammy – why did she always let him creep into her thoughts? She had been trying not to think about him since his proposal earlier in the week. In fact, she had been deliberately avoiding him by staying indoors every time she heard the sound of his tractor either leaving the yard or coming up the lane. Perhaps he had been keeping out of her way too, for she discovered he had put the longer screws into the hinge of the gate as promised, but hadn't called in to say the job was done, the way he normally would have, and then waiting for the customary cup of tea.

Tomorrow would tell the tale, she decided. Tomorrow was Sunday, and Sammy and his father always gave her a lift to church. At this stage in her thinking she suddenly remembered how Sammy always joked that it would be more convenient if they both attended the same church, playfully telling her that if she would go to church with him it would save having to stop at the top of the village to let her out of the car before making his way to the Church of Ireland at the other end of the hamlet. It was a joke he had frequently made. Or at least, Martha had always assumed it was a joke and had treated the remark accordingly, by saying he would save petrol if he went to the Presbyterian Church with her. Now she was wondering if perhaps he had been considering marriage for quite some time and was hoping she would catch on to what he was hinting at. Perhaps her light-hearted banter had given him the idea that she was thinking along the same lines and that was why his proposal was so straight forward – no waffle or romantic gestures leading up to such an important question. Perhaps he thought it was a foregone conclusion that she was expecting a proposal and was prepared to accept it.

Wow! This gave the situation a whole new image and it was probably all her own fault. But that was the way she and Sammy had always been – always teasing each other about something and neither of them taking anything seriously that the other said. That's what she liked most about Sammy. With him she could be as silly as she wanted to be and her behaviour was always acceptable. From throwing a bucket of water over him when she discovered him asleep behind a hay stack to hiding the keys of the tractor, Sammy never condemned anything she did. Sammy always accepted her as the fun loving girl she was, the fun loving girl who lived under a strict set of rules on Daisy Farm, where laughter or any form of frivolous behaviour was frowned upon. A place where she became another version of her true self and, gradually and without being aware of what was happening to her, she had accepted the situation as normal and behaved accordingly. Then it dawned on her – she had become a carbon copy of her mother. Suddenly she realized that she didn't want that same rigid life style

– a life that was ruled by duty, the clock and the seasons. At present there were no rules to abide by - she could make her own decisions, she was answerable to no one. But now when she had that freedom, the first big decision she was presented with had left her startled and confused and, subconsciously, she longed for the time when her decisions were made for her. That way she couldn't be blamed for making the wrong ones – it was an easy way to live – just do what was expected of her and ask no questions.

But things had changed – her *life* had changed, and now she had to take control of that life, and that meant *making* decisions and living with the consequences. Although Sammy was her major query there was another matter she had to resolve. Something she had wondered about since her father's death – the possibility of buying a car. She liked driving - had driven her father's tractor and the Land Rover for many years, but that was only through the fields. That met with his approval, but a woman behind the steering wheel of a car 'gallivanting all over the place' as he described it, was something Henry Sloan definitely did not approve of. According to him, a woman's place was either in the kitchen, working in the fields or attending to the animals. Martha smiled at the thought of how he would react if he was there beside her now and discovered what she was considering doing. He would be flabbergasted, she decided. The very thought of her driving a car around these wee narrow country roads would, in his opinion, be sheer fantasy. But this was reality, and all of a sudden her mind was made up – come hail or high water, she would buy the wee red Mini she had seen in Village Cars – she would get a licence and she would be independent. Then she wouldn't need anyone to take her to church, and she wouldn't have to wait for the grocery man or the bread man on their twice weekly visit – she could go to the shops herself. All of a sudden she felt brave and confident. She had made a decision without the dread of being contradicted or scorned for being silly with high flung ideas in her empty head. Then, just as suddenly, her confidence deserted her. Would she have the courage to drive a vehicle on the main road? she wondered. And, most importantly, would she pass the driving test? She decided she would ask Sammy for his advice. He would know the best thing for her to do. Sammy, Sammy, Sammy. Why did she always need Sammy? Why did she always run to Sammy when she needed advice or was feeling unhappy? Why? Why? Why? And why could she not make up her mind about marrying him when he held such an important and necessary place in her life? What would she say to him tomorrow if he mentioned their last meeting? Would he expect an answer? On reflection, she assumed that he wouldn't. With his father there the conversation would probably be about the usual day to day things that everybody talked about - the weather and the crops and the state the world was in, with all this flower power and rock and roll, and, if there was enough time, then Senior would probably go on about how, in spite of the war and the rationing, the forties were good times in comparison to these so called 'swinging sixties'.

Maybe Sammy wouldn't be going to church tomorrow, she mused. Sammy was known to miss the occasional service when something unexpected happened on the farm. Although there were occasions when Martha suspected that staying too long in Murphy's bar the previous night had more to do with his absence than any great emergency with the live stock. His father was a stickler for regular attendance at their house of worship and Martha assumed he was the reason Sammy attended as well as he did. At this point Martha started to wonder what Sundays would be like if she and Sammy did marry. Would he go to her church or would he expect her to go to his and would he go to either of the churches when his father wouldn't be there to keep shouting at him to 'get up or you'll never be ready in time.'

That train of thought brought her to another query. Where would they live? If Sammy moved in with her, that would leave his father on his own, and that wouldn't be practical or fair, and she didn't think she could live in the McCracken household. It had been a

21

male domain for too many years, and too many untidy habits had been established. Martha's opinion of 'a place for everything and everything in its place' would probably drive the men folk round the bend, and their attitude of 'it'll do all right for now' would drive her up the wall. Even if all those problems could be solved, there was still the matter of Saturday nights. Would Sammy still want to go to Murphy's?

Martha always thought that drinking on a Saturday night and going to church on Sunday morning with a hangover was a strange contradiction, but when something didn't meet with her approval she always recalled Matthew, chapter seven, verse one: 'Judge not that you be not judged.'

Martha's mother had been a very religious woman – never missed a church service and always took Martha with her, refusing to listen to the occasional, 'But I've just been to Sunday school and I've heard it all before and I'm tired."

Apart from being ill, really ill, excuses were brushed aside. Sunday was a day that had to be respected; a custom Henry Sloan thought was a waste of time.

"Sure, isn't God everywhere all the time," he'd argue when church was mentioned. "There's no need to make a big show of it. Grand clothes and big hats – it's only a waste of money. I can pray in the fields or the byre or anywhere else and it costs me nothing."

Martha smiled at the memory – the memory of the two people who had loved her, each in their own individual way. A mother with Christian values that she instilled from an early age – a mother who had tucked her into bed and told her how much she loved her – a mother who sang and played games with her - a mother who had always been there when she needed her.

"Oh Ma, I wish you were here now," she whispered into the gathering gloom, feeling like a deserted child – her eyes bright with unshed tears as her thoughts drifted to her father. He had loved her too, she assured herself - he just had a different way of showing his love. He didn't think hugs and fun and laughter were important. In his opinion, if a man provided for his family and kept a ruling hand over them, leaving no opportunity for silly mistakes, then that was all that was needed. Martha thought differently - Martha did a lot of thinking – a lot of observing. Martha often wondered what her life would have been like if she had been given the opportunity to fulfil her dream of becoming a nurse. A dream that her father had scorned, calling it the silly notion of a silly girl who thought she was something, and anyway, she was farming stock. All their ancestors had been the same – hard working honest people who didn't need uniforms to prove what they were. Then he resorted to the old saying, 'You should never forget the bowl you were baked in."

When she protested, he had laughed and said, "I don't know why you would want a job cleaning other peoples' back sides when you could be helping me to clean out the byre any evening."

After tossing and turning for most of the night Martha woke with a headache and was tempted to use it as an excuse for missing the service and delaying the inevitable first encounter with Sammy after 'that day' - the day Sammy had thrown her world into confusion with his unexpected proposal – a day that would be forever printed in her memory regardless of the final outcome. However, after taking two pain killers and her usual tea and toast, common sense had prevailed – she was going to church and she would go with Sammy and his father and do as she'd often heard Nancy Shaw advise when the outcome of anything was uncertain, *'Just play it by ear'.*

At the sound of the horn honking Martha stole a quick glance in the mirror to make sure her hat was at the right angle. Martha hated hats – hated wearing a hat – thought they were silly, stupid looking things perched on top of anyone's head. But they were considered compulsory, a sign of respect when entering church. She wore hers with a certain degree of endurance until the service was over, but always removed it at the church gate on the way out. Another, more urgent toot of the horn as she brushed imaginary fluff from the lapel of her neat, navy two- piece, ensured she was on her way.

Sammy reached over, opened the back door of the car and remarked how good the weather was.

His father remarked, "And your wee lodger has gone," as if Lorna had been their current topic of conversation.

"Aye," Martha replied, pushing aside various newspapers and farming magazines that were scattered over the seat, thinking, 'when I get my own car it won't ever be in this untidy state.'

"You'll miss her," Arthur continued. "Sure, everybody needs a bit of company."

"The house is strangely quiet without her," Martha admitted, and suspecting Arthur was hinting at the possible match between her and Sammy, she added, "It was nice to have female company for a while – that's what I missed so much when my mother died. I'll maybe advertise for another lodger, or if I see Tam Lorimer first I might mention it to him for he's usually in the know."

The silence from the front confirmed Martha's suspicions.

He can put that in his pipe and smoke it, she thought, feeling quite pleased with herself for her quick reaction to Arthur's comment.

Sammy cleared his throat a few times and made another comment about the weather. A nice, safe topic, she decided, and prolonged the nice, safe topic with comments about the forecast and how it would affect the spuds.

"Don't wait for me today," she said, as she got out of the car. "It's Children's Day so the service will be longer than usual on account of the wee ones getting their Sunday school prizes."

Sammy said waiting for her wouldn't be a problem – sure it was Sunday and they had nothing better to do. His father made similar comments, but Martha was adamant, saying that she'd probably get

24

a lift with someone else going her way, and, if not, she would enjoy the walk as it was such a nice, sunny day, and laughingly added that a couple of miles of fresh air would do her the world of good – blow the cobwebs away.

At that stage Sammy seemed to get the message and said, "OK, then, have it your own way, bossy boots."

The comment was made in a good-humoured way. She was glad of the easy familiarity with which he tossed the words at her. In the last few days she had been dreading the possibility that their friendship could never get back to the uncomplicated way they had always been able to enjoy each other's company. So, if today's attitude was an indication of how he would handle rejection, then all would be well. The only problem being, maybe he wasn't expecting a refusal – maybe he thought she was following the romantic route and keeping him guessing. If that was the case then why had he been avoiding her during the week? Maybe he had been busy, or maybe he had decided to give her more time to think about things. After all, it was a major decision and Sammy knew she wasn't the sort of person who would rush into anything. All these maybes. She had to admit that if any avoiding had been taking place, she was as guilty as he was. Staying out of his way – hiding behind the curtain – it was a ridiculous thing for a woman of thirty five to be doing. She should have more sense, she chided herself, and, after all, it wasn't the first proposal of marriage that she had got, although even that one had been rather unusual too. She must not dwell on the past – it was the present that she had to deal with, and so far she didn't feel that she was making any progress. She'd just have to put all the wondering out of her head for the time being, she decided, or she wouldn't get any enjoyment or enlightenment out of the service, and if there was one thing that she desperately needed, it was enlightenment.

"Do you think she's just keeping you guessing?" Arthur commented as he and Sammy made their way into the church.

Martha's name hadn't been mentioned since she got out of the car, but it was obvious to the older man that she was very much on Sammy's mind.

"What do you mean, 'keeping me guessing'?" asked Sammy. "Sure I haven't set eyes on her all week."

"All the same now, son, you have to accept that sometimes women can be hard to understand –take your mother for an example, I never figured her out. Women just don't think the way we do, they're more devious."

"Ugh Da, would you catch yourself on," Sammy said. "This is Martha we're talking about. Sensible, no nonsense Martha – it would never cross her mind to be devious. She just needs time to weigh up the pros and cons. That's why I stayed out of her way all week to give her time to figure it all out in her head."

"Figure it all out in her head," Arthur repeated, and then muttered under his breath, "Very romantic!"

There wasn't time for any further discussion as they took their places in the pew and the service was about to start. A service that Sammy paid little attention to as his thoughts were elsewhere, especially after his father's comments about his mother - the fact that he had never been able to figure her out. He couldn't figure Martha out either, so maybe there was the possibility that she would pack up and leave him some day, the way his mother had done. A feeling of abandonment crept over him. Although he could only vaguely remember the tall, slender woman with the thick auburn hair so like his own, he was always aware of the space she had left behind. There was only the annual Christmas card addressed to both his father and himself and signed Peggy/Ma, with no return address, but postmarked in a different part of the world each year. Sammy had long since given up hope of ever seeing her again.

Arthur often thought about her and wondered where she was and who she was with. He had tried to find her the only way he knew how, by writing to her parents, but they couldn't help. Whether it was a case of 'couldn't' or 'wouldn't, Arthur wasn't sure, for he knew that they hadn't approved of the marriage. They said she was a city girl and wouldn't survive in the country. She had said she loved him and he had loved her – probably *still* loved her, though he refused to let himself consider that possibility. Yet, each December, when the envelope with the familiar handwriting dropped onto the mat he opened it with trembling fingers, hoping there would be an address or a note, or maybe an explanation. Each year he was disappointed. He couldn't understand why she had to be so mysterious. What puzzled him most was that the Christmas Sammy was in England the card was only addressed to him and signed Peggy. He never mentioned this to Sammy when he returned. He had just replied, "Canada this year," when Sammy asked, "Any post from our *loved* one?" in a mocking tone.

The small boy who had often cried himself to sleep had grown into a man who harboured a great deal of resentment towards the woman who had deserted him when he needed her most. Things could have been much worse, Sammy often admitted to himself. Martha's mother had been good to him when he was growing up, tried to mother him without taking his mother's place, and Henry Sloan was the best friend any man could have.

"Weren't the wee pets lovely," Nancy Shaw said to no one in particular. Martha was behind her as they came down the steps of the church.

"They certainly were," Martha replied, "and they were all so excited to get their prizes. Doesn't it take you back?"

"Doesn't it just," Nancy agreed. "Don't you wonder where the years go."

Martha nodded her agreement – a wistful smile on her face.

"No sign of your usual lift," Nancy commented.

"I told them not to wait for me on account of our longer service and, anyhow, it's a nice day for a walk."

"Of course it is."

When Martha made no further comment Nancy continued, "Listen, pet, there's no point in me beating about the bush and pretending I haven't heard the gossip or the rumours. You can call me an 'oul busy buddy if you like, but don't forget, I helped to bring you into this world so I'm entitled to be concerned about you."

Dear, loveable Nancy, Martha thought – *her* life hadn't been all sunshine and roses either.

"You're on your own now," Nancy continued, "and you don't want to go making any hasty decisions."

"I know, but, oh why can't life be simple? Why can't things just stay the same?"

"But pet, they don't," Nancy said. "We just have to make the most of each day – take it as it comes – *play it by ear.*"

'Play it by ear.' Martha smiled, remembering that those were the words that had encouraged her to travel with Sammy and his father earlier in the day when she had no idea what path the conversation would take.

"I just wish my mother was still here," she said. "I still miss her so much."

"Of course you do, pet."

A comforting hand was placed on Martha's shoulder.

"You were her best friend," the younger woman said. "You knew her so well. What do you think she would say about Sammy and me? What would she advise?"

"Probably the same as I will. Follow your heart. It's what I did and I never regretted a minute of it."

Nancy linked her arm through Martha's.

"I'm just having soup for my lunch," she said. "I don't go to a lot of bother with the cooking since my Charlie died, but you'd be welcome to join me. I'd be glad of the company."

"I'd love to," Martha replied, thinking about the salad she intended preparing and not looking forward to another plate of rabbit food, as her father used to call such meals. But, like Nancy, when there was no one to cook for, then there wasn't any desire to make an effort.

With arms linked, the two women made their way down the village street to Nancy's two up, two down. The snow-white lace curtains and brightly painted red door gave an indication of the neatness and welcome within.

Once inside, Nancy busied herself in the tiny kitchen that had been added on when Charlie's wee endowment policy with the Pearl had matured.

"The extra space is great," Nancy always said to anyone who commented on the improvement. Now that statement was usually followed by, "But when you've nobody to share it with, then it's not the same."

Martha felt a strong empathy with Nancy. She had no one to share anything with either – at least not at the present time, but one single word could change all that. Perhaps she *should* say yes, perhaps that would be the wisest thing to do. Just stop hesitating and accept Sammy's proposal and let all the tomorrows and possible problems take care of themselves. Be irresponsible for a change – jump in at the deep end – right or wrong. What difference could it make? At least it would be interesting finding out, and if it wasn't a success there was always the divorce court as an escape route. Suddenly her hand flew to her throat. What was she thinking about? What had got into her? Considering accepting a proposal of marriage and figuring a way out of that marriage all at the same time. She really must get a grip on reality. She had always admired people who were independent and able to make their own choices without having to consider anyone else – people with no commitment or sense of allegiance to anyone – people who were free spirits. Martha had spent all her adult life being sensible, doing the right thing, doing what was expected of her, and all for a *quiet* life. Sometimes she longed for the freedom to just be herself, to have the courage to put herself first. That had never been her way, and now when she had that freedom, she was faced with a huge and unexpected dilemma and she didn't know how to cope with it.

Martha didn't realize how deeply she had sighed until Nancy said, "That sounds serious," as she beckoned her through to take her place at the blue and white gingham covered table. Martha smiled at the kind-hearted woman, who was placing the bowl of vegetable soup in front of her. She knew Nancy cared – knew she wanted to help, but there was nothing she could do. This was her problem, and she would have to live with the consequences no matter what choice she made.

"Do you love him?" Nancy asked.

"I suppose so," Martha replied. "I care about him, he's a good man, he would take care of me, and he has always been there for me through the good times and the bad."

"He has," Nancy agreed, "but pet, true love is to love in *spite of*, not *because of*."

This all sounded very philosophical, and Martha wasn't sure how to react to her friend's statement, or if she was even expected to comment at all as Nancy continued. "Take my Charlie and me for example – everything was against us. We were from different religions, he was fifteen years older than me, and both our families bitterly opposed our marriage. The fact that we went to England and got married in the registry office fuelled their wrath. 'You've let us all down,' 'you're not married in the eyes of God,' 'you should have got married in church' 'you should have got married in chapel,' we heard it all. That's why we left Donegal. With partition the Protestant community was in the minority. Jobs were hard to come by, and you can imagine how it was for Charlie; he wasn't popular with either side. But we didn't blame them; it was just the way things were at that time. But Charlie and me, we loved each other in spite of everything and everybody, and neither of us ever regretted a single day we spent together."

Martha understood what Nancy was saying. Hadn't she also loved *'in spite of'* but that was a long time ago, and as nothing could change the past, she recalled a comment a customer had made one day while she was working in the village shop.

"I prefer the other brand, but, when you can't get what you want, then you just have to take what you can get."

As if reading her thoughts Nancy said, "You know, pet, taking what you can get isn't the same as getting what you want."

LATER THAT DAY

"Want a lift?" Tam Lorimer's soft, friendly voice broke into Martha's thoughts.

Her mind had been so far removed from her present surroundings that she had been only vaguely aware of the vehicle pulling up beside her.

"I'd *love* a lift," she replied. "These shoes are *killing* me."

"Then hop in," he told her, "this is your lucky day."

Martha was quick to obey, throwing the despised hat ahead of her as she exchanged pleasantries with Tam's missus. "Heading off somewhere nice?" and "Great day for a run out." The usual bit of chit chat that fills a few unexpected minutes in someone's company.

"It's not often I see you out walking at this time on a Sunday afternoon," Tam remarked, joining in on the casual conversation.

"Nancy Shaw invited me to have lunch with her after church," Martha said, and went on to tell how much she had enjoyed the company, adding that they had done a lot of reminiscing, though not disclosing what they had reminisced about. Tam wondered if a certain someone had been included in their recollections, or did he no longer hold a place in Martha's memory? But that was unlikely, he decided, for Martha wasn't the fickle type – the love 'em and leave 'em sort of girl like some he had encountered during his many years of taxi driving. If she decided to marry Sammy McCracken while still having the other guy on her mind, it could be a recipe for disaster, especially as he was about to return to the area within the next few weeks. Yes, things could get very complicated indeed. Tam wondered now, as he'd often done before, if it would have made any difference if he hadn't been so discreet - so good at minding his own business. There were so many times when he could have spilled the beans, but maybe that would have made matters worse, he consoled himself, although it was hard to watch people he cared about settling for second best.

"Thanks very much for the lift," Martha said, reaching for her hat. Tam changed down through the gears as he approached the end of her lane.

"Sit where you are," Tam said. "I'll take you on up to the house."

Before Tam could turn the steering wheel, the honking of a horn drew their attention, and Sammy's Austin 18 appeared in Tam's rear view mirror. Tam got the message and pulled up beside the milk stand. Sammy parked behind him, jumped out and rushed up to the side of Tam's car, yanked the back door open and said, "Where the devil have you been all day? I thought something had happened to you."

"I was visiting Nancy Shaw," Martha told him.

"Well, don't ever pull a stunt like that again," he ordered. "The next time you decide to go walkabout, have the decency to let me know where you're going and then I'll not be running the roads looking for you."

Martha made no reply. It was as if she hadn't heard a word he had uttered.

"Enjoy your evening in Portrush," she said, patting Tam on the shoulder as she got out of the car, obviously taking a lot longer than was necessary, "and buy the good woman a nice big ice-cream in Morelli's."

"Good idea," Tam replied laughing. "I'll maybe even get one for myself."

Martha walked past Sammy as if he was invisible.

"Sammy has just made one very big mistake," Tam said to his missus as they drove away.

"Get in," Sammy said, nodding towards his own car.

"No thanks, I'll walk – I like walking."

"In those heels?" Sammy raised his eyebrows as he pointed to the navy stilettos.

Neat ankle, he thought, but didn't dare voice his opinion.

Martha ignored his comment as she removed her shoes, tucked them under her arm and proceeded to walk on the soft grassy centre of the lane, refusing to step aside to let Sammy pass. He drove behind her until they reached the junction where she turned right and he turned left. By then the initial irritation she had felt was starting to wane, for Martha wasn't one to hold a grudge. But she wasn't going to let anyone boss her around either – she'd had enough of that sort of behaviour, and the sooner Sammy McCracken realized it the better.

Later that afternoon Martha reflected on her visit with Nancy. She had enjoyed the time they spent together, and although they had chatted about the usual mundane things that most women talk about – the cost of living – who was getting married – who had had a baby and who was just 'a-waiting on', a lot of their conversation was based on recollections. Nancy's particular viewpoint on certain events was giving Martha food for thought. It was something in the tone of Nancy's voice when she commented that if she married Sammy it would be like history repeating itself, which set Martha pondering and questioning some of her previous assumptions. Now she was wondering if perhaps her parents' marriage had been based on convenience and familiarity rather than some romantic moment of sudden awareness that they were meant for each other the way the characters in women's magazines always do. Martha knew that her mother and father had gone to school together - were both from farming backgrounds, and as he was an only son it was the accepted thing that when he married he would bring his young bride home to live with his parents. But she'd never know the true story now. They were both gone. The pages of time couldn't be turned back, and, on reflection, she was sure her mother had been reasonably content, in spite of the strict regime she lived under. But was she ever *really* happy? Martha wondered. Or did she yearn for fun and excitement the way she herself had so often done before *she* learned to accept her lot? Perhaps her mother simply went along with what she felt was expected of her out of some sense of duty. If she did, then Martha was certain that Grandmother and Grandfather Sloan would never have wanted her to feel that way.

Martha thought of the gentle couple who had treated her like a little princess and wished that they could have lived long enough to see her grow up. Perhaps if they had, they would have been able to convince their son of the importance of education and Martha wouldn't have ended up working in Gallagher's cigarette factory where the smell of tobacco made her nauseous most of the time. So, sick, and with no prospects of another job at that particular time, she readily accepted her father's idea of staying at home and helping on the farm – a decision that she frequently regretted.

Must not dwell on the past, she chided herself, reaching for the kettle. Tea was the solution. Martha always felt there was something comforting about holding a cup of tea between both hands and letting the hot steamy fragrance float upwards as if it was taking all the cares of the day with it to disappear in the misty swirling vapor.

Martha's train of thought was broken by Sammy's arrival.

"Is it safe to come in?" he asked, poking his head around the side of the door, "Or are you still cross?"

"As if that would make any difference to you," Martha replied.

He hesitated, unsure of her mood, not knowing what else to say or what to do. He stood there, holding onto the latch – one foot on the kitchen floor, the other one still on the doorstep as if ready for a quick getaway. For several seconds neither of them spoke another word, until eventually Sammy couldn't cope with the tension any longer.

"If you're going to throw that kettle at me," he said, "then would you just get on with it, or else set it on the stove and make us both a 'drap 'o tay."

He emphasised the country dialect hoping to add humour to the situation.

"Come on in and close that door," she said, "and sit down before I change my mind."

He breathed a sigh of relief. This was familiar ground – this was the Martha he knew so well – the Martha who was totally at ease in his company – able to say anything and in whatever tone of voice she chose, knowing that he would never take offence or even take her comments seriously. He liked her that way – the way she had always been; but if only she would take him seriously concerning the big question. The suspense was really starting to annoy him. Why was she wavering? Why couldn't she just make up her mind and give him an answer and put him out of his misery? It had been a simple enough question, so, to Sammy's way of thinking, the answer should be simple too. Yes or no, that was all he needed and then he could get on with whatever the outcome happened to be. He was hoping she would say yes. That would really please his father, he reflected, for he knew that senior had big plans - big ideas. But if she said no, then he would have to accept her decision, and his life would go on the same way it had always been since the day he left school. Apart from the time he went off in a huff to England after having a disagreement with his father, Sammy had spent all his thirty nine years on the farm. He often thought about that brief spell in Liverpool, but that was the past, this was the present and Martha's happiness was important to him. He cared about her and wanted to make her happy. He'd seen her tears on too many occasions – tears that only he knew about, since he was the one she always ran to when she was upset.

As Martha busied herself making the tea she was having thoughts of her own – considering all her options, of which she had three.

Option one - Johnny Connery, a neighbouring farmer, had called with her during the week to inquire if she would consider selling the land. He had offered her a fair price and Martha found the

36

suggestion very tempting. If she took him up on his offer, she mused, it would mean she could move away from the area and make a fresh start. An exciting idea, but how would she cope on her own in a strange place? She wouldn't know anyone and she wouldn't have Sammy to run to if a crisis occurred. Option two was the safe one. Just carry on as she had been doing, living in the house she had been born in, living amongst the people she knew and keeping Sammy as a friend. Of course, there was always option three. She could marry Sammy, and it wouldn't really make all that much difference to her life once the living arrangements were sorted out. Admittedly, there would be extra work with two men to cook and clean for, but Martha had never been afraid of hard work so that prospect didn't concern her. It was the question of whether she really wanted to be married to Sammy. That was the stumbling block. Did she want to share his life? Did she want to share his bed?

"I'm sorry about earlier this evening," Sammy said, reaching across the fleece backed tablecloth and taking her hand. "I didn't mean to shout at you, but I was worried out of my mind when I couldn't find you, and I was just so relieved when I turned the corner and saw you in the back of Tam's car."

"Forget it," Martha said, pouring tea into the blue and white striped mug, "I suppose I over reacted a bit myself," she continued, "but sometimes I don't know how to cope with everything that's going on."

"It'll take time," Sammy assured her, "it's only been two months, but you *will* cope, I know you will. You always do."

He recalled the day he'd been coming up the lane when he saw the ambulance, and Martha, white-faced, walking beside the stretcher that was carrying her father. He'd rushed to her side, but all she said was, "They think it's a heart attack, I have to go with him."

He admired the way she had coped with the suddenness of it all. Martha was a strong woman. There was no one else quite like Martha.

Then in a sudden change of conversation, Martha announced, "I've something to tell you."
Sammy's hand with the slice of buttered fruit loaf halted half way to his mouth. At last he was going to get an answer. She was going to tell him that she would marry him. Or maybe not.
"Well, go on," he urged, still clutching the piece of uneaten bread.
Her reply was a surprise he could never have anticipated as she unfolded the story of Johnny Connery's offer to buy her property. If she did decide to sell, she assured him, he and his father would get first refusal.
This was the last thing Sammy expected to hear. What about his proposal of marriage? Where did it fit into the scheme of things? If there was the slightest possibility that she was considering selling then she couldn't be thinking too seriously about accepting his proposal. What would his father think? What would his father say? He knew the old codger had big plans for Daisy Farm – had it all figured out.
Martha would be married to Sammy and she would be established in the McCracken household, making both their lives considerably easier. They would never have to worry about cooking or cleaning ever again, although cleaning was never one of their priorities. The thought of everywhere being neat and tidy and a clean shirt in the drawer was a major bonus, and, as Sammy's wife, she would combine her house and land with theirs. It would be wonderful and they could take on a permanent farm hand to help cope with the additional yield that would be produced from the extra acres and, hopefully, let the house to the same guy, keeping him close at hand for any emergencies that might occur, or late hours, depending on the weather. Of course, everything would be hers and Sammy's when he departed this scene of time, although he didn't expect that

event to happen in the foreseeable future. No, definitely not. Life was taking on a whole new meaning for Arthur McCracken and he wanted to hang around as long as possible to enjoy the fruits of his scheming.

"Are you going to eat that?" Martha asked, nodding towards the uneaten piece of loaf. "Or are you just going to sit there with your mouth open waiting to catch flies?"

Martha had never seen Sammy stuck for words before – this was definitely a one off, and, although she found the situation quite amusing, she managed to curb the giggle that threatened to escape.

Finally he spoke. "But what about us? Are you going to marry me or are you not going to marry me? What sort of a game are you playing?"

"I'm not playing any game," Martha replied, "I'm just not sure, I think I need more time."

"More time!" Sammy exploded, "How much more time do you need? You've known me all your life. '*More time*' says she - well if that doesn't beat all."

Sammy pulled a hanky from his pocket and mopped his brow. "I don't understand you," he continued, "I really don't."

"Drink your tea before it gets cold," Martha advised, "and then go home and get a good night's sleep – tomorrow's another day."

It was another restless night for Martha as she lay in the darkness and listened to the steady tick and half hourly strike of the old grandfather clock in the hallway below. She longed for sleep to claim her and give her respite from the torrent of confusing thoughts and images that raced across her mind, especially Sammy's attitude when she wouldn't give him a definite answer about marrying him. Although she had brushed aside his earlier apology, his unexpected outburst when he encountered her in Tam's car still puzzled her, and she wondered if perhaps this was another side of Sammy that she'd never seen before. Was this the real Sammy who would expect her to abide by his rules and his way of thinking and no longer the Sammy of carefree childhood, good friend and neighbour? It was not a pleasant or reassuring thought.

Martha sighed and wished for the umpteenth time that she could turn back the hands of time. But how far would she want to turn them? Would it be to the day her father had scorned her hopes and dreams? Was that the time she should have defied him and let him know she had a mind of her own? Probably not, for back then she wouldn't have had the courage to cope with the aftermath of his disapproval. What about the night she could have snatched her chance of real happiness? There was no need to ponder that one, for in her heart she knew that even given the same opportunity now, she would still make the same decision. So there was nothing to be gained by dwelling on the past– nothing to be gained by dwelling on what could never be altered as she recalled how often she had heard Nancy Shaw saying, "Whatever's for ye, won't go past ye."

Then there was her father's firm belief that everyone was exactly where God intended them to be – that it was all preordained the day they were born.

1930

6th April 1930. The day Martha Sloan was born. A memorable day in more ways than one, for although her birth was a great source of joy to her young mother, the event was somewhat overshadowed by the drama that was taking place in the neighbouring farmhouse.
Arthur McCracken had woken to the knowledge that his life would never be the same again. The note on the dresser gave him the message that every man must dread. Although, in Arthur's case, the possibility that his beautiful young wife was unhappy and would eventually leave him, had never entered his head. He read the last sentence over and over again: *'This life just isn't for me. I can't take Sammy with me, but tell him I love him.'*

"What's that Da?"
"Nothing important, son, it's just a piece of paper. Now eat up your breakfast."
"I don't like bread and butter," the four year old Sammy protested. "Ma makes soldiers to dip in my egg. Where is Ma? I want Ma."
"She had to go away for a day or two."
"When's she coming back?"
"I don't know son – I don't know."

The news that Arthur McCracken's wife had *flown the coop* made the usual rounds of the nearby village and surrounding countryside with lightning speed. Most folk were surprised, having assumed that the pretty girl from the city had easily accepted her role as a farmer's wife. She was often seen in the fields helping to stook corn or gather potatoes, and could compete with any of the men as far as speed or skill was concerned. She could always be relied upon to produce delicious cakes and pastries for any church or social event that was taking place in the village, and any compliments were quickly brushed aside with the statement that it all came from being the daughter of a restaurant owner and having to help in the kitchens during school holidays. To the majority of those who observed her behaviour, she was a typical young married woman who was happy and content with her lot. But a few of the other more observant locals were less convinced by her apparent happy state, and feared that some day she would grow tired of the routine and domesticity. Although they had their doubts they were, nonetheless, surprised that she had deserted in such a sudden and callous way, leaving a small boy behind – a small boy who would undoubtedly shed many tears and ask many questions – questions that his father would have difficulty finding answers to.

The only person who wasn't surprised when the news broke was Tam Lorimer. Against his will and sense of decency he had collected Peggy McCracken at the bottom of the lane at five thirty in the morning and driven her to Belfast harbour. Where her *final* destination would be, Tam didn't know nor didn't want to know. Being involved in her departure was enough to feel guilty about. But it was his job – his livelihood. Apart from 'Where to?' a taxi driver didn't ask questions his father had advised him the day he retired, and handed over the keys of the business to the young Tam.

"A taxi driver merely follows orders," the older man told him. "They respect their passengers' privacy and they don't repeat anything they overhear."

There were times when Tam wasn't comfortable with what he was privy to, and this was one of them, although he knew Peggy was going to leave anyhow, regardless of who drove her to the docks. Her final comment as she got out of the car confirmed her determination beyond any shadow of a doubt. "Don't think too unkindly of me, Tam," she said, reaching for the old battered suitcase. "I tried. God knows I tried. But the day I saw the photograph of me walking across the yard wearing a bag apron and carrying two buckets, I knew I couldn't pretend any longer."

Unaware of the turmoil that was taking place in her neighbour's house, Mary Sloan assisted Doctor McGoldrick and Nancy Shaw, the new young midwife, as her daughter-in-law struggled to bring new life into the world. It had been a long stressful night, and fear was mounting that Ruby wouldn't survive the strain of such a lengthy, difficult delivery. Even if she did, there was a strong possibility that the baby wouldn't.

Henry Sloan was in the next room, maintaining that babies and all those sorts of goings on were women's stuff and men shouldn't be involved. He tried to sleep, but for most of the night his efforts were in vain. He was used to new birth as it was a regular occurrence on the farm and usually presented no problems, but this was different – this was the son he had hoped for – a son who would grow up and be the same help to him as he was to his father. The possibility that it might be a girl never occurred to him.

He rose at his usual time since there were essential chores that had to be carried out each morning and his father would already have made a start. As he passed the room where his young wife had spent the most traumatic night of her life, he heard a faint whimper. He hesitated outside the door and listened as that first cry grew to the full scale howl of a new born baby. In spite of all the problems, Martha Sloan had arrived, a healthy seven pounds of energy, and Ruby, though exhausted, insisted on checking every tiny finger and toe.

"It's safe to go up now," Mary said. "The coast is clear and Ruby is asking for you."

"Is he all right?" Henry asked, looking up from the Ulster Fry.

"She's fine," the proud grandmother announced.

"But the wean," Henry said. "What about the wean?"

"She's fine, I told you, and she's beautiful!"

"She? She?"

43

His disbelief and disappointment were so obvious that Mary had difficulty holding back the tears. Poor Ruby, she thought, after all she had been through to give him a child, and now all he could do was show displeasure.

"Yes, she," his mother said, "and she's a wee darlin'. You should be down on your knees thanking God for her, because she almost didn't make it."

Henry made no comment as he placed another piece of crispy bacon in his mouth and continued to chew. Mary gripped his arm tightly, ensuring she would get a response to her next statement.

"Ruby's life hung in the balance too," she told him, "so I would advise you to wipe that scowl off your face and get up those stairs and give your wife some consideration."

Henry rose from the table without replying to his mother's outburst, and made his way to the room where Ruby waited expectantly to show her husband their pretty little girl. But it was obvious to the young mother as she watched him look into the cradle that he wasn't as pleased as she was, and she knew this was not a good time to tell him that she could never have another child.

"It's a girl," Henry told Arthur McCracken when he met him coming across the lane with wee Sammy by the hand. "It's a girl," he repeated, when his neighbour didn't respond. "I'm the father of a girl!"

"She's gone," Arthur said, ignoring Henry's announcement, and so caught up in his own problems he didn't notice the look of disappointment on the other man's face. "She's gone," he said again.

"She didn't make it then," Henry said, assuming Arthur was talking about one of the cows that had been causing concern.

"It's Peggy," he said. "My Peggy. She's gone."

"Where's she gone Da. Where's Ma gone?" Sammy asked, tugging his father's hand.

"Run you on ahead and make sure that the hens are all right," Arthur told him, avoiding the question.

Sammy ran off as fast as his short, chubby legs would carry him. He was thrilled to be allocated such an important task. This would be something to tell his Ma when she came home, he thought. He was sure she would be pleased, because she was always telling him that he would have to be a big brave boy, and a boy had to be very big and very brave to be trusted with the important job of checking on the hens.

"She's left me," Arthur said, pulling the crumpled piece of paper from his pocket and reaching it to Henry.

For a long time both men stood in total silence – each locked in their own private thoughts. In the space of a few hours both their lives had changed beyond anything they could ever have imagined.

"Come on back to the house with me," Henry said, when he finally found the power of speech. "Ma will put the kettle on. It'll take her mind off me, for she's in one of her bossy moods, lecturing me on how I should be feeling about this new wean."

"You don't know how lucky you are," Arthur replied. "A nice wee wife who won't let you down, and now a wee ba. What did you say it was?"

"A girl," Henry said, "a girl."

Mary reached for the kettle the minute Henry and Arthur and wee Sammy walked into the kitchen. It was obvious from their expressions that something wasn't quite right, and there was more to it than Henry's disappointment at not getting a son.

Bit by bit the story of Peggy's unexpected departure unfolded. Part of the tale was related through spelling some of the words, trying to keep as much information as possible from the four year old, hoping that the runaway Mum would see the error of her ways and return before he became aware of the situation.

Mary had her doubts about that possibility and promised that, no matter what the outcome would be, wee Sammy would never be lonely, adding that, in no time at all, Arthur's wee girl would be running around and she and Sammy would be company for each other.

How right she was. Time has a habit of flying past on a farm, as one season drifts into another. She had also been right about Sammy and Martha. They became inseparable.

1941 THE HEARTBREAK OF WAR

A cloud of despondency hung over the village. Two years of war and no sign of it ending. Supplies of food, clothing and petrol were rationed, and iron gates were taken to make ammunition. Blackout blinds were a must, and gas masks were issued because of the threat of chemical warfare. Everyone tuned into the BBC Home Service for news from the front line, and although there was no conscription in Northern Ireland, countless men of all ages volunteered. Some joined the Army, some the Air Force, others the Navy; some survived and others never came back. Children from the city were evacuated to the countryside. Willie Rossborough was one of those children.

Martha looked across the scrubbed kitchen table at the young boy sitting opposite her. His pale complexion was evidence of the twelve years that he had spent living in a small tenement whose tiny windows obscured most of the light, while the air outdoors was polluted by smoke from the factory chimneys. He smiled, a cautious, uncertain smile, not knowing if he was welcome, or a burden to the family who had accepted him into their home.
"Can you play Snakes and Ladders?" Martha asked.
He nodded.
"Oh, good," said Martha, "that's great. Da hasn't time and Ma only plays sometimes because she says I should spend more time outside in the fresh air and I'm sure granny and granda cheat."
Martha giggled on the last part of the sentence, knowing she would get a reaction, and she did, as her grandmother came up behind her, pulled her ear and winked at Willie.
"If anybody is going to cheat, you can be sure it'll be this rascal here, so keep a close eye on her."

"I will," said Willie, his smile lighting up his dark brown eyes. He was going to like it here he decided. The elderly lady's sense of humour and the possibility that Martha could be a challenge were something he knew he would enjoy. All his dread of being unwelcome had vanished and, for some reason he couldn't explain, he suddenly felt as if he belonged.

The days drifted into weeks, and the young evacuee rapidly grew out of the clothes he had brought with him. His face had lost the pallor and had taken on a healthy glow from the hours spent running through the fields. His legs, exposed below the short trousers, bore scars from numerous scratches obtained on his happy-go-lucky trips through the thick thorny hedges that separated the fields. He could never understand how Martha managed to engage in similar activities and escape without a graze. But Martha was a country girl – Martha knew where the hedge was thinner, where it hadn't produced as many thorns. Martha knew that going through backwards saved her face. She also knew that it was a good idea to let someone else go first, and then follow close behind. On the other hand, Willie was a city boy with a lot to learn about the country-side, but he was adapting much better than had at first been expected. He was fond of the animals, particularly Ned, a young donkey that a farmer on the other side of the river had bought on the spur of the moment and then decided he didn't need or want. After overhearing her father and Arthur tut tutting about the man's stupidity, Martha decided she would like to have it. She had always liked the story about Jesus riding into Jerusalem on a donkey, and decided she would like to ride on one too. Her pleading and fake tears finally resulted in her father agreeing she could have it, but only on condition that she would be responsible for it.

"I'll help you to look after it!" Willie offered. "This is great, I can't wait."

"You'll just have to wait," Sammy announced, but no one was listening.

So, the morning the grey animal with the cross on its back arrived at Daisy Farm was a big event. The word had spread about the expected time of arrival, so the usual troop of children who often joined Willie and Martha on their rambles was there to meet and greet. Willie had become popular with the local children, fitted in as if he had lived in the area for years. He was especially popular with Victoria Burnside, but Willie was quite unaware of the extra attention she paid him. Willie was also unaware of how the sunshine had bleached his fair hair to various shades of blonde. Willie Rossborough had become an extremely handsome boy.

Apart from his enforced separation from his parents and the dread of what could happen to them if they didn't get to the shelters in time, everything else in Willie's life was good. He had been enrolled in the local school and was making good progress. He had also joined the Sunday school, and never refused to attend church with Martha and her mother immediately afterwards, although there were times when he would have preferred to go straight back to the farm, for by then the hunger pangs would already have started. Willie liked the meals that were cooked on the big black range and, although food was rationed, the benefit of living on a farm meant there were plenty of eggs and potatoes and milk and they always had roast chicken on a Sunday.

Willie's only problem was Sammy. Sammy was always hanging around and Willie got the impression that he didn't like him spending so much time with Martha. Then Willie started to wonder if perhaps Sammy was Martha's boyfriend. He hoped not, but decided to ask her anyway.

"Don't be daft," she exclaimed. "Sammy is fifteen and I'm only eleven. Girls of eleven don't have boyfriends."

"Girls of eleven at my school in the city say they have boyfriends," Willie told her.

"Catch yourself on," Martha said. "They're takin' a hand out of you."

Martha didn't wait for Willie to comment as she continued to give him the benefit of her opinion. "You're a right mug if you believe all that garbage. They're talking a load of bunkum. By the way, are you anybody's boyfriend?"

"Of course not," Willie replied, "I'm only twelve."

"Well, then, does that not tell you something?"

Willie gazed across the field to the mountain beyond, puckered his lips for a few seconds as he considered the facts, then he turned to Martha and said, "When we are older I could be *your* boyfriend."

"Aye," Martha replied, twisting a section of her long brown hair round her finger until it became tight.

"We could even get married some day," Willie continued.

"I suppose we could," she agreed, "but I think the fellow has to ask the girl first to see if she *wants* to marry him."

"All right then," said Willie. "Will you marry me? When we're older of course."

"Aye, all right. Now what about a game of marbles?"

"OK," Willie agreed, "but I bet you a jelly baby that I win."

"I bet you two jelly babies that you don't," Martha threatened, as they ran off towards the house to fetch the jam pot of tiny round pieces of multicoloured glass.

There was a car parked in the yard that they had never seen before so they went to investigate.

"Come inside, both of you," Henry called from the open kitchen door.

"We were only looking," Martha said in defence of their actions.

Henry didn't reply, but they knew from his expression that he expected them to do what they were told. Once inside they saw a man and woman whom neither of them recognized. The woman slowly approached Willie.

50

"You have to be very brave," she said, placing her hand on Willie's shoulder. Willie knew what she was trying to tell him – knew that his worst fears had been realised. "You can be very proud of your parents," the stranger continued; "they would have made it to the shelter in time if they hadn't turned back to help an old lady who had stumbled and fallen."

Willie didn't speak as he stared at the sad face of the stranger who had brought him the tragic news. Martha glanced at her grandparents who were standing together holding on to the back of a chair. Then she looked at her mother whose face was strangely white and her father kept running his finger around the inside of his shirt collar as if it was too tight. Nobody cried – nobody except Martha, as the horror of war invaded her young mind.

Mainland Britain had suffered numerous attacks, but the previous evening Belfast had been the main target. In an attack that had lasted for over five hours, 35, 000 homes were destroyed, 900 people killed and 600 seriously injured.

Martha ran from the house – ran to the field where her new friend brayed a greeting when he saw her approaching.

"Oh Ned, Ned," she wailed. "Something terrible has happened."

She clung to his rough neck, tears streaming down her face as she told him the awful news that the strangers had brought to Willie. Then hearing the rustle of footsteps in the long grass, she turned.

"I think you might need this," Sammy said, reaching her a hanky. She shed the rest of her tears on Sammy's shoulder.

A week later Martha was shedding more tears, but for a different reason. Willie was leaving Daisy Farm. Martha knew she was going to miss him, they'd been such good friends, and had spent so much time together. She would still have her other friends, she consoled herself, although she didn't really care whether Victoria came to play or not, because she was unpredictable and always tried to get her own way. She liked Jean and Mary. They liked to play the same games as she did, and Bobby and Davy always made her laugh with their antics, climbing through the trees. She knew the summer would soon pass and the days would get shorter, then they wouldn't be allowed to stay very long because their mothers insisted they had to be home before dark, except for Bobby's mother who didn't seem to mind how long he stayed out. But Bobby always left with the others because he said he was afraid of the shadowy shapes of the trees when he couldn't see them properly. Henry Sloan didn't encourage other peoples' children to come into the house. He said they were only a nuisance, with the exception of Sammy McCracken who was more like one of the family, and he only accepted Willie because it was his patriotic duty – his contribution to the war effort. Bobby said he had overheard somebody saying that people had to take these weans whether they wanted them or not, or the police would put them in jail. Of course, nobody paid any attention to anything Bobby said. But, compulsory or not, the true fact remained. Willie Rossborough was only residing in the Sloan household because he *was* an evacuee. Ruby would have loved all the young people around her, but Henry's word was law. Even his mother and father had stopped trying to change his mind about anything, having accepted the fact that Henry was stubborn by nature and becoming more so, since the farm had been signed over to him. Arthritis and various other aging complaints were catching up on the older generation, so it had seemed the sensible thing to do, although there were times when Mary wondered if her son's position of authority was, at times, making life unpleasant for his pretty wife. Henry sometimes appeared not to notice that she was around, and, although Mary knew Henry loved Martha in his own undemonstrative way, she was, nevertheless, the little girl who had been a big disappointment to him because she wasn't a boy. Now, in the matter of a few short days, that little girl was discovering that life isn't all about fun and laughter and carefree summer days. The little girl had discovered the heartache that war can inflict on innocent people; she was also experiencing the misery of losing someone she cared about. Yes,

Martha was going to miss Willie. Martha was going to be very lonely without him.

Willie's parents had left instructions that if they didn't survive the war, he was to stay with Elsie, his mother's sister who lived in County Cavan. A reasonable enough suggestion, for Southern Ireland was a neutral country – had declared its neutrality on 2nd September 1939. Dublin had been bombed once, but apparently that had been a mistake so there was no need to be concerned. Willie would be safe on the other side of the border. Willie had never met Elsie and didn't know anything about her except for snippets of conversation he had overheard between his mother and his granny before the old lady had died. Things like, let bygones be bygones, and something about religion. Willie assumed that whatever the problem had been it couldn't be resolved, and that was why he'd never met the relative who was now to be his legal guardian.

The big car with the Southern registration pulled into the yard and a woman bearing a striking resemblance to his mother got out. She had the same wavy fair hair, blue eyes and ready smile. She came towards Willie, who was standing at the door with Martha.

"I'm your Aunt Elsie," she said, "I've been looking forward to meeting you."

"And I'm Sean," the man said in his soft, lilting, Southern brogue as he came to stand beside his wife.

Willie didn't know what to say so he just nodded his head, and then turned to receive all the hugs and good wishes from the family that he had come to think of as his own. Then, as he stooped to pick up his suitcase, Sean said, "Sure give that to me, young fellow, and I'll put it in the boot for you."

Ruby invited them to stay for tea, but they graciously refused. It was obvious they were anxious to be on their way, back over the border to the safety of their neutrality.

"We couldn't save anything from the house," Elsie told Willie as they made their way to the car. "The whole row went down."

Still Willie didn't speak, but he was glad his mother had insisted that he take the family Bible and the shoe box containing family photos and birth certificates with him when he was being evacuated. This was his identity - his link to the past.

Willie waved through the back window of the car as it slowly moved away. His eyes were bright with unshed tears, but Martha knew he wouldn't cry while anyone was watching. Willie never cries, everyone thought. Martha knew differently, for during the last week she had heard his muffled sobs through the partition that separated their two rooms. To-night there would be no one in that room to hear *her* sobs because it would be empty, but probably not for long. There would be another evacuee to take Willie's place, but he wouldn't be like Willie – no one could ever be like Willie.

Sadly, Martha's new experience of heartache didn't finish with the departure of Willie, for three months later her beloved Grandmother passed away peacefully in her sleep, and six weeks after that her grandfather was also gone. A severe attack of Asthma followed by pneumonia was too much for his elderly body to cope with.

Friends and neighbours shook their heads and agreed that he had died of a broken heart – just couldn't live without the woman who had been his wife for nearly fifty years.

It was the morning of the funeral and Martha was distraught. All her mother's comforting words about how granddad and granny were together in Heaven, happy and free from all suffering, didn't do anything to ease the pain that the young girl was suffering.

"I don't want them in Heaven," she protested, "I want them here, with us. I want granny to help me with my knitting. She promised to show me how to do feather stitch and she went away before I got a chance to find out how to do it."

"I know, darling," her mother said, putting her arms around her, "but I'll show you how it's done."

"You won't be able to do it the same way as granny and I want granddad back too, for he was able to tell me stories about things that happened long, long ago that nobody else could tell me because they weren't there. It's just not fair – they shouldn't have left me."

The tears were starting again as she broke free from her mother's embrace and rushed out the door.

Ruby made to follow her.

"Let her go," Henry said. "There's only so many tears a person can cry. Let her work it out on her own, she'll be all right."

Ruby wondered if Henry ever cried. She'd never seen him shedding tears, but of course men were expected to be strong in a time of trouble – expected to take charge of unpleasant situations, while it was quite acceptable for women to dab their eyes with their lace hankies and appear useless.

"Where's Martha?" Sammy asked, coming through from the parlour where he had been spending a few moments in quiet reflection with the remains of the elderly gentleman he had been so fond of.

"She ran out about five minutes ago," Henry said. "She's probably down in the field talking to the donkey. That's where she usually runs when things aren't going her way."

"I'll go and see if she's all right," Sammy said, not waiting for any further comments.

Ruby found it a great comfort to know how much Sammy cared about Martha. He had always been there for her, even when she was a toddler playing on the floor with her rag doll, wiping away her tears when she fell over and banged her head or grazed her knee. He'd ruffle the top of her hair and make funny faces, and within minutes he'd have her chuckling with laughter. But it would take more than a funny face to fix Martha's anguish today.

PEACETIME   1946

With the war over and life getting back to normal, people were beginning to enjoy the freedom of peace time. Blackout blinds were abandoned, gas masks were tossed to the backs of attics, and those who could afford the price of a bus or train ticket were swarming to Belfast to view the shops and the scenes of devastation that were still evident as a result of the numerous bombs that had been dropped on it.

But Martha wasn't interested in a trip to the city. To-day was her sixteenth birthday and that was much more exciting than trudging through the crowded streets. Sixteen was a special age as far as Martha was concerned – she was feeling all grown up, especially as her father (after a lot of persuading by her mother) had agreed, as a treat for her big day, to let her go to a party and dance being held in the village hall that night, but only on the condition that Sammy went too and kept an eye on her and brought her home no later than twelve o'clock.

"That's not a problem," Sammy agreed.

Henry was pleased that his orders had been so readily accepted – it had obviously escaped his mind that it was Saturday, and on a Saturday night the last dance always finished at a quarter to twelve to allow enough time to play the National Anthem and have everyone out of the hall before midnight. But twelve was Henry's deadline on any night and Martha thought it was a bit early. She'd heard some of the girls who came into Mrs Smyth's grocery shop where she had a temporary job, talking about how, during the week, these village hops usually went on into the wee small hours. It sounded like a lot of fun and Martha often wished she could be like them, but with a father like hers it wasn't a good idea to argue. Better to obey the rules and keep him sweet, because if anything or anybody annoyed him, it usually meant an awkward atmosphere in the house for days after and she knew that upset her mother.

"Sweet sixteen and never been kissed," Sammy teased, and threatened to rectify the matter if she didn't pour him another glass of milk.

Martha wrinkled her nose at him, the way she used to do when they were children, and called him a silly big lump. Sammy grabbed a piece of bacon from her plate and ran out the door closing it behind him and holding tight to the latch, preventing Martha from following and attempting to carry out numerous threats about how she would pay him back. Sammy made funny chicken sounds until they were both laughing so much that there was little chance of either of them being able to play any more tricks – or so Sammy thought!

"Come on in," Ruby called to Sammy, "that silly daughter of mine is all talk and your spuds will be turning black."

Ruby had cooked the mid-day meal. It was spring time and there was a lot to do on the farm. Sammy and his father were helping - returning the favour as Henry Sloan had helped them the week before.

Sammy returned to the table, pulled out the chair, but the second he attempted to sit down Martha pulled it from beneath him. Sammy stumbled – caught his foot on the leg of the table, and only for quick thinking by the two fathers, several plates and a jug of milk would have followed the surprised Sammy onto the red tiled floor.

"That's enough of that nonsense!" Henry bellowed. "Any more of your gipein and you'll be at no dance the night."

"But Da!"

Ruby frowned and conveyed by shaking her head from side to side that it would be better for Martha to keep quiet. The rest of the meal was eaten in silence except for the occasional 'pass the salt' and the polite 'thank you.'

Martha viewed her reflection in the long mirror on the wardrobe door and was pleased with what she saw. She had plaited her long, brown hair earlier in the day, and now, combed out, it was hanging in soft waves around her shoulders. But her dress was the main focus of her attention. She thought of the hours her mother had spent at the old treadle sewing machine creating this beautiful frock for her special birthday. She smiled as she recalled the times her mother had said the machine was her valuable and irreplaceable friend – always ready to obey her commands as she patched overalls, turned the collars of shirts and made bed sheets and pillowcases by stitching together the unravelled Morton's flour bags after they had been steeped for a week in cold water and pennies to remove the picture of the crow that was the firm's logo. They were all good housekeeping skills that were practised in almost every home. Nothing was disposed of if it could be mended or made into something else. But the making of Martha's dress hadn't been merely a matter of doing what was necessary – it had been a labour of love, and Martha was delighted with the end result. The deep shade of pink, slightly flared skirt, elbow length sleeves and square neckline trimmed with brown ric rac, was everything a young woman could dream of. The new, brown high-heeled shoes that she had saved for weeks to be able to afford, along with the nylons that Sammy had bought her, completed the look. Martha was ready for her big night. Now she only had to wait for Tam Lorimer to arrive in his taxi to take her and Sammy to the hall, and, knowing Tam, he would probably be picking up a few others on the way. Tam always had a full load both to and from these events. Sammy was already downstairs in the kitchen – she could hear him chatting to her father, and suddenly she realized how deep his voice had become, especially when he came through to the hall and shouted, "Are you goin' to be titavatin' up there all night?"

Ruby watched as Sammy and Martha got into Tam's car. They looked so right together – Martha, small and slim, and Sammy tall, broad shouldered and his brown suit complimenting his auburn hair.

"That could be a match," Ruby commented.

"What?"

"Sammy and our Martha. I wouldn't be surprised if they decided to get married some day."

"To each other?"

"Aye."

"Have a bit o' sense woman; sure our Martha is only a wean."

"She's not a wean any more," Ruby told him. "She's sixteen, and they have always been close."

"Well, you can put that idea out of your head," Henry said. "That definitely won't be happening."

"I thought you liked Sammy."

"Of course I like Sammy, but he's too old for her."

"There's only four years between them," Ruby stated.

"It doesn't make any difference," Henry argued. "They'll not be marrying, for Martha's not the marrying kind."

"What makes you think that?"

"She's a country girl," he said. "She belongs on the land. All this talk she goes over about how she loves working in the shop, and then dear knows where else she'll think of heading off to, none of it'll last. She'll end up here, helping you in the house and doing her duty on the farm. She'll not have time for boys an' all that nonsense."

Ruby let the matter drop, the future would take care of itself, but in the meantime she was glad Martha had Sammy as a friend.

"All ready for the big night out?" Tam said as Sammy and Martha hopped into the back of Tam's car.

"As ready as I'll ever be," Sammy replied, "bearing in mind I'm responsible for this scallywag in the new dress – thinks she's no goat's toe."

"She's a nice wee girl," Tam replied, "if only I was twenty years younger!"

Tam's comment was the start of a lot of good-natured banter as Sammy announced that Martha would have to sit on his knee and the weight of her would probably kill him. Mary and Jean were already in the car and either one of them would have been quite happy to change places with Martha, especially Jean, who had admitted to Martha that she had a wee liking for Sammy. Bobby Birch was occupying the front seat, as if it was his God given right to sit beside the driver, and when they stopped to collect Davy, Bobby thought he should also squeeze into the back. But Davy wasn't easily out-manoeuvred.

"Slide over a bit," Davy said, giving Bobby an almighty shove. Fortunate for Bobby that the gear stick was beside the steering wheel, not positioned between the two seats as would have been normal in a newer model.

Strains of 'Roll out the Barrel' reached the friends as they tumbled out of the car.

"Big Danny's getting well into the swing of things tonight," Tam remarked.

"He certainly is," Sammy agreed. "He knows that wee accordion inside out."

"Aye, and Matt Hamilton isn't bad on the drums either," said Tam. "He can fairly keep up."

Sammy agreed with Tam's opinion, but the girls weren't interested in the hows and whys of the men's musical abilities as they rushed into the hall, eager to make the most of their night out.

Victoria was already there, keen to tell her friends that daddy had driven her to the dance. Apparently daddy thought girls should be properly chaperoned to such events. After all, daddy was a solicitor and he knew everything.

"Clever daddy," Sammy murmured out of the side of his mouth, assuming Martha would be the only one who could hear him.

"What was that you said?" Victoria demanded.

"I said, the weather's hardy," Sammy replied turning away as he took Martha's arm, leading her onto the dance floor for the last part of the Quick Step, almost knocking over Bobby Birch as he dusted the floor with the dreaded powder that made the surface really slippery, resulting in many a tumble. An occurrence that was always a great source of amusement to the onlooker, but a huge embarrassment to the individual who had difficulty regaining their balance, not to mention their dignity.

Martha was on the floor for every dance. Sammy had taught her well, the teaching having taken place in the barn or down the lane when her father wasn't in close proximity, for Henry Sloan didn't approve of such shenanigans. He said it was grossly indecent for girls to be held so close by boys. So, with no knowledge of Sammy's coaching skills, he assumed Martha would be sitting at the back of the hall listening to the music and refusing any offers of taking to the floor because she didn't know one dance from another. In Martha's opinion it was a matter of, *what he doesn't know will do him no harm.*

Sammy took turns dancing with Mary and Jean, but only if someone else had already asked Martha, which was quite often. Martha was a very pretty girl, a fact that hadn't gone unnoticed by the local lads, especially Bobby Birch who was obviously very sweet on Martha, but of course Bobby was inclined to be interested in any girl who so much as looked in his direction. Unfortunately, his manner did little to encourage any of them, especially his notorious way of asking a girl to dance. His predictable '*wud you hit this a clatter way us*?' made the other guys' question of '*are you getting up?*' seem very polite.

"Are you enjoying yourself?" Sammy asked as he and Martha twirled around to an old time waltz.

"I'm having a great time," Martha assured him.

"I've never seen you looking so happy," Sammy informed her. "You have a real twinkle in your eye tonight."

Sammy didn't know that it was the secret Martha had in the pocket of her new dress that was the cause of her high spirits. The piece of paper inside the envelope that had been addressed personally to Miss Martha Sloan and not the usual 'Sloan Family' as was Willie's custom when writing to the inhabitants of Daisy Farm with an update on the progress of his education and ending with best wishes to everyone. It was only a short note.

Hope you have a great birthday – thinking of you often. ***Love Willie.***

PS. Hoping to get into Queen's University.

Just a few words but they meant a lot to Martha.

"So much for daddy's chaperoning," Sammy said, nodding towards the door as Victoria left on the arm of a young man whom neither of them recognized. But Martha wasn't listening – wasn't particularly interested in anything concerning Victoria Burnside. Martha was still counting her blessings that *she* had met the postman that morning instead of her father. Something that she could never remember happening before, as he was always in the yard when Paddy McGrath came panting up the lane pushing his old squeaking bicycle, but today the delivery had been earlier than usual. Paddy had gone to his uncle's funeral in Randalstown and the stand-in guy hadn't taken time to chat to everyone he met.

THE UNEXPECTED

"Just like his mother – just her all over again!"

"Arthur McCracken!" Ruby exclaimed, reaching out to steady the distraught man as he staggered into the kitchen waving a piece of paper above his head. "What's wrong? What has happened?"

"Our Sammy," Arthur replied, "taken off just like the woman I was foolish enough to marry. He'll likely not come back either."

"What's all the commotion?" Henry asked, pulling his wellingtons off at the back door as he followed his neighbour inside.

"Our Sammy," Arthur repeated. "Here, read this."

Henry reached for the note that Arthur thrust towards him – Ruby reached for the kettle.

"Read it out loud so Ruby can hear it," Arthur ordered.

Sorry if I have upset you, but I have to get away. Don't worry about me I'll be all right. Tell Martha that I won't forget her. Your loving son, Sammy.

For what seemed like hours, although it was only a few seconds, nobody spoke. Then Henry broke the silence.

"Where's Martha?"

"She's still in bed," Ruby replied. "I didn't waken her. I decided to let her have a wee lie-in. I thought she would be tired after being at the dance last night."

"She'll not be lying in much longer," Henry announced. "They were together last night; she's *bound* to know something."

"Come down those stairs at once," Henry shouted, banging the banister with his fist.

"It's all right Da, I'm coming now. Ma didn't waken me, but I'm up now. I'll be down in a minute."

"Make it a very short minute," he ordered.

"Do you know anything about this?" her father demanded, holding the note in front of Martha's face as she came into the kitchen rubbing her eyes with the backs of her hands.

Martha blinked as she stared at the scribbled message, and then looked at her father. It was obvious he was waiting for an answer, but she didn't have one and she didn't know what to say or what to think. Then she looked at Arthur. He was sitting with his elbows resting on the table, his head in his hands. He still had his cap on, unusual for him, because normally he always removed it the minute he came through the door. 'Poor Arthur,' Martha thought, 'he doesn't deserve this. What has come over Sammy? How could he be so cruel?'

"Tay's no use on its own at a time like this," Henry shouted at his wife as she filled the striped mugs with the strong dark liquid. "Reach me down that bottle of brandy." He nodded towards the cupboard at the side of the fireplace.

"At nine o'clock in the morning?" Ruby exclaimed. Her husband didn't reply but his silence was her answer. She fetched the bottle and brought it to the table. Henry poured a generous amount into Arthur's tea and a similar amount into his own.

Martha was still holding the crumpled piece of paper, unable to comprehend what she had read. Why hadn't Sammy said something last night? Why hadn't he told her what he was going to do? If he had, then perhaps she could have talked him out of it, or at least been given the opportunity to understand why he was leaving. Without doubt, he must have realized what this would do to his father, for he had grown up with the aftermath of his mother's actions, and now he had done the same thing.

"I asked you a question," Henry's voice startled Martha out of her reverie. "Do you know anything about this? Did you know Sammy was leaving?"

"No, I didn't, honest, I didn't. He never said anything to me about leaving. If he had, I would have tried to stop him."

It was obvious from the expression on the young girl's face that she was telling the truth.

"Get her some breakfast," Henry told her mother. "I think she's as shocked as the rest of us."

"This has been an awful day," Martha told old Ned as she patted his rough, grey back. "What are we going to do without Sammy?"
Ned nuzzled her arm as if to say, 'I'm still here, I won't leave you.'
Martha sat down on the grass beside her beloved donkey. Apart from Sammy, he was the only one she could talk to without worrying about how silly she might be sounding. Admittedly, her mother was always prepared to listen to her problems and daydreams, but she was a practical woman, who could, at all times, see the bigger picture, but that wasn't necessarily what Martha always wanted. Sometimes Martha just wanted to talk nonsense and to be silly and laugh at the impossible things she said she was going to do, and those were the times she talked to Ned, because he couldn't tell her she was crazy. Those were also the times she talked to Sammy, because he would join in on the unattainable plans and they would both laugh and call each other mad.

Martha pondered over the events of the previous evening. She was sure there had been no indication of anything unusual on Sammy's mind. He had just been his typical self, laughing and chatting to everyone. She couldn't think of anything that had been different. Admittedly he had said something about his father being a stubborn oul goat who always wanted things done his way, that his way was the only way. But Martha hadn't paid any particular attention to his comments, assuming it was just Sammy being in one of his *gernin moods* as she often told him he was in when he was having a gripe about the weather or the cows or anything else that happened to be irritating him.

The days that followed were strange for Martha as she frequently thought of something she wanted to either ask Sammy or tell him, and then suddenly remembered he wasn't there. If only he would get in touch to let them know he was all right. Martha wasn't sure if he had their phone number, as the equipment had only been installed the day before he left, but that wasn't a good enough reason for not making contact. A letter, no matter how short, would have been an enormous comfort to Arthur who was getting more convinced as each day passed that he would never see his son again. But still he waited, and hoped, and watched for the postman every morning. Unfortunately the seasons don't wait for anyone or anything, and, although Henry Sloan did all he could to help his neighbour, more man-power was needed. So Bobby Birch was hired to partly replace Sammy. Bobby wasn't the most intelligent of people, but he was a good worker and willing to tackle any tasks that were given to him, and although not always in tune, he was frequently heard singing or whistling as he went about his daily chores. It was refreshing to have someone around who sounded happy and wasn't continually complaining or trying to change the way things were being done. Things had been done the same way for years, even before Sammy had been born, so why the sudden notion to alter everything – a tractor indeed! Doesn't the younger generation have some grand ideas, Arthur mused, although he had to admit to himself that the grey four-wheeled machine Sammy had set his heart on and didn't get had probably been the final straw.

"Open it," Martha's father ordered as he handed over the letter with the Liverpool postmark.
She hesitated. Could this be from Sammy? It had to be from Sammy. Of course it was from Sammy – she'd know that spidery handwriting anywhere, and anyhow, she didn't know anyone in Liverpool, unless Willie had gone over there for a few days on some course or other. But no, that was only wishful thinking. The letter was from Sammy, there was no doubt about it. He had been

gone for more than three weeks and this was the first contact he had made. Would it be good news? Would she be able to run across the lane and tell Arthur what he would want to hear? Or would she have to tell him that Sammy wasn't coming back? But maybe Arthur had got a letter too, she thought. Maybe he already knew what she was about to find out. Maybe it would be better not to know. Maybe she should just wait and see if Sammy had written to his father too and then she wouldn't have to be the bearer of bad news. That's if it was bad news. But maybe it was good news. So many thoughts and so many possibilities were running through Martha's mind that she had forgotten her father's earlier order.

"Did you not hear what I said?" Henry's voice had taken on an edge of urgency.

Martha looked at her father, her eyes conveying a mixture of fear and hope.

"Open it," he said again.

"It's my letter," Martha said, holding it against her chin as she struggled to reach a decision as to what was the best thing to do with it.

"Are you trying to disobey me?"

"No, Da, it's just that I don't know what to do. What if Sammy's not coming back? How would I tell Arthur? Maybe I should throw it in the fire."

Martha was close to tears. Ruby came over and put her arms around her.

"Go easy, Henry, can you not see how upset she is?"

"Everybody's upset," he said, "and if I could get my hands on that Sammy boy I would happily wring his neck."

Martha couldn't hold back the tears any longer.

"Stop that snifflin'", her father told her. Then, quite unexpectedly, he took another approach to the situation which wasn't his usual way of dealing with Martha. He came across and pulled her away from her mother and put his arms around her and stroked her hair back from her tear-stained face.

"Easy on, wee M, don't distress yourself, let me sort it out."

He hadn't called her 'wee M' since she was a tiny child, and the out of the blue endearment resulted in another flood of tears.

"I do love you, daddy," she said, resting her cheek against the bib of his old dungarees, feeling the outline of the packet of cigarettes and box of matches inside the pocket. She clasped her arms around his waist and could quite happily have stayed there forever. She wanted him to tell her that he loved her too, but love wasn't a word that came easily to the tall, rugged farmer.

"It's only a letter," he said, disentangling himself from Martha's hold. "There's no need to get yourself into a pucker. Do you want me to open it for you?"

"Aye, maybe that would be a good idea," she said, then immediately changed her mind. If Sammy had wanted Henry Sloan to open his letter, then he would have sent it to Henry Sloan. But he had sent it to her, and it was her duty to deal with whatever it contained.

"No Da, I've changed my mind. It's all right. I'm OK now. I'll open it myself."

Martha sat down on the chair beside the stove and slowly ran her thumb nail below the seal, then removed the single sheet of paper.

Dear Martha, Sorry for not writing sooner but I was waiting until I got a permanent address. I've got a job on a building site and lodgings with a nice family that love anybody who comes from anywhere in Ireland. Apparently the woman of the house is a great great granddaughter of a man who was born in County Down. So how's that for a bit of good fortune. I haven't written to my Da because I'm supposing he's still mad at me, but I hope he's managing all right. I suppose your Da is helping him out. I hope you're keeping well and your Ma too. I'll write again when I have more to tell you. It's up to you whether you tell the oul fellow you have heard from me. You'll know best what to do. Best Wishes. From Sammy.

"Well?" Her father urged.

"He's all right; he's got a job and lodgings."

"And?"

"I don't know what to do. I don't know what to tell Arthur or what not to tell him."

She hesitated for a few seconds, and then reached the letter to her father. "Take it," she said, "and do whatever you think is right."

He scanned it briefly to get an overall insight into its contents, and then read it again, slowly this time as if he was digesting every single word.

"I'll let Arthur know that he's all right," Henry said, folding the letter and putting it in his pocket.

Martha and her mother waited anxiously, wondering what way Henry would broach the subject of Sammy without causing the other man too much distress.

Finally they saw the two men coming across the lane, both heads drooped and their hands pushed deep into their pockets.

"Are you all right?" Ruby asked Arthur as soon as they came in, and then indicated for him to take a seat at the fire.

"I'll cope," he replied, "I'll have to cope; there's nothing else I *can* do."

"Can I have the letter back please?" Martha asked her father.

He gave it to her without comment and she immediately sat down at the end of the table with a pen and a writing pad. She started to write and never halted until she was signing her name at the bottom. It was obvious that whatever Martha had to say didn't need too much consideration. She placed it in an envelope, licked the gummed section of the flap and stuck it down, then banged the edge with the side of her hand. She copied the address from the top of Sammy's letter, took a stamp from the bowl of miscellaneous objects that sat on the window sill and stuck it on. Then she reached across the table and placed her completed task against the window pane.

"I'll put it there," she said to her father, "so as the postman will see it in the morning in case you miss him."

Sleep eluded Martha for most of the night as she tossed and turned, wondering what Sammy would think when he got her letter. She had been totally honest in everything she had written and didn't regret a single word of it. She had told him of the distress he had caused his father. She also informed him that the next letter he decided to write, should be sent to the man who was missing him, the man who was doing his best to cope without him. She didn't tell him that Bobby Birch was helping out. She thought it best to let him think that his father was having too much to do, and maybe that would poke at his conscience and make him come home. She finished off by saying that if he couldn't write to her to say he was coming back, then to not bother writing at all.

His letters sat on the mantelpiece, behind the clock, opened and read but unanswered. There were so many things she would like to tell him, but she was still angry - angry that he had gone away without telling her and angry that he still hadn't come back.

"How long are you going to hold out?" Ruby asked.

"Sorry, Ma, what was that you said? I wasn't listening."

"You were miles away," her mother said. "Why don't you write to him? You know you want to."

"I do not indeed!" Martha retorted, tearing her gaze away from the pile of correspondence that had been occupying her thoughts. "There is no way I am going to waste ink writing to Sammy McCracken. He can stay in England till the desert freezes." Then she went into a rant about how she told him in her one and only letter that she didn't want to hear from him unless he was writing to say he was coming home, but he was such a stubborn big lump that he kept writing anyway, and she knew he was doing it just to annoy her and to let her know that he wouldn't be told.

"Well, at least he's writing to his father now," Ruby said, "and I think from what Arthur has been saying that they're getting over whatever wee tiff caused the problem, so maybe Sammy will be back sooner than you think."

"I hope so, for his father's sake."

"*Only* for his father's sake?"

"Oh, all right," Martha conceded, "I wish he was home too for I miss the company. I was always used to him being around and it seems strange without him, but I wouldn't give him the satisfaction of knowing that."

"Would it be possible that you have a wee liking for Sammy?" her mother inquired.

Martha looked genuinely surprised at her mother's implication.

"Ugh Ma! That remark doesn't even deserve an answer. Sure Sammy is more like a brother than even a neighbour. Wasn't he practically reared in this house. You were as good to him as his own mother could ever have been."

"I felt sorry for the wee soul," Ruby sighed. "According to your granny, it was the most pitiful sight she had ever seen. Poor Arthur standing in the middle of this kitchen with the good bye letter still clutched in his hand, and wee Sammy looking all puzzled because he couldn't understand what was going on."

"Where were you that day?" Martha asked.

"I was upstairs holding a new born baby."

"She left the same day as I was born?"

"The very same, although, as far as I know, she was gone an hour or two before you arrived. Yes, it was quite a day," Ruby continued. "I suppose the folk in the village didn't know which topic to discuss first, although I would be surprised if the runaway wife didn't take priority over a new birth."

71

Her mother was right, Martha admitted to herself during the wee small hours when sleep was eluding her once again. She *did* want to write to Sammy. She wanted to tell him that even with her father's help and Bobby Birch's efforts his father still had to hire two casual workers off the dole to get the harvest in before the weather broke. She wanted to tell him that it wasn't fair because he should be at home where he belonged, instead of posing around Liverpool acting the toff (the fact that he was labouring on a building site didn't impress Martha.)

She wanted to tell him about the folk who came into the shop and said, "Suppose there's no word of Sammy coming home?" and "Sammy's not back yet?" Comments that were made in the hope that she would either confirm or deny them, assuming she would know all the details. Martha also wanted to let him know that she was leaving that job at the end of the month and going to work for Doctor McGoldrick, just to do a bit of cleaning in the house, and it was only part time, just similar hours to what she was doing in the shop. She wanted to know what he thought about her decision. Was she doing the right thing or was she making a mistake? She had been talking to Jean and Mary the other day and they were telling her that they were getting a start in Gallagher's cigarette factory at Lisnafillan. They said they were looking forward to it for they thought they would have a lot of fun with the confusion they would create being twins. Maybe she should try for a job there too, but it was a very early start and she would have to go on the bicycle to the village to get the bus. All these decisions! She needed Sammy's advice – she needed Sammy's opinion. She could ask her mother or father what they thought she should do, but she knew what their answers would be, so what was the point? Her mother would say, "Whatever you think is best, whatever makes you happy." And her father would make some comment about how she didn't know her own mind from one minute to the next. It was Sammy's opinion she wanted. Sammy always told her the truth whether she liked it or not. Yes, she definitely needed and wanted

Sammy's advice. She definitely wanted Sammy to come home for she felt lost without him. But there was nothing that would persuade her to go back on her word. She was not going to write to him. He could send her as many letters as he wanted to but she would not relent. She could be as stubborn as he was.

If only she had known that Arthur was unwittingly keeping Sammy up to date with current events. The casual queries of 'What's Martha up to these days?' always resulted in his father telling him all he needed to know, including the fact that Martha appeared to be missing him. Arthur hoped that little bit of news might encourage Sammy to come home. So far Arthur hadn't asked him if, or when, he might return, thinking it was better not to put too much pressure on him in case it would strengthen his resolve to stay away. The only incentive he had offered was to make a casual remark that Henry Sloan was talking about getting a tractor and maybe it would be a good idea, for eventually everybody had to move with the times.

It was one of those wee jobs that Arthur had done many times before. He was repairing loose bits of zinc on the barn roof before the arrival of the inevitable winter gales. He thought the ladder was secure. Fortunately Ruby heard his cries for help when she went to bring in the washing.

The ambulance arrived in record time and whisked Arthur off to the Waveney Hospital, where it was confirmed that he had broken his leg, and, in spite of all his protests, he had to finally accept the fact that a hospital bed was going to be his home for the next few days, if not weeks, depending on his progress.

Martha was determined that she wouldn't write to Sammy, but desperate situations call for desperate actions.

Dear Sammy, Your father is in hospital with a broken leg. I think it's time you came home. Martha.

Sammy was on the next boat after receiving Martha's letter. Now life could get back to normal.

ANOTHER BIRTHDAY 1951

"Twenty one is a really important birthday," Martha said to her father, coming to his rescue when he was struggling to attach a collar stud.

"Hurry up, girl," he told her. "I haven't got all night."

"If *you* hadn't been in such a hurry today you wouldn't have banged your thumb with the hammer," Martha retorted, "and you wouldn't have that bandage getting in your way, so just have patience and sit at peace."

Ruby held her breath as she waited for the inevitable onslaught. She knew her husband didn't like to be challenged, but to her surprise he just muttered something about how accidents will happen.

"So. what about my birthday?" Martha asked again, patting his collar into place.

"To hear you prattlin' on you'd think nobody ever had a birthday before," he said, pulling on his checked sports coat as he walked across the kitchen to view his image in the mirror that hung on the back wall. He pulled a comb from his top pocket and combed his hair. He had good hair – strong and thick and dark, with streaks of grey starting to show at the temples. He viewed his reflection and seemed content with what he saw, then placed his cap on his head, pulling the peak forward, then from side to side until it felt comfortable.

"But Da, this one is special." she continued. "It's twenty one, it's sort of different, the key to the door and all that sort of thing."

"What do you need a key for?" he asked, winking at his wife behind Martha's back. "Sure the door is never locked except at bedtime."

"I know that, but it's still, well sort of, you know what I mean, sort of a land-mark and I'd like it to be special – maybe a party… or…something."

"A party? What put that silly idea into your head?"

"It's not silly, it's, oh I don't know what it is, but I just know that it's what I would like."

"Well, I haven't time for all that fool talk now," he said. "You know it's lodge night and I'm already late and this bandage is getting slack. Go and get another bit of thread."

After he had gone the two women sat down, either side of the big black range, to savour their cups of tea and a slice each of the oven loaf that Ruby had baked earlier in the day.

"I'm fed up and browned off and scunnered!" Martha declared. "That man treats me like a two year old when I want something for myself, but he never forgets how old I am when he wants me to help him in the evenings and on a Saturday."

"I know, darling, but that's just your Da. It's the way he is. There's nothing in his mind except the farm. The farm comes before anything else."

"But it's not fair," Martha declared, putting strong emphasis on each individual word. She knew she sounded childish – these were the same words she had uttered on the morning of her grandfather's funeral. They didn't alter anything then and they couldn't alter anything now.

For the next few minutes mother and daughter sipped their tea in silence.

"If you could have any wish granted for your birthday what would it be?"

Martha was so engrossed in her own thoughts that her mother's question startled her and she couldn't think of an immediate answer.

"There must be something, apart from a key to an open door," Ruby smiled, trying to bring humour to the situation.

"Lots of things," Martha said.

"Name one," her mother suggested.

"I'd like to do something that my father would approve of, something that would really make him proud of me."

"But he is proud of you. Why wouldn't he be? You're a lovely young woman."

"But I never seem to do anything that pleases him. He didn't like it when I was working in the shop; he said I would be listening to gossip all day, and he didn't like it when I was working for Doctor McGoldrick; he said I would be poking into peoples' private business. What he thought I would find out while cleaning the house or answering a few phone calls beats me, but I think he just doesn't like the doctor anyway. Sometimes I think he blames him for delivering a girl instead of a boy."

"Don't talk such nonsense; you know your father loves you."

"But he'd love me more if I was a boy, a big strong boy like Sammy, a boy who would continually talk about farming. Sometimes I think he would rather have Sammy than me, for they're always talking and sharing opinions about the farm and the cows and everything. They're even away together the night."

Ruby started to laugh. "Oh, Martha, you really have got yourself into a right pucker. They haven't gone out together and left poor wee you behind. Your Da has gone to a lodge meeting with Sammy and his father."

"I suppose," was all Martha could say.

"More tea?" Ruby asked, lifting the brown enamel pot from the back of the stove.

Martha nodded. "He doesn't like me working in Gallaghers' you know. What I could be doing wrong there I don't know, although, I must admit, I don't like working there either."

"Why?"

"The smell can be a bit overpowering and the noise is deafening, and sometimes I feel hemmed in, for I can't see out. I don't even know when the sun's shining or when it's raining."

"I didn't know you were feeling like that. Why didn't you tell me before?"

"Ugh Ma, you know me, I don't like giving in, and anyway, what's the use of complaining? It wouldn't change anything."

"You don't want to prove your father right, that's your problem. Come on, admit it."

"Well….Maybe…."

Ruby started to laugh. "What are we going to do with you?"

"No idea," was the reply, as both women held up their cups and said, "Cheers."

In spite of the humour that had crept into their conversation, Ruby felt sure that Martha had other things on her mind apart from her place of employment.

Ruby was right – there was one particular thing on Martha's mind that she didn't know how to go about suggesting to her parents, but it was something that she wanted above all else. And she felt certain that he wanted the same. The letters with the veiled hints about hoping to see everyone soon, and how he probably wouldn't recognize Martha now, seemed to go unnoticed by both parents, but it was obvious to Martha. Willie Rossborough hadn't forgotten the people he had become so fond of during his brief stay during the war, and was hoping to be invited back to Daisy Farm for a visit. Martha thought about how often he had written during the intervening years, always keeping them up to date with all the major events in his life, the most exciting being his acceptance into Queen's University where he was studying to be a doctor. Although he had only ever sent one note specially addressed to Martha, she still felt that the letters that included everyone were still in some way meant more for her. Just a silly romantic notion, she often told herself. After all, they had only been children and their friendship had been brief. Recalling that friendship, she smiled when she thought about the day he had asked her to marry him. Such childish innocence, but if they were to meet again, who knows what might happen? Daydreaming again, she chided herself and

78

decided she'd probably just been reading too many Ruby M. Ayres novels. But perhaps her daydreaming was the reason she never got romantically involved with any of the local lads who showed more than a passing interest in the girl who could be friendly while still making it obvious that she wasn't attracted to any of them. So eventually, one by one, they gave up hope of ever being able to call her their girlfriend, assuming Sammy was her special someone. A natural assumption, because no matter where Martha went, Sammy was usually somewhere close by. But it wasn't Sammy's company she was thinking of to be her special birthday treat. First on her list was a party, with a few of her childhood friends, which of course included Sammy, and then the highlight of the evening would be Willie. It would be great to see him again – it would be like old times. She wondered if he still liked jelly babies or a game of Snakes and Ladders. Extremely unlikely, she decided, as neither would be considered essential in the life of a young student doctor. But it would be interesting to see what he looked like now. Would he still look the same or would he have changed so much that she wouldn't recognize him? Would he still be as fond of the countryside as he used to be, or would he have become a city boy again with city ways and attitudes? Maybe she wouldn't even like him now. Maybe he had become what Nancy Shaw always called Victoria Burnside, 'a right wee upstart,' but it would be exciting finding out and what could be a better time than a twenty first birthday party?

"Would you really like to have a party?" Ruby asked in a sudden change of conversation.

"Of course I would!"

"And who would you like to invite to this party?"

"Everybody!" Martha giggled, then continued. "What I would really like is maybe not exactly a party, more of a get together with some of my friends from school days and you and Da and Arthur and Sammy and maybe even mention it to Willie when you're answering his next letter."

"Willie?" Ruth looked at her daughter over the rim of her cup.

"Aye," Martha replied. "Sometimes I think he's dropping hints about wanting to come back for a visit for he has often remarked in his letters about how there are times he just stays at Queen's during breaks because it takes so long to travel down South to his Auntie's, so maybe what he's really saying is that he would like to come here for a change."

"I suppose you could be right," Ruby said. "I'll mention it to your Da and hear what he thinks."

"He could come on the train and Tam Lorimer could meet him at the station and he could sleep in his old room. Of course it would have to be well aired for nobody has used that room since the war ended."

"So you have it all worked out," Ruby said, a smile forming at the sides of her mouth.

"Well, I suppose it's just a matter of common sense. By the time the party would be over the last train would have gone."

Martha had chatted excitedly since getting into Tam's taxi about how it would be like old times having Willie around the house for the next few days and how surprised she was that her father had agreed to the whole thing.

"I could hardly believe my ears," she said, "when Da told me he had sorted it out with the committee to let us have a party in the hall. It's just not like him because he's usually so involved with farming things that he never thinks about anything else."

"Your Da obviously wants you to enjoy your special birthday," Tam managed to remark before Martha went on to inform him that everyone would be welcome, any one could drop in. Danny McAuley and Matt Hamilton were providing the music as they usually did at all village functions, and her Ma was baking a cake and Nancy Shaw was going to help with the making of the sandwiches. There was no need for an invitation, although of course he was especially invited, along with Sammy and his father and Jean and Mary and Bobby and Davy.

"Willie wrote by return post," she said, "as soon as he got Ma's letter to tell him about my birthday and to invite him to stay for a few days, so I had been right all along. I knew he had been dropping hints about coming back, but neither Ma nor Da seemed to catch on."

"Ah well," Tam said, "sometimes these things have a way of working themselves out, but we're here in good time anyway."

"There he is! That's got to be him, or is it?"

Martha was out of the car in a flash.

"You have to come with me," she pleaded, "in case it's not him."

Tam did as he was asked, for he was also looking forward to seeing Willie again, although he found it hard to believe that the wee lad who came to the village as an evacuee in 1941 was now a student doctor. Where had the time gone?

Tam looked in the direction Martha was pointing.

"Is it him?" Martha gripped Tam's arm. "Maybe it's not - maybe it's just somebody who looks like what I think he will look like."

Tam wished that it *wasn't* him. Wished he was somewhere else amongst the crowd that was still spilling out of the carriages - wished he was *anywhere*, except walking towards them with Victoria Burnside clinging to his arm. He could feel Martha's grip tightening – could feel the tension that was surging through her, for it was a well known fact that, although they were part of the same group of children who had spent lots of their free time together, Martha didn't particularly seek out Victoria's company. Victoria always thought she was a cut above the others because her father was a solicitor. Martha thought she was a pain in the back side and hadn't hesitated to tell her so on several occasions.

"Martha!" Victoria gushed. "How good to see you again."

Martha didn't reply, so Victoria continued, "This is Willie. You remember Willie, our *little* friend from the war years?"

Funny how the word *wee* turns into little when you spend a while in the city, Martha mused.

Willie's face couldn't have looked sterner if it had been carved out of stone.

"Of course Martha remembers me," Willie said as he shrugged Victoria's hand off his arm and reached out for Martha. "And I remember her," he added.

Martha went willingly into his outstretched arms as she looked up at the handsome face now wreathed in smiles.

"Welcome back," she said.

"Should that not be *welcome home*," he said, and kissed the top of her head.

"Welcome home," she whispered into the softness of his tweed sports coat.

If Tam had been asked to describe those few seconds, he could have answered with one word – magic! But not to be outdone by the poignant reunion, Victoria prattled on, directing her comments to Tam.

"If we had known sooner then there would have been no need for you to come, because Willie could have got a lift with Daddy and me." A well manicured finger pointed in the direction of the big black shiny car where Daddy sat smoking a cigar. Tam ignored her comment as he shook Willie's hand. Willie's other hand stayed on Martha's shoulder.

"Good to see you again, lad."

"Good to see you again too," Willie replied, "and I can't wait to see the village. I hope it hasn't changed too much."

"You'll still recognize it," Tam chuckled. "There's not too much changes in our wee part of the world."

Realizing she was being left out of the conversation, and with a false smile pasted across her thin lips Victoria said, "OK folks, got to go, mustn't keep Daddy waiting."

"Cheerio then," Tam said. Martha and Willie were still smiling at each other. But Victoria wasn't the sort of girl who liked to be ignored.

"Oh, by the way," she said, turning to look at Willie, "if you want a change of lodgings you can always come to our house – we have *loads* of room."

No one commented on her suggestion. Daddy honked the horn and the spiteful girl walked away, swinging her hips in what Martha assumed she thought was a provocative manner. Martha thought she looked ridiculous.

Back at Daisy Farm Ruby had prepared an Ulster fry. Although such meals were more common for a winter breakfast, she knew Willie would appreciate it at tea time. Willie had always loved a fry, and anyhow, it was something that wouldn't spoil while keeping warm in the oven of the big black stove as she wasn't sure what time they would get back.

Tam's car pulled into the yard. It was quite a reunion. Ruby was delighted to see Willie and couldn't believe how tall he had grown and wanted to hear all his news, but not until he had a good meal inside him, for she was sure young people didn't eat enough of the right food when they were at University. Willie agreed, and said he had been looking forward to a farl of her home-baked fadge ever since he got the invitation to come and visit. Martha could see that the compliment pleased her mother. Poor Ma, she thought, she never gets any praise for anything, no matter how much she does.

Tam was invited to stay.

"There's plenty for everyone," Ruby said, swinging open the oven door. "You must be starving with hunger by now, for you've been gone for ages."

Tam knew his missus would probably have something keeping warm in their oven too, but it would be something healthy; worse still, it wouldn't be in the oven at all, it would be a salad. He could picture it now, everything on the plate would be green except for a tomato and half a hard boiled egg, and it would be covered with an upside down plate to keep it clean, and it would be sitting on the marble slab in the back kitchen to keep it cool. His better half had decided he was putting on too much weight. Apparently she had been reading an article in some magazine about a man who had put on a lot of weight and he had taken a heart attack. Tam knew several thin people who had taken heart attacks but that argument didn't hold up against the evidence of the printed word.

"It smells good," Tam said, sitting down at the big farmhouse table. "Thanks very much, Ruby, I'm partial to a bit of a fry now and again."

"Where's Henry?" Willie inquired as he sat down on the chair beside Tam.

"He went over to Arthur's about something, but he said to ring the bell as soon as you got here," Ruby replied. "So I was keeping an eye out for you and I rang it the second I saw the car turning in at the end of the lane."

"So you still use the big bell," Willie said, his face beaming with the memory of the times its tones had summoned them to return to the house, and the many times they chose to ignore its first command because they were having so much fun. But they always obeyed the second ring – it was the definite order. It meant your food is getting cold, or it's time for supper and then bed.

"Oh, couldn't do without the old bell," Ruby declared, as Henry walked in the door, with Arthur and Sammy following close behind.

"See what I mean," she said, nodding in their direction. "It works every time."

There followed the inevitable greetings and eventually everyone settled at the table, including Sammy and his father. Ruby had invited them earlier in the day for she thought it would be nice for Willie to have a real get-together with the folks he had known, and she had cooked accordingly plus a bit extra – just in case.

Martha observed the gathering of the people she knew so well. They were all taking a great interest in Willie's decision to become a doctor. He explained that, although no one was able to save his parents when Belfast was bombed, there were many others still alive because of the skills of the doctors and nurses, and that was what had inspired him to pursue a career in the medical profession – he simply wanted to save lives. Sammy didn't appear to be impressed. Martha assumed that if Sammy had got the education and the opportunity he would probably have been a vet. But the object of Martha's main observation was Willie. He had changed – that was to be expected. Gone was the unruly windswept fair mane, now replaced with a neat tidy hair cut, and gone was the wee boy who sat in that same chair all those years ago, doing his homework while she sat at the other side doing hers. Now he was replaced by a very handsome young man who became aware of her scrutiny as he looked across and caught her gaze, and for a brief second the wee boy was back with that same bright smile that seemed to come from within and light up his face and his big brown eyes.

In the midst of all the friendly conversation, Tam Lorimer was also observing the assembled gathering and drawing a few conclusions of his own. He knew it was assumed by many that Sammy and Martha belonged together, but Tam had his doubts. Admittedly it would be a natural progression – the farmer's daughter and the farmer's son. They had grown up together and they knew each other so well. There would be no unpleasant surprises, not for Sammy anyway, for Martha was a good honest girl. What you saw with Martha was what you got. But what Tam had never seen before was Martha looking at Sammy the way she looked at Willie, and it was obvious that Willie was looking at Martha the same way. But what about his train journey with the notorious Victoria Burnside? In Tam's opinion, Willie didn't appear to be too pleased with her company, but Victoria was known for her selfish and scheming ways and what Victoria wanted, Victoria usually got.

Heaven forbid, Tam thought, that the self-centered wee twerp would ever get her clutches into the unsuspecting Willie. Then he silently chided himself for pondering the matter. After all, it was none of his business, but he just hoped everything would turn out all right for everyone concerned.

Then, as if Martha had been reading his thoughts, she enquired.

"Is Victoria in your part of the college?"

It was obvious the question was meant for Willie, although Martha never lifted her gaze from the piece of bread she was placing the prongs of her fork into.

"No," was Willie's reply. "She's studying law. She said something about wanting to be like *Daddy*."

Willie put strong emphasis on the word Daddy, and Martha seemed content with his reply, although Tam had a feeling that, before long, Martha would want to know more, such as how they came to be on the same train on the same day and at the same time.

Sammy unwittingly gave her the opportunity to keep the conversation exactly where she wanted it to be – firmly fixed around Victoria, as he remarked, "I hear they're leaving the area."

"Who is?"

Arthur had obviously lost interest in what was being said.

"The Burnsides," Sammy informed him. "Victoria's mother and father."

"Who told you that?" his father wanted to know.

Sammy wasn't completely sure, as it had only been some snippet of chat he had overheard in the bar the previous Saturday night, and when Henry remarked, "It's not all gospel that's quoted in Murphy's," there was no one to contradict him. It could quite easily have been the end of the discussion only for Martha's quick thinking.

"If they go, Davy won't be too well pleased," she said.

"Why not?" Sammy inquired.

"Davy's obsessed with Victoria," Martha informed him. "Don't tell me you don't know?"

"Never noticed," Sammy shrugged.

"Even when we were children," Martha continued, "he always took her part when the rest of us were fed up with her trying to get her own way and then huffing if she didn't."

"Never noticed," Sammy said again, "and even if he does have a notion of her, then her people moving away won't make that much difference, for I don't think she comes home that often anyway."

Willie didn't enter into the conversation and Martha couldn't make her mind up if that was a good sign or a bad one, but decided to keep on with the subject to see what the outcome would be.

"Suppose you're right Sammy," Martha conceded, "for I hadn't seen her in ages until today. Of course, with me not being in the shop now I'm a wee bit out of touch with the day to day happenings in the village."

"Did she say anything to you about her folks moving?"

This question was directed to Willie.

"No, she never mentioned it," Willie replied, apparently more interested in dipping the end of a sausage into the soft yolk of his fried egg.

Did his answer mean she never mentioned her folks any time they were together, Martha wondered, or did it mean she didn't mention them today when they had only met by chance?

"Why the sudden interest in Victoria Burnside?" Henry asked. "I thought you weren't all that fond of her."

"I'm just thinking about Davy."

Tam had difficulty keeping a straight face. For all Martha's straight- forward, honest ways she could be quite cunning, and he couldn't help wondering how far, or how long she was going to pursue the subject until she got whatever information she was looking for.

"I don't think Davy stands much of a chance anyway," Willie announced.

"Has she somebody else in her eye?" Sammy wanted to know.

Martha got the distinct impression that he thought Willie was the 'somebody else' and seemed quite pleased with the prospect if the smile on his face was anything to go by.

"Of course she has," Willie replied.

Martha held her breath but Sammy kept smiling and Willie continued, "One of the fellows who attends the same lectures as me."

Perhaps that was the explanation, Martha thought. Maybe Willie had commented to this chap about his plans for the weekend and he had innocently passed on the information to Victoria, and, discovering there was going to be a party, she had decided to pick that weekend to come home, and of course travelling with Willie would be an added bonus. Tam had reached the same conclusion, but like Martha he knew it was best not to comment.

"It must be serious then," Sammy commented.

"It might be," Willie said, "although I get the impression that she is keener than he is."

"More tea?" Ruby asked.

The subject of Victoria was closed and the conversation turned to other matters. Willie wanted to hear all about the farm and the animals and Martha's job in Gallaghers'. Henry readily filled him in on all aspects of farming, but when it came to discussing Martha's place of employment she didn't have much to say except that the pay was good but the work was very repetitive and boring, but she liked the long weekends because they got off early on a Friday. Then she added, "If I fall asleep half way through the party tonight you can blame the early start this morning."

"A bucket of cold water would soon cure that," Sammy threatened.

"Don't even think about it," she warned.

Then Willie inquired about Ned, but a visit to the old donkey would have to wait until the next day, because, as Ruby said, 'time was marching on' and they would have to think about getting ready for the big event in the hall and the cake with the twenty one candles.

"Oh Ma, you must be worn out. You look exhausted," Martha declared as her mother came through from the tiny kitchen at the back of the hall with another plate of sandwiches.

"I'm enjoying every minute of it," her mother replied. "It's great to have a get together like this and everyone has been so kind. Nearly every woman who has come through that door has brought either buns or biscuits, and Mary and Jean's mother brought a loaf of egg and onion sandwiches."

It was the best night Martha could ever remember having. All her friends were there, plus Victoria Burnside, although she wasn't quite sure what category she would put her in, but, nevertheless, everyone seemed to be in a good mood. Even her father appeared to be enjoying himself as he moved through the crowd, stopping to chat to several people as he went. Martha assumed their conversation would be about the crops, and their possible success or failure depending on the weather. But she got quite a surprise when he made his way to the kitchen, returning seconds later carrying her birthday cake and announcing, "Quiet everybody while this special wee girl of mine makes a wish and blows these candles out. That's if she has enough puff left after all the running around she has been doing all day."

That met with a huge cheer and a round of applause as he placed the cake on a small table in the centre of the floor. Martha was quite overcome by it all. This wasn't the way her father normally behaved and she didn't quite know how to react. In fact, she wasn't even sure how she felt. Everyone started to clap and kept repeating "blow, blow, blow." She could feel her cheeks going red with embarrassment and she was wavering between nervous laughter and tears of joy as she leaned over the flickering candles and made her secret wish.

"Now I think you'll need this," Sammy said as he reached her a knife.

She hadn't noticed him approaching, but she was glad he did. She always felt safe when Sammy was nearby – felt confident and able to cope with any situation just so long as he was there.

"Can I have a candle for a keepsake?"

Martha turned as Willie put his hand on her shoulder.

"Of course you can," she said, pulling one out of the pink icing and reaching it to him. "It'll come in handy if you ever have a power cut at the University."

With the cake cutting event over and all cups empty, Bobby Birch, the self appointed M.C. for the evening, got up on the small stage and announced that it was time for a few party games and decided 'The Farmer Wants a Wife' would be a good one to start with.

"Everybody in a big circle," he shouted, "and then push somebody into the middle."

There followed a lot of laughter as several people rushed onto the floor holding tight to the next person's hand, determined that they were not going to be the first farmer in the circle. More laughter ensued as additional folk were dragged reluctantly to join the others, including Martha's parents. Wee Davy, as he was always referred to, was the farmer as the music started up, with Bobby singing as loud as his vocal chords would allow, to make sure that everybody understood what part of the game they were in.

The farmer wants a wife, the farmer wants a wife, hey oh my dearie oh, the farmer wants a wife.

Davy chose Victoria. No surprise there!

The wife wants a child, the wife wants a child, hey oh, my dearie oh, the wife wants a child.

Victoria Chose Willie. No surprise there either.

The child wants a nurse, the child wants a nurse, hey oh my dearie oh, the child wants a nurse.

Willie chose Martha. Victoria's face went white.

The nurse wants a dog. The nurse wants a dog, hey oh my dearie oh, the nurse wants a dog.

Martha chose Sammy. Sammy seemed pleased.

The dog wants a bone, the dog wants a bone, hey oh my dearie oh, the dog wants a bone

Sammy chose Ruby. Martha had never seen her mother look as happy as the usual chorus of 'and the bone is left alone' followed, leaving Ruby in the middle as the farmer, and it all started up again.

The farmer wants a wife, the farmer wants a wife, etc. etc.

Who will she pick? Martha wondered in those few seconds where it is customary for the farmer to keep everyone guessing for as long as possible. When she chose Henry everybody went 'Ahhh' resulting in hoots of laughter, and when *he* in turn chose Martha, she felt as if her heart was going to burst with happiness.

The fun and games continued, with Bobby deciding that there should be the occasional waltz or quick step thrown in.

"Are you getting up?" Bobby asked Martha, after jumping off the stage the minute the music started.

Martha hesitated because her father didn't know she could dance, so any indication that she had the slightest knowledge of the procedure could really put the cat amongst the pigeons and ruin the whole night. Bobby didn't appear to notice her reluctance as he caught her hand and announced, "The birthday girl has to dance with the first man who asks her."

Bobby always made up his own rules as he went along. But Martha needn't have worried about her father's opinion of her dancing skills, as Bobby's translation of a Quick Step was to rush around the floor as quickly as possible with little regard for the rhythm of the music. When that dance was finished he rushed back to the stage and Martha breathed a sigh of relief.

"I think we'll have a waltz now," he announced, and before one note of music was played Henry said to Martha, "You'll have to dance this one with me."

"But Da, you know I…."

"I know you can," he said and led her onto the floor to the strains of 'On top of Old Smokey'.

Martha was gobsmacked. How did he know? Or was he just guessing?

Would he be angry tomorrow when the party mood was over? Would he accuse her of deceiving him? But there was no point in pretending, so she matched his steps to every beat of the music as he twirled her around the floor. She never knew he could dance, she had never even thought to ask. He was just her father – the man who owned the farm – the man who had very little to say unless it was necessary, and then he would either agree or disagree depending on the circumstances. When the music stopped he smiled down at his mystified daughter and said, "You're a quick learner." Martha couldn't be sure if he meant it, or was trying to tell her that she couldn't fool him. But with the effort he was making to keep from laughing she decided it was the latter.

"This next part of the dance will be a general 'Excuse me,'" Bobby stated as the music started up again. The Tennessee waltz this time – Martha's favourite.

"Excuse me," the young man said, tapping Henry on the shoulder and reaching for Martha.

"No problem," Henry said, "for this is all getting a bit too much for an oul' boy like me."

Martha didn't hear the last of her father's comment as she drifted into Willie's arms.

Tam Lorimer wasn't a dancer, but he loved music and liked to see people enjoying themselves, especially the young folk. So between other fares to different locations around the country he stopped off at the hall to see how the party was going. In his estimation everyone was having a good time apart from Victoria Burnside and Sammy McCracken. It was obvious that Sammy was feeling a bit deserted as Martha was spending most of her time with Willie, and Victoria appeared to be having the same problem. But, never one to miss an opportunity, when Bobby announced A Lady's Choice, Victoria was across the floor like a sheet of lightning to ask Willie to dance. Martha asked her father and Sammy still didn't look pleased.

Tam caught part of Victoria's comment as she and Willie danced past where he was standing, 'Sammy and Martha are made for each other and it's natural that they will..'

The little minx, Tam thought, for although he didn't hear the rest of the sentence he knew what it would be. Then he remembered a comment his grandmother had made when he, as a teenager, had arrived home with a very unsuitable potential girlfriend. 'All the turf in the bog wouldn't warm me to her.' Tam smiled at the memory – she was a wise old bird, his granny, and suddenly he understood what she had meant.

AFTER THE PARTY

Martha couldn't sleep. Every time she closed her eyes they popped open again in spite of her efforts to keep them shut. It was the sounds from the other room that she couldn't ignore - the creaking of the floorboards as Willie tiptoed across the floor trying not to wake her parents who had left the party early, declaring that late nights were only for the young. Then further creaking as he lowered himself into the familiar bed that he had spent so many comfortable nights in when he was just a boy. Willie sighed, a contented sigh. It was good to be back among the folks he had known, and everyone seemed pleased to see him again, although he had some doubts about Sammy. Maybe Victoria was right, maybe there *was* an understanding between him and Martha, but from past experience of Victoria's tales, they weren't always the most reliable – not like Martha. Anything Martha said could be relied upon at all times regardless of the outcome. He hoped Victoria was mistaken and that she had got the wrong impression and was adding two and two and probably getting six. Willie liked Martha. He liked her a lot. Her big green eyes and ready smile had been something he had never been able to forget. Ever since the evening his Auntie and her husband had taken him to the safety of County Cavan there had never been a day where he didn't think about her. First as the wee friend he had spent so many happy times with, and then, as he got older, he pondered the possibility that they could be something more. The memory of the time he had asked her to marry him and she had accepted, often brought a smile to his face. But that was the evening they had run down the hill as happy, carefree children to be met with the news that his mother and father wouldn't be coming to take him home when the war would be over. If only he had got to stay on Daisy Farm, but life is full of 'if only' as Willie had discovered, when he recalled how his parents had met their death on the streets of war-torn Belfast. If only they had got to the shelter in time. If only they had decided to visit the country that day. If only, if only. But Willie had learned to accept that you can't bring back a single second that has gone. If it was possible, he knew he would bring back those precious minutes he had spent with Martha in his arms as they danced around the hall. But would she ever be his? That was the big question. All this uncertainty was hard to cope with. He wondered if perhaps he should ask her if she intended marrying Sammy, and then he would know one way or the other. It would be better than wondering. But what if she told him she was in love with Sammy and had set a date for their wedding? And what would he do if she asked him to be best man? Oh no, that scenario didn't bear thinking about. He'd have to put that image out of his head if he was ever going to get any sleep. He switched off the bedside light and drew the covers up to his chin. The bed creaked again. Martha knew he was still awake and the memories came flooding back. She decided to do what she had always done when they were children. She reached above her headboard and banged her hand against the wall.

"Are you awake?"

"I am now."

He remembered!!

She giggled and shouted, "Go to sleep."

"Night night," he called.

"Night night," she replied, "God Bless."

"God Bless," he repeated. "See you in the morning."

"See you in the morning," she said.

Willie felt he had come home. He smiled and snuggled further below the bedclothes as sleep was starting to claim him.

Martha smiled and snuggled further below her bedclothes, but sleep still evaded *her* as she recalled the feel of his arms around her, the scent of his after shave and the way he smiled down at her. Willie was home at last.

Saturday morning and afternoon flew past with Willie enjoying a trip into the village, a walk through the fields, a visit with old Ned and savouring the mouth-watering meals that Martha's mother prepared. Martha was always there by his side, but so was Sammy, and Saturday evening was no exception.

"I was down in the far field checking on the sheep," Sammy informed them, "so I thought I'd call in and see how everybody was doing. That's a cool one," he continued, rubbing his hands together, and then holding them over the top of the range. "That weather would cut you."

"Aye, it's hardy enough," Henry agreed.

When the topic of the weather for that day, and what was expected for the rest of the week, had been exhausted, Sammy turned to Willie and asked, "What are you going to do with the rest of your evening?"

Willie said he was considering going to the pictures in Ballymena. Sammy said that was a good idea and inquired about what was on.

Willie consulted the Observer and discovered that the war time classic 'Mrs Miniver' starring Greer Garson and Walter Pigeon was showing in the State.

"I've heard a lot of talk about that film," Sammy said. "I think it was made some time during the war, but I've never seen it. It must be back by popular demand, as they say, so I'll give my Da a shout and make sure he has nothing urgent lined up for me to do this evening and then we'll be on our way."

"Well, actually," Willie said, "I intended taking Martha."

"Aye, surely, why not?" said Sammy. "We daren't leave the wee scallywag behind or she'd never forgive us."

"Just talk about me as if I'm not here," Martha said, her cheeks pink with a mixture of emotions. Pleased that Willie wanted to take her out; irritated that Sammy was going too, then feeling guilty for not wanting him there.

"Will we walk into the village and get the bus?" Sammy asked. "Or should we get Tam Lorimer to take us?"

"Whatever you think best," Willie told him. "I'll leave that to you."

"No, no, it's up to you - after all, you're the visitor."

"It doesn't make my opinion any more important," Willie stated.

It was obvious to Martha that Willie was a bit miffed at the way Sammy was railroading the event to suit himself, and his offer to let Sammy decide their mode of transport held a slight note of sarcasm. But Sammy didn't appear to notice anything unusual in the comment and immediately made the decision.

"Well then, we'll get Tam to take us, for I think it's going to rain."

"I'll phone him," Martha offered, making her way through to the hall.

Most girls would have been flattered in such a situation, but not Martha. In her opinion, Sammy was trying to out-manoeuvre Willie, while Willie was fool enough to let the other fellow's tactics annoy him. Martha had no patience with such childish behaviour.

"It's not very often I get such a pretty girl in the front seat beside me," the friendly taxi man declared.

"Well, Tam," Martha replied, "there's no sense in three of us squeezing into the back when there's a spare seat in the front, and anyway, I'm sure the boys will have lots to talk about."

She folded her arms and turned her head to view the passing countryside.

Someone has rattled her cage, Tam thought, and decided Sammy was probably the most likely candidate.

They sat three rows from the front – Martha in the middle – Sammy on her right – Willie on her left. When it came to the really emotional part of the film where Mrs Miniver discovered that her daughter-in-law was dead, Sammy reached Martha his hanky, declaring that the wee dainty lacy affair that she was discreetly dabbing the corner of her eye with was no use at a time like that.

Meanwhile, Willie was holding her other hand in his and trying to reassure her that it was only a film.

On the way home Martha sat in the back – in the middle – Sammy on her right – Willie on her left.

With the memory of their childhood behaviour having been recalled the previous night, Martha couldn't resist, as once again she reached up and knocked the wall, "Are you awake?"

"I am now."

Then suddenly they were both laughing so much that neither of them could continue with the rest of the exchange.

"We're all awake," her father called from across the landing.

His comment added to their amusement, and with great difficulty the laughter had to be restrained.

Ruby was delighted the next morning when Willie inquired if the church service was still held at the usual time, and announced that he would like to go with them. He had brought his good suit and was looking forward to seeing the Rev. Murdock again.

"You'll see a big change in him," Martha informed Willie. "The black hair is white now, what's left of it, and he must be two stone heavier."

"Don't be so disrespectful," Henry chided. "He's a good man and can preach a good sermon."

Martha looked at her father with raised eyebrows as much as to say, 'How would you know?'

"He took the service the Sunday of the Orange Parade." Her father said in answer to the silent question.

Martha made no comment. This was so typical of her father. Church was just a convenience, a place for a funeral, a wedding, a baptism or the annual parade.

"Sammy always gives us a lift now," Ruby said, eager to change the conversation. "It's a bit far for me to walk these days."

"We've an extra passenger today," Martha said as she approached Arthur's car with her mother and Willie close behind.

"The more the merrier," Arthur said. "Hop in the lot of ye."

The Rev. Murdock was pleased to meet Willie again, although at first he didn't recognize him until Ruby reminded him of the little boy who had stayed on Daisy Farm during the war.

"Yes," he said enthusiastically. "You were the little guy who could always be relied upon to know his catechism, and one of our best singers in the Sunday School choir."

Willie was delighted that the minister remembered him, but a little embarrassed by the words of praise.

"Have you heard the news?" Victoria Burnside gushed as, with little regard for the fact that she was breaking into their conversation, she pushed in between Willie and the minister. "Tam Lorimer," she continued. "He's been taken into hospital – they think it's his heart."

"Oh no," Martha exclaimed, "how awful! And he was fine last night when he drove us home. He was joking and laughing and there didn't appear to be anything wrong with him at all."

"Well, don't worry," Victoria said, turning to Willie. "I suppose you were expecting him to take you to the station this afternoon, but Daddy will take both of us the whole way to Queens', because he's going to Lisburn to view a house he's considering buying, so it won't be that much out of his way."

"Actually, Sammy has offered to drive me to the train," Willie told her.

"Why bother with the smelly old train when you can travel in comfort with Daddy and me?"

Willie didn't relish the thought of spending an hour, or maybe more, depending on the traffic, listening to Victoria's endless, senseless chatter, but in the circumstances he couldn't refuse.

"That's very kind of him," Willie said, trying to look grateful.

"Daddy's thinking about retiring," she told them, "and obviously he will want to move somewhere more upmarket."

"We better move somewhere out of the way," Martha said. "We're blocking the doorway."

"See you about half past six," Victoria called to Willie, giving him the benefit of her most radiant smile and perfect white teeth.

Willie shook hands with Martha's father, and Sammy and Arthur who had come over to say goodbye. He hugged Ruby and thanked her for the lovely meals and for inviting him to the party. Then he hugged Martha, a little longer than he did her mother and promised to return very soon. Mr Burnside's car was purring at the top of the lane and Martha was pleased to see that the gentleman had insisted that Willie sit in the front, leaving Victoria alone in the back to probably sulk.

It was obvious to Martha who knew her so well that her face had that same familiar look that she had carried from childhood when things weren't going her way.

Willie waved to the assembled friends as the car started down the lane. He had enjoyed his visit to the place he had so many fond memories of. He had also discovered something that had previously been a maybe, but was now a certainty. He was in love with Martha Sloan, but what about Sammy McCracken? What about the comment Victoria had made about him and Martha the night of the party.

"Well, that's that over," Henry said, flopping down on the chair beside the range. "Now everything can get back to normal. Is there any more tea in that pot?"

Everything back to normal! For her mother and father and Sammy, yes, everything would be back to the usual routine, back to normal as her father had expressed it, but not for Martha, who, just like Willie, had also discovered something important. Willie Rossborough was the fellow she loved, but what about Victoria

Burnside? It was obvious she had designs on him and Victoria was a very persuasive girl.

The next day brought better news about Tam Lorimer. His suspected heart attack had been a false alarm. The pain in his left arm was caused by a pulled muscle. Apparently he had been doing some repairs to the taxi that would have been better left to a mechanic using the proper tools. But the unexpected check up was what his better half described as 'a blessing in disguise' for during the tests it was discovered that he had high blood pressure. So a change of lifestyle was a definite must – more exercise, a healthier diet and off the cigarettes.

Amazing what one wee mistake can lead to, Tam thought, the first day he had to do without his Woodbine. That wee mistake had also resulted in Victoria having Willie as a captive audience on their journey to Belfast, giving her plenty of time to comment on the suitability of Martha and Sammy and their inevitable union.

LATER THAT SUMMER

Willie paced the floor with the letter still clutched in his hand. It had been quite a day. After he had passed his driving test the previous week, his Aunt Elsie, as promised, had provided him with a car. It was a two door Morris Minor, but, as far as Willie was concerned, it might as well have been a Rolls Royce. Dear Aunt Elsie, she had done her best to take the place of his mother. And Sean – Uncle Sean as Willie had come to think of him – what a pity he had never been accepted into the family.

"Couldn't be helped," Elsie explained. "I made my choice, but your mother never turned her back on me – she always kept in touch – good thing she did or we wouldn't have you to be so proud of – you're the son we never had."

And truly, he had been treated like a son as they showered him with love and all the material things that money could buy. Their hotel was a thriving business and he had loved the advantage it gave him of meeting interesting people from all over the world. Now his plans to visit there more frequently were being realized with the arrival of the little black car. It was the beginning of the summer break and he had intended spending most of it in County Cavan with Elsie and Sean where he would have the opportunity to get his emotions sorted out without the constant comments from Victoria about the suitability of Sammy and Martha. Although he never sought her company, she had a habit of turning up unexpectedly, but as she was still going out with his pal Clive, it was impossible to avoid her completely. The rest of his plans included coming back up North and accepting Ruby's invitation to spend a few days on Daisy Farm before starting the new term in September. But the letter he was reading for the third time was making him want to change his plans, for he knew he wouldn't be content so far away from Martha when perhaps she needed him. But maybe she didn't need him – maybe she didn't even want him there. Sammy would be the man of the moment, taking charge, knowing what to do, providing a shoulder for her to cry on. Willie scanned the page again hoping that there was some hidden message that she did want him with her – that would be why she had written, giving him a reason to go there. But maybe she was just being polite by replying to his news about passing his driving test and getting the car, the way Ruby would have done if she hadn't taken the unfortunate tumble.

He folded the letter and held it to his lips, and then he unfolded it and placed it on the table and read it again.

Dear Willie, I'm sure you are surprised that I am replying to your last letter as it is always Ma who does the corresponding, but unfortunately she is unable to write to you as she has had a fall and broken her right arm and her left leg. She can't remember how it happened, but insists that she must have caught her foot on the top step of the stairs. However, the doctor is of the opinion that it is more likely that she took a dizzy turn. She has a few other bumps and bruises, but her arm is expected to take quite a while to heal as it is broken in three places. Her leg has just the one break but seems to be causing her the most discomfort. She's still in hospital and not liking it one bit. Da has decided it's time I gave up my job in Gallaghers and take over Ma's role in the house. Considering the circumstances I feel I must agree with him – bow to the inevitable – be a true farmer's daughter.

Ma sends her love and is delighted with your news about the car, and she says you are to be careful and not drive too fast.

Hope you have a good summer. Martha

PS. The invitation to visit is still valid. I know I'm not as good at making soup as Ma is, but I promise I won't poison you. Ha! Ha!

There *was* a hidden message there he decided. That was why she had mentioned the earlier invitation that her mother had made. Or was she just being polite? He couldn't be sure, but either way his mind was made up – he was going to go to Daisy Farm the next day. He would phone his Aunt in the morning and tell her his visit would be delayed, and then he would ring Martha and tell her he was on his way. It would be nice to hear her voice again. He'd never rung the farm before as he knew Ruby had never taken to the new piece of equipment. She said it didn't feel right talking to somebody she couldn't see, and she only answered it when there was no one else around to do it. Ruby liked to get a letter and she liked to reply in the same way. Willie respected her wishes and although there were times when he would have loved to make a call and talk to Martha he had no viable excuse to do so, until now. He could hear it ringing – could picture the black shiny apparatus sitting on the highly polished half-moon table in the corner of the hall. But there was no answer, so there was no other option – he would just have to arrive unannounced.

"And where are you off to so early in the day?" Clive asked, as Willie was putting his bag into the back of the car. Victoria was clinging onto Clive's arm. Willie related the unfortunate events that had taken place on Daisy Farm and told them he was going to pay a visit there before going to Cavan.
"You're one great mug," Victoria declared. "Rushing away there just because old Ruby couldn't stand on her own two feet."
"Victoria!" Clive exclaimed. "That's very insensitive."
"Maybe it is," she retorted, "but somebody needs to talk a bit of sense into this big fool. It doesn't matter what he does, or how nice he is to that family, he hasn't a hope of getting Martha. Catch yourself on," she continued, turning towards Willie. "How many times do you have to be told, Martha is Sammy's girl and you have no chance."

Willie ignored her comments as he slid in behind the steering wheel and pulled the starter.

The house seemed unusually quiet as Willie pulled into the yard. Then the door opened and Henry came across with his hand outstretched in greeting. "This is a bit of a surprise," he declared. "We thought we wouldn't be seeing you until the end of the summer."

Willie explained that when he got the news about Ruby's mishap he felt he wanted to come and see if there was anything he could do to help.

Henry assured him there was nothing he could do, but his visit was greatly appreciated, and he was sure Martha would be delighted to see him.

"She's at the hospital now," Henry informed him. "Sammy went with her for there were things I had to do here."

Willie didn't reply. He'd heard Sammy's name mentioned enough to last him a lifetime.

"That's a great wee motor you've got there," Henry said, rubbing his hand across the bonnet, "but we'll get a better look at it later on when you've had something to eat. Come on in and I'll see if I can make a start – Martha and Sammy shouldn't be much longer."

There it was again – Martha and Sammy. It was starting to sound like some sort of a double act, like Laurel and Hardy, or Fred Astaire and Ginger Rogers.

Henry had been right. Martha *was* delighted to see Willie, and just *how* delighted she hoped wasn't too obvious. Willie wanted to hear all about Ruby's progress and he made the appropriate comments – remaining non-committal. At this stage it wouldn't be helpful to either Martha or her father to enlighten them to the fact that Ruby's recovery would be a long and painful process.

As the evening wore on it was decided that Willie should keep to the original plan of visiting his Aunt and Uncle first, which would mean Ruby would be home and able to enjoy his visit when he came back up North before the start of the next term. So, a good night's sleep for Willie was a must, as he had a long and tiresome journey ahead of him the next day. Martha would make up his bed, Henry told him, and pop a hot water bottle in between the sheets. A warm cosy bed was essential for a good night's sleep.

After Martha did the necessary bed making for their unexpected guest Willie was encouraged by Henry to 'get away on up there before the bottle gets cold.'

I'll talk to Martha in the morning, Willie decided – perhaps take her to visit her mother. That way he would get a chance to speak to her alone, and it would be nice to see Ruby again and wish her all the best for a speedy recovery.

The aroma of frying bacon was the first thing Willie was aware of when he woke the next morning.

"Do I hear you getting up?" Martha called from the bottom of the stairs.

"On my way," Willie replied.

"Breakfast's ready," she announced.

Willie smiled – lost in daydreams of how nice it would be if he and Martha were married and she was busying herself in the kitchen while he was preparing for his day at the hospital (always supposing he passed all his exams) and in the evening she would still be there waiting for him to come home, and they would sit by the fireside and tell each other all about their day with no Sammy or Victoria meddling in their lives.

The familiar sounds from the kitchen below brought him back to the present. It had just been wishful thinking, he chided himself, but it had been *pleasant* wishful thinking.

The magnificent view of the mountains and surrounding countryside went unnoticed by Willie as he sat on the ditch eating the packed lunch Martha had prepared for him earlier in the day. Willie wasn't interested in the scenery, for his thoughts were elsewhere as he recalled the look on Martha's face when her father said how nice is was of him to suggest taking the time to visit Ruby before heading off on his summer break, and offering to take Martha along was very generous, so it was only fair that he shouldn't have to drive her back again.   Hence his idea that he would go too, and when they would be ready to come home they could ring Sammy from the pay phone in reception and he could come and collect them. Willie was sure he could detect a slight irritation in Martha's voice when she said, "Well now, Da, it wouldn't take you very long to sort everybody out."

Was she annoyed because they couldn't spend time together, or was she just fed-up with her father continually organizing her life? He couldn't be sure, although he hoped it was the first possibility. Regardless of all the evidence pointing to a union between Martha and Sammy, Willie felt that there was a spark between himself and his childhood friend.

"Ah, sure, isn't it great to see you again," Sean declared as he held out his hand in greeting to the travel-weary Willie. "And I do declare you've grown another foot!"

"Nope, I've still only got the two," Willie replied, entering into the friendly banter that had always existed between them.

"Here, sure won't I take this," Sean said, lifting Willie's case out of the car. "An get a move on, for it's as sure as there's two eyes in Paddy Maginty's oul goat, that woman in there has been counting the days."

"It's great to be back," Willie said, as his Aunt Elsie greeted him with the usual big hug and a flood of questions about his health, and was he eating properly and how was university etc. etc. After reassuring her on all accounts the next statement was, "Go and get freshened up – dinner will be ready in five minutes."

The days drifted by in the usual way. Willie helped out when and where he could, and when there was some free time he and Sean went fishing. Other times they drove to the next town where Sean had a great fondness for a particular pub. Though not a heavy drinker, he enjoyed a 'wee haffin' an a bottle, where he could sit back and be served instead of doing the serving, and the fact that Willie was driving meant he could indulge in an extra glass if he so desired. He knew Elsie would be cross if he came back the worse for the wear, but, as she never stayed angry with him for very long, he considered it well worth the lecture, and, anyway, he loved the way her eyes glistened when she was in a lather. In fact, he loved her no matter what state of mind she was in. She was just his Elsie and he had loved her from the first day he had met her and there wasn't a thing anybody could do to change his mind.

Willie had often observed them, how right they seemed together – how they belonged together and hoped that some day he could be as happy and contented as they were.

"It's just a matter of finding the right person," Elsie had often said when the topic of marriage came up.

Willie knew he had found the right person, but was he the right person for her?

"Yer miles away," Sean declared, when he had spoken to Willie for the second time and still hadn't got a response.

"Sorry, Sean, what was that you were saying?"

"Nothing, nothing atal," Sean replied, "but whoever she is, you've got it really bad."

Willie just smiled as he continued sweeping the path that led down to the little private garden at the back of the hotel. He liked it there – it was out of bounds to the guests, so he didn't have to make small talk with strangers. It was somewhere he could think his thoughts and dream his dreams.

"Tea's ready," Sean said, heading back towards the house. "Its salad, so there's no rush, it won't get cold."

Sean's attempt at humour escaped Willie as his thoughts were elsewhere.

As the end of his summer break was drawing to a close Willie couldn't quite make up his mind if he was sorry or glad, and the more he thought about it the more confused he became. Normally he would have bade goodbye to Elsie and Sean with a certain degree of regret that the visit was over for another few months, but also with a huge degree of excitement at getting back to his studies. But this time was different. While he was in Cavan he could think about Martha and almost make himself believe that Sammy didn't exist, but when he got back up North he would be paying a visit to the Sloan household, and then he would have to face reality.

It was the evening before his departure. His bags were packed and he had gone outside to escape the activity that was taking place inside. A lot of the guests were leaving the next morning and they were all settling their bills and then crowding into the bar area for one last night of relaxation before they returned to their various homes, places of employment and stress.

Willie was deep in thought as he sat on the steps that led from the patio area to the orchard. The evening was balmy with a slight mist draping itself over the distant hills, and with only the faint twitter of the birds to disturb the silence he was suddenly jolted out of his reverie.

"So you're the famous Willie."

"Pardon?"

"The famous Willie."

"I wouldn't say famous," Willie replied.

"Ah, well now, I wouldn't be too sure about that, if what Mrs O'Reilly says about you is true," the slim, red-haired girl declared, parking herself beside him on the step.

She put her head to one side and viewed Willie from head to toe as if she had decided to make her own judgement.

Willie found her scrutiny uncomfortable, and, eager to avoid any further discussion on the subject, he said, "Are you new around here? I don't think I've seen you before."

"Molly's the name," she informed him, offering her hand. "Molly the maid," she continued, "and you don't need to introduce yourself for sure haven't I already guessed."

Then she went on to tell him that she had worked in the hotel during the winter, but had to leave at the beginning of the summer because her mother was in the family way *again*. She emphasized the *again* with a deep sigh and added, "High blood pressure, and swollen ankles and all that sort of thing, and as I'm the oldest I was told that I would have to take over and look after the wee ones, but number ten arrived last week so I said, 'I'm out of here.' My head was ready for going, having to cope with all them squalling weans. Working here is like a holiday compared to our house." She sighed again and continued. "One thing I am sure of, I will never marry, for it's nothing but a mug's game."

Willie just smiled. He wasn't interested in continuing with this seemingly useless conversation.

"Be gorra, I'd say you're a fella with something on your mind."

"Pardon?"

"You're miles away," Molly declared. "Sure it's obvious you're not here atal."

"What makes you think that?"

"It's that faraway look in your eye that's the telltale," she informed him.

Willie wished that she would go *away*, but, as that possibility seemed unlikely, he excused himself on the pretext of having a lot to do before leaving the next day.

"I know about these things," she called after his retreating figure, "because I've got the gift."

The gift of the gab, more likely, Willie thought as he made his way back across the patio.

The journey north seemed endless. The few phone calls he had made to Daisy Farm had done nothing to ease his mind about Martha and Sammy. Ruby was out of hospital and improving, and yes, everybody was looking forward to seeing him again. Everybody wasn't what Willie wanted to hear, but of course that had been Ruby's comment when he rang the day before. Any other calls he made to the farm had been answered by Henry and once by Sammy, which Willie found irritating. Apparently he was keeping an eye on Ruby while Henry took Martha into the village for some messages.

But today was make or break time, Willie decided. He couldn't go on with the uncertainty – he was going to find out, one way or other, what the situation was between Sammy and Martha. How he was going to manage it he didn't quite know, or how he would react to the outcome was indeed a bigger mystery. The only thing he was sure of was the fact that he loved Martha and her happiness was what he considered the most important thing.

Alone at last! The setting was perfect. If he had planned it, it couldn't have been any better. A pleasant September evening, a full moon, the faint twitter of the birds as they settled for the night and Martha by his side. They made their way through the long grass to where old Ned greeted them in his usual friendly way as he turned his attention from the trough of fresh water and came towards them.

"I hope you still know me," Willie said, patting his scruffy mane.

"I don't think he'll ever forget *you*," Martha ventured. She would have liked to add, 'and neither will I' but she didn't have the courage. What if Willie laughed at her – made a joke of her comment? It would be better not knowing how he felt than having to cope with rejection. If only she had known the jumble of thoughts that were going through Willie's mind at the same time. Was she in love with Sammy or were they just good friends? What would she say if he told her he loved her? Would she laugh at his admission? If she did, he knew he would be devastated, and if she

111

told Sammy then that would add to his humiliation. He sighed as he looked at her face – that pretty face with those big green eyes. But there was something in those eyes that he hadn't seen there before. It was as if they were telling him something that her lips had never uttered. Then it all happened so quickly. He didn't know who made the first move – she didn't know either – perhaps it was a mutual decision, for suddenly she was in his arms. Their lips met, and for what seemed like an eternity they were in another world - a world that belonged exclusively to them where no one else existed.

The chirping of the birds faded and Ned's usual loud bray sounded a long way off, and then, also from a long way off, Martha heard her name being called. Willie had been repeating her name over and over as he held her close and ran his fingers through her long brown hair. But this wasn't Willie's voice.

"Martha, where *are* you?"

"Sammy's calling me," Martha said as she broke free from Willie's arms and ran towards the gate that led onto the lane and back to the house.

In her urgency she didn't take time to explain to Willie that she thought her mother had fallen again or some other disaster had occurred during her absence. But Willie didn't know that it was panic that had driven her from his arms.

He followed her at a much slower pace. He had got his answer. Sammy had called and Martha had obeyed. Their special moments together had been nothing more than stolen moments, the sort of moments that belonged to Sammy. As he made his way along the lane he wondered if she guessed how he felt about her and had just been playing games with him – a bit of fun to lighten her mundane existence. In his heart he couldn't believe that Martha was that sort of girl, but still, the facts spoke for themselves. Willie knew when he was beaten. What he didn't know, was the anger Martha felt when she rushed into the house and saw Sammy sitting at the end of the table engaged in a game of draughts with her father.

"What's wrong? What has happened?"

112

"Nothing," Sammy replied, and then turning to his opponent he said, "That was a crafty move."

"That's what you get for leaving the board for a couple of minutes."

The two men laughed, obviously enjoying the game.

A couple of minutes, Martha thought, just a couple of minutes to destroy my *special* minutes.

"Why did you call me?" she demanded.

"I was just wondering where you were," Sammy told her, without lifting his eyes from the board.

"Well, as there seems to be no emergency, I'm having an early night."

She stormed out of the kitchen as Willie came in.

She couldn't face him just now – she would talk to him in the morning before he left. Regardless of Sammy or anyone else she would take him aside and explain.

There was no childish knocking on the dividing wall that night, just the creaking of the bed as Willie tossed and turned, unable to erase the memory of those special minutes when he had held Martha in his arms. The faint aroma of her Jasmine perfume still clinging to the jacket he had hung on the bedpost added to his misery. Sleep eluded Martha too, until, exhausted with the tears she shed below the covers, she finally dozed off around 3 am. She overslept the next morning.

"I didn't mean to sleep so late," Martha said, rushing into the kitchen. "Why didn't you call me?"

"Your Ma said to let you sleep, and she's having a lie in herself this morning. She said she was still feeling tired."

"She has been complaining a lot about tiredness these last few days," Martha replied. "I better go up and see what she wants for breakfast."

"Let her sleep for a while first," her father advised.

"Willie must be tired too," Martha said, "for he's usually up and about at this time."

"Willie's gone."

"What?"

"He's gone."

"Gone where?"

Henry lifted the piece of paper from behind the clock on the mantelpiece and reached it to Martha. She read the scribbled words aloud.

Decided to make an early start. Many, many thanks for all your hospitality. Willie.

Henry watched as the colour drained from his daughter's face, but that was the only evidence of how she was feeling. No one would ever know that her heart was breaking, especially Sammy, for it was his entire fault and she would never forgive him.

"What time did he leave?" she asked.

"I don't know. He was already gone when I came down at a quarter to six."

"So what about you?" she asked, immediately changing the subject. "Have you had any breakfast yet or do you want me to swing the pan?"

Henry declined the offer, saying that he had already eaten and he'd better be making tracks; the farm wouldn't look after itself.

Martha was relieved when he put on his boots and went out closing the door behind him. Now she could give in to the tears that had been so determinedly kept under control. Now she could ponder all the questions that were crowding her mind. Why had Willie left so suddenly? Did he regret what had happened between them the previous evening, or had he been deliberately toying with her feelings? Was it some sick joke he had been playing to boost his ego? But no, that couldn't be possible, for Willie wasn't that sort of person. But he *had* crept away in the early hours of the morning

114

like some sort of a criminal, so it was hard to know what to think. Perhaps she'd *never* know the real reason for his speedy departure, but what she did know was that she loved him and probably always would.

"Martha, are you there?" The voice was faint, but in the quietness of the kitchen it was loud enough for Martha to respond instantly, knowing there was urgency in the few words her mother had uttered.

The events of the next hour took priority over any queries Martha had about Willie's behaviour or intentions, as the doctor diagnosed a possible heart attack. Martha had never seen her father so distressed, and her earlier decision to hate Sammy for the rest of her life vanished when, once again, he became a shoulder for her to cry on as her mother was carried into the waiting ambulance.

Gradually the residents of Daisy Farm got into a comfortable routine. Ruby was back home and her prospects quite good, providing she took care of herself and did not get overtired. Nancy Shaw became a regular caller, and Ruby looked forward to her visits as she always had a good story to tell, and, coupled with her mischievous sense of humour, a lot of laughter ensued. Ruby frequently declared, "That Nancy woman is as good as a tonic."
Martha looked after her Mum the way an over indulgent mother would pamper a delicate child. But all the care and attention was freely given. Martha was happy to take over the running of the house, plus feeding the hens, tending to the vegetable plot etc.etc. She also created a small flower garden at the front of the house. Her father didn't approve. He said ground should only be broken when something useful or edible was being planted. He also said it was a waste of time because no one ever came to the front door, so it wouldn't be seen. But Martha intended it as a quiet place for her mother to sit out on warm evenings where she could enjoy the

fragrance of the flowers and be undisturbed by the normal activity that regularly took place in the farmyard. When the chores of the day were over Martha often joined her mother on the front porch where they sat in companionable silence reading their magazines. Ruby had a fondness for Peoples' Friend, Martha preferred Red Star Weekly. But once read they always swapped publications.

Willie Rossborough's name had never been mentioned since the morning Martha came down the stairs to be given the note he had left, so she assumed her father must have put a ban on any reference to him, either because he was angry at the way he had left without saying goodbye, or else he realized Martha had been hurt by his actions and wanted to spare her any more misery. The fact that there had been no letters from Willie since his hasty departure probably added to Henry's resolve. Martha found it hard sometimes to know what her father was thinking, although, in spite of his usual unconcerned manner, there were occasions when his softer side was apparent, especially the way he had organized her twenty first birthday party and the affection he had shown her on the night. But she didn't like to dwell too often on that particular event, for it hurt too much. Willie had been there that night; Willie had taken her in his arms as they danced around the hall and that memory always reminded her of the next time he had drawn her into the circle of his arms. If Sammy hadn't called her at that particular moment would the outcome have been any different? When she queried him later about why he had come looking for her, he just shrugged his shoulders and said that Ruby had been wondering where Martha had gone, so he decided to find out on her behalf. It seemed such an innocent explanation, yet it had such far-reaching consequences and Martha knew she would always wonder. What if?

The weeks turned into months and Christmas was just a few days away. The new guy who drove the bread van had taken a liking to

Martha and asked her to accompany him to a dance that was being held in the Town Hall in Ballymena. Apparently somebody famous was providing the music, but he wouldn't tell her who it was. He said he wanted it to be a surprise. She could quite easily have found out who this so called celebrity was by reading the local paper, but, as fame didn't impress her, she didn't bother, and the fact that this young man didn't have a car and expected her to make her own way to the town and meet him at the venue didn't impress her either. So the invitation was turned down and she went to the dance in the village with Sammy instead, but only after her father promised that he would stay with her mother in case she took 'another wee turn' as they always referred to her previous attack.

No dandering over to Arthur's for a chat and probably a wee glass of something to celebrate the festive season had been the firm instructions before Martha left the house.

Tam's taxi was, as usual, their mode of transport, with the inevitable pickups along the way. It was good to get back to normal, Martha thought. The predictable, good-natured banter about who would sit where, and who was taking up too much space resulted in plenty of laughter and name-calling and this was the highlight of their conversation on such journeys.

This is how it used to be, Martha mused, before Willie came back on the scene. She wished she had never suggested to her parents that they should invite him back for a visit. It would have been so much better to have let him remain a memory. A pleasant memory of a young boy who was evacuated out of Belfast during the Blitz and came to reside with her family for a time until he went to stay with his Aunt down South. The fact that he kept in touch was very kind of him and it was nice to know that he hadn't forgotten the folk who had been so good to him. Yes, that would have been the simple way, to just let life take its own course instead of interfering. She would never do anything like that again she vowed, but what she would do was pretend he had never come back, and if he eventually decided to write to the family she would take no interest in his news, because his present or his future had nothing to do with her.

With that decision firmly fixed in her mind she had an exceedingly good time and was on the floor for every dance, and not always with Sammy. There was a good-looking young man there who came from the next village. He liked dancing, especially the Quick Step and especially with Martha.

Martha agreed to go out with him the next evening.

Who was Willie Rossborough? She couldn't remember!

DECISIONS 1951/52

Willie Rossborough viewed his reflection in the mirror and tried to convince himself that the tiny lines now creasing his forehead were the result of too much study, but the real reason was the amount of self examination he had been carrying out on his common sense or, perhaps, lack of it. But there was no point in trying to reach a satisfactory conclusion now, when he had failed for so long. It was his wedding day and he had to smile and pretend he was happy. But he shouldn't *have* to pretend, for he was marrying a beautiful girl who had declared her undying love for him. A girl who had forsaken a previous boyfriend and offered to be his wife, a girl who had taken responsibility for all the wedding arrangements so that his studies wouldn't be interrupted. Admittedly, there wasn't a lot of arranging to do, for he had been adamant that there would be no big flashy cars and expensive photographers. It would be a quiet, short ceremony in the registry office, with no guests and only her parents there as witnesses. She had agreed to all his wishes and he knew that very few would be happy with such an arrangement, when it was every young girl's dream to float down the aisle in a cloud of white satin and lace with all her friends and relations there to share in her special day. There were many who would say that he was an extremely lucky guy to have found such a gem. He had to admit they were right, for everything was going his way, so why this sinking lurch in the pit of his stomach when he should have been feeling on top of the world. Reaching for his fourth cup of coffee that morning, he spoke aloud to the empty walls, "She just isn't Martha."

But Martha didn't want him. Martha wanted Sammy, and Willie didn't know what was happening on Daisy Farm. Perhaps by now Martha was married to Sammy or, at least, was making plans for her big day. He hadn't heard from any of them since the morning he fled before anyone was awake and he hadn't written to them either, because he didn't know what to say.

He often wondered if he had been too hasty in accepting defeat and what would have happened if he had turned the car and gone back, as he had considered doing along every mile of the road that was taking him further from the girl he loved. But his pride was hurt and that prevented him from following his heart and persuaded him to put as much distance between them as possible.

He was tired by the time he got back to the city, for he had completed the journey without taking a break, and then there was the party- there always seemed to be a party to celebrate something. He hadn't been in a party mood – he had too much on his mind, but he was surrounded by several students who dragged him along. There was no sign of Clive, his usual pal, but Victoria was there, eager to tell him that Clive had got transferred to another college. She didn't know where, because she wasn't interested; she was just glad he was gone. They were finished, she informed him, implying that she had done the finishing. She stayed by Willie's side all that evening, making sure that his glass didn't get empty. Willie wasn't a lover of drink. Its effects on the human body had been one of the subjects he had paid particular attention to during his studies, and never intended to indulge in the habit. But he was in a reckless mood, not caring much about the outcome, and when Victoria declared that she had always been in love with him and suggested that they should get married Willie had said, "Yes, why not? Let's do it."

At least she loved him, he argued with himself the next morning. She cared about him. She was willing to marry him under any circumstances. That would prove to anyone who was interested that Willie Rossborough wasn't anybody's cast-off. Perhaps the effect of the alcohol was still ruling his assessment of the situation at that time, because a few hours later he started to question his

120

sanity, but by then it was too late. The news of the forthcoming nuptials had travelled the length and breadth of the college, especially as several of his friends had witnessed his acceptance of Victoria's proposal. He couldn't back out now, it would break her heart, and she would be the laughing stock of the college. He couldn't do that to her, for, in spite of her callous and irritating ways, Willie was prepared to give her the benefit of the doubt. There was bound to be some good qualities hiding behind her hard exterior, so he may as well go through with it since there was no chance of him ever getting the opportunity to marry the one he really wanted. That door had been firmly closed.

The wedding was a very sombre event with Victoria's parents making no attempt to disguise the resentment they were feeling at being denied the pleasure of having a big flamboyant affair in the village church. Although they had moved to Lisburn, Mrs Burnside would have loved the opportunity to go back and show off their style and wealth. So it was with a great deal of relief that Willie bade them goodbye after having a meal in a nearby restaurant and headed South to where his Aunt Elsie had promised them the bridal suite in the hotel.

On their journey they stopped off mid-way for something to eat. Victoria said she wasn't very hungry and added that sometimes she was troubled with travel sickness when travelling in such a small vehicle.
"I'm sorry it's not a Rolls," Willie retorted. She didn't reply and just kept staring out of the window.
Then he regretted being so sharp with her. After all, it wasn't her fault. Lots of people had the same problem and he supposed her parents' attitude had been as upsetting for her as it had been irritating for him.
"Sorry," he said, reaching across and taking her hand. She looked so vulnerable and he felt guilty for the way he had deprived her of

121

what should have been her big day. "We'll both feel more human once we get a plate of Aunt Elsie's Irish stew inside us," he continued, trying to lighten the mood, but she turned up her nose as if he had suggested eating grass.

Elsie met them at the door in her usual gushy, friendly way, congratulating both of them and hugging Willie, but she didn't get the chance to greet Victoria with the same enthusiasm, as a slender cold hand was presented, and an equally cold voice said, "It's nice to meet you, Mrs Reilly."

"Oh, please," Elsie said, "call me Elsie, even *Aunt* Elsie if you wish."

The comment was accepted with a weak smile and Willie was mortified on his Aunt's behalf. Sean came through from the dining room and was greeted in the same formal way, but he took control of the awkwardness by declaring, "Be gorra, isn't it nice to see a young lady with such good manners."

Molly showed them to their room, but Victoria made no comment about how beautiful it was. She just ran her fingers along the top of the dressing table, then went to inspect the bathroom. Molly shook her head, then gently touched Willie's arm. "I really do wish you all the best, but she's not the one that was on your mind the last time you were here."

When Willie was about to reply, she reached up and put her finger to his lips. "You don't need to say anything," she informed him. "It's your eyes," she continued. "I can tell by your eyes."

Willie took her advice, for there are times when silence is the best answer, especially as Victoria returned to stand beside him. Molly stated that she hoped everything would be to their satisfaction and left the room.

Elsie had laid on a meal fit for a king, but Victoria picked through every course. Willie made her excuses, explaining about the travel sickness. Elsie sympathised saying that she was the same on a boat. Shortly after the meal Victoria said she was tired and could feel a migraine coming on, so perhaps she should go on up to bed, but not to let that spoil their evening for she was sure they had a lot of catching up to do.

Willie breathed a sigh of relief, for he was in no hurry to consummate their marriage and, it appeared, neither was Victoria. With every hour that passed Willie realized he had made the biggest mistake of his life, and, being here, where he had spent so much time thinking about Martha, confirmed it. He longed to hear Martha's voice and toyed with the idea of ringing her, but if he did what could he say? Tell her he had got married and accept her congratulations? No, he couldn't bear that. Maybe he could just inquire about how things were on the farm and apologise for not writing because he was busy with his studies, but that would be a lie and he would never lie to Martha. It was stupid to even consider getting in touch with her, he finally admitted, for if there had ever been the slightest chance that they could be together, then he had signed it away that morning in a dreary, depressing registry office in Belfast.

"Do you fancy going into the town a wee run?" Sean said. "Give the bride time to sort herself out."

"Sean!" Elsie declared. "Have you taken leave of your senses? It's the boy's wedding night, for goodness sake."

"Sure he has the rest of his life for all that sort of thing," Sean replied. Then turning to Willie, "Come on, ye boyo, let's go."

They were out of the door before Elsie could utter another protest.

The two men took their seats in the snug – their favourite place in the town's popular bar - Sean with his bottle of stout and Willie with his glass of pure orange. Then the barman came over.

"Your Elsie's on the phone," he said to Sean. "She seems to be in a bit of a panic, so you better come over and speak to her – she's still hanging on."

Sean rushed over to where the receiver was dangling against the wall.

"What's wrong? What's happened?"

"It's Victoria," she told him, "she's been rushed into hospital, so you two better get over there as fast as you can."

Willie turned as the white-coated figure entered the room.

"Mr Rossborough?"

"Yes."

"I'm Doctor Harkness," the tall, grey-haired man said, reaching out his hand to Willie.

Willie waited for what seemed like an eternity as the doctor glanced in Sean's direction. Willie understood.

"It's Ok,"he assured him. "This is Sean, my uncle. What's happening? Is she going to be all right?"

"She will be fine. She's resting now. But..."

The doctor stared at the floor.

"But what?" Willie urged.

"I'm sorry, Mr Rossborough, but there's no easy way to tell you this."

There was another long pause, and then he continued. "She's lost the baby."

"The baby?" Willie declared. "She's lost the baby?"

"Yes, I'm very sorry, but there was nothing we could do."

Willie's face went deathly pale as he slumped down on the nearest chair clutching his head in his hands.

"I really am very sorry," the kindly doctor said.

Willie looked up, his eyes bright and staring.

"Can I see her now?"

"I'm afraid not. She has specifically requested no visitors."

"But..."

"Try not to get too upset. It's quite common in situations like this. Sometimes the young wife feels confused and thinks she has let her husband down, but I'm sure with time you will be a great comfort to each other."

Willie didn't speak, didn't know what to say, so the doctor continued, "She will need all the love and support you can give her."

Willie knew the rules, but he still insisted that he wanted to see her, needed to talk to her, needed to make some sense of it all. But the wishes of the patient always got priority.

"Try and get some sleep and come back tomorrow," the doctor advised. "Things always look better in the morning."

"Come on, there's nothing you can do," Sean said, placing his hand on Willie's shoulder. "Let's go home."

Very little was said during their journey apart from how unpredictable life can be and several comments about the weather – how quickly it had changed from warm and dry to wet and windy.

"Willie dear," Elsie declared. "You look exhausted. Is she all right? Come and sit by the fire; the kettle's boiling. I'm sure you're dying for a cup of tea. Have they taken her to theatre yet? Are *you* all right?"

Willie gathered his Auntie into his arms. Loveable, caring Aunt Elsie. What a treasure she was.

"I'm fine," he told her, "and she's fine and you should be in your bed. It's past 2 am."

"I couldn't go to bed without knowing. It all happened so quickly. I didn't know anything was wrong until the ambulance pulled up at the door and there she was, poor thing, standing at the bottom of the stairs, doubled in two with the pain and a blanket wrapped round her. She had phoned the hospital and never said a word to me. Apparently she didn't want to annoy me, but she said her appendix had been bothering her for a while and she supposed it had all come to a head."

Willie assured his Aunt that everything would be all right and persuaded her to go to bed, promising that he would do the same as soon as he finished his tea.

With their mugs cupped between their hands and the tea going cold, the two men sat either side of the table, heads bowed, both pondering the events of the previous few hours.

Sean broke the silence. "You didn't know about the ba, did you?"

Willie nodded, indicating that Sean's assumption was correct.

"And it wasn't yours."

Again Willie nodded to imply that Sean was right, and then asked, "How did you guess?"

"It was obvious by your reaction."

Willie ran his fingers through his hair, and then thumped the table with his clenched fist.

"The lying, conniving, cheating…"

"Keep calm," Sean advised. "Getting yourself all worked up won't do any good."

"But it all makes sense now," Willie said. "She didn't dump Clive. He has scarpered when he found out she was pregnant. I don't think he ever cared about her anyway – he was just using her. If I ever get my hands on him I'll…"

"Oh Willie, Willie," Sean interrupted. "How did you ever get yourself into this state of affairs?"

Willie shrugged his shoulders. "It's a long story. Short version – the one I wanted didn't want me; Victoria swore she loved me instead of the chap she was seeing, so I suppose it's what's called 'marriage on the rebound' and anyway, I had been drinking."

Marry in haste, repent at leisure, was more appropriate Sean thought, but refrained from voicing the words. Poor Willie, he really had got himself into quite a pickle.

"I'd rather this was kept between you and me," Willie said. "I don't want Aunt Elsie finding out and getting upset. You know how she worries about me, so as soon as the doctor allows Victoria out of hospital I'll take her straight back to Belfast."

"But it's your honeymoon, so Elsie will expect you to bring her back here and give her time to recover. After all, she thinks the girl has had major surgery."

"I couldn't face it," Willie said. "Watching Victoria deceiving her, taking her sympathy and her kindness. It would be too unfair, and anyhow, the quicker I get her back to Belfast then the quicker I can get this horrible mess sorted out."

Willie took another sip of the tea, then shook his head in disgust as the strong cold liquid trickled down his throat.

"Forget about that," Sean said, taking the cup out of Willie's hand. "This situation calls for something a bit more substantial."

It was the 'something more substantial' that had got Willie into the situation in the first place, but the deed was done, so why worry about his liver now?

"Fill it up," he told Sean, holding up the glass. "Fill it up to the brim."

Willie entered the hospital with long purposeful strides and made inquiries on the whereabouts of Mrs Victoria Rossborough, stating that he was her husband. The sound of her name on his lips irritated him, for she didn't deserve the title, she had only acquired it by manipulation and deception.

"If you just come this way," the rosy-cheeked nurse said as she led him down a long narrow corridor.

"How is she?" Willie felt compelled to ask.

"A wee bit more settled now, compared to what she was during the night."

Willie didn't comment, waiting for her to continue.

"She was very distressed, quite delirious in fact, and kept saying how sorry she was and that her husband would never forgive her."

Sorry! Willie thought. A million sorrys wouldn't right the wrong she had done. He had his speech prepared – the list of names he would call her, and the threats he would make about how he would shame her in front of her family and friends and how an annulment of their marriage would take place at the earliest possible opportunity. Oh yes, this was going to be quite an encounter for the deceiving Mrs Rossborough.

"We tried to reassure her," the nurse said, "explained how these unfortunate miscarriages take time to come to terms with."

"Yes," Willie said.

What he really meant was, there's more to come to terms with than an unfortunate miscarriage.

"But you are both young, so there's plenty of time for more babies."

Willie made no comment, for the very thought of inflicting a mother like Victoria on an innocent child was way beyond his imagination.

Reaching the ward door, the nurse informed him, "Her blood pressure is still very high. She's quite fragile at the moment."

The nurse returned to her other duties leaving Willie to enter the room alone. It was a small room, what was sometimes referred to as a side ward, a place where a very ill patient would be put to prevent them from being disturbed. What he saw there wasn't what he expected, for there was no sign of the defiant, confident, young woman he had married a little over twenty four hours ago. In her place was a sobbing, heart-broken, pathetic slip of a girl who looked lost and bewildered. She raised her head from the pile of white pillows and reached across to catch Willie's hand, but he wasn't close enough as he sat down on the chair beside the bed.

"I'm sorry," she sobbed. "Please let me explain."

"Explain!" Willie said. "Please do. Was it going to be premature? Did you think I was that stupid that you could get away with that? Or maybe it was going to be another immaculate conception?"

When she turned her head away from him and the tears began to flow again, Willie realized that his sarcasm had probably hurt her more than all the cruel things he intended to say.

He waited for what seemed like hours, when it was really only a few minutes. Then she started to speak again. He decided to let her have her say, there was plenty of time for him to have his when she would finish.

"I was always in love with you," she told him, "but you didn't want me, you wanted Martha, so I settled for second best. Then, when I told Clive that I was pregnant, he said I would have to get rid of it, and the next day he gave me a name and an address of a woman who could sort it all out. But I didn't go to her because I couldn't take my baby's life and, when I told him that, he said all sorts of terrible things and called me all sorts of terrible names and then I never saw him again. I don't know where he went."

She was unable to say any more and started to sob again. Willie took a hanky from his pocket and reached it to her. Silence fell until Willie couldn't stand it any longer. "And then I came to your rescue," he said. "You knew I was in a reckless mood that night or I wouldn't have been drinking and you made sure that I drank plenty. And, hey presto, you had found a fool to solve all your problems."

"It wasn't like that."

"No! Then tell me what it *was* like."

"I didn't want to deceive you, so when you agreed to marry me I went the next day to the woman who fixes things. I thought I could go through with it and you and I could be happy together, but as soon as she opened the door I ran away. I still couldn't kill my baby and now it's dead and that's my punishment and it's all my fault."

Suddenly Willie started to think of the life that had been lost and a great sense of sadness came over him. He had been so consumed with his own hurt and anger that he hadn't given a thought to how Victoria was feeling. Regardless of what she had done, she had lost her child and there's nothing can hurt a woman more than to end up with empty arms. Willie felt guilty, couldn't think of anything to say except, "I better be heading back to the hotel."

As Willie reached the door she called his name – he hesitated for a second, and then kept on walking, back the way he had come, then out into the chilly air. It had started to snow and the ground was already quite slippery. A young couple was carefully making their way towards a waiting taxi. The girl was carrying a baby and the young man had his arm draped protectively round her shoulder.

Willie spent his journey pondering over how much or how little he would tell his Aunt about the dilemma he found himself in, but Sean had other ideas about the *'how much'* and the *'how little'*.

"You'll have to tell her the whole story," he insisted, when Willie broached the subject. "Sure she knows you're hiding something and she'll not rest until she gets to the bottom of it. You know what she's like. You might as well be trying to smuggle daylight past a rooster as trying to hide anything from *her*."

Willie was surprised at how patiently Elsie listened as he unfolded the sorry tale. She never interrupted once and listened intently to everything he told her.

"I won't bring her back here," Willie said, when he had finished his account of the last two days. "I'll take her straight back to her parents, and then I'll start proceedings to get her out of my life."

"Oh no, no," Sean exclaimed. "You can't divorce her. Sure it wouldn't be right in the eyes of God."

"Ugh Sean," Elsie declared, waving her hand in a 'go away' motion. "Don't be so Catholic!"

"It's nothing to do with being Catholic," he protested. "It's you Protestants! Have you no sense of Christianity about you atal?"

The question was asked with mock severity.

"It's nothing to do with being Protestant either," Elsie informed him. "It's just because we have enough sense to know that he doesn't need a proper divorce, he only needs an annulment."

"And why would that be?"

"Well now, my dear man, you should know why," Elsie replied, "for weren't you the boy who encouraged him to go to the pub on his wedding night."

Sean pulled a face that admitted defeat, but the gesture seemed to ease the tension and Willie started to laugh.

"If ever a match was made in Heaven," he said, "it's you two."

"I'll match him any day of the week," Elsie declared.

Then turning to Sean she said, "Put the kettle on, sweetheart, we could be doing with another wee cup of tea."

"Yes, madam; of course, madam. Will there be anything else, madam?"

He avoided the cushion she threw at him and left the room calling over his shoulder, "Missed."

With the short respite of humour gone, it was back to the serious matter of what to do next.

"You have to be sensible about this," Elsie declared, knitting her brows together. "First of all, you can't consider driving all that way back to Belfast in this weather with a girl who has just come through what she has suffered."

When Willie attempted to interrupt she held up her hand to silence him and continued, "In spite of all the wrong she has done, she's only human, and she'll be suffering the loss of that baby, and that's not a pleasant experience."

Her eyes misted over with tears but she quickly wiped them away with the back of her hand. "Bring her here," she continued. "I'll look after her until she's feeling better, or, at least, until the weather improves, and then we'll see what happens after that."

In spite of the hurt and anger Willie was feeling, he knew his Aunt was right, and if he was ever going to be the kind of doctor he always wanted to be, then he had to accept the fact that there would be times when the welfare of a patient would have to take priority over any personal problems he might have. So, if he could think of Victoria as a patient, then maybe that would help him to cope, he decided. But bringing her back to the hotel as his wife? That was another matter entirely. As if reading his mind Elsie said, "Room five is vacant. Maybe you would want to move your things in there."

"Room five?"

"Aye," Elsie replied. "It has two singles."

Willie spread the rug across Victoria's knee, and then tucked it around her legs.

"That's very kind of you," she said, looking up at him with eyes that were having difficulty holding back the tears.

"It was my aunt's idea," he told her, closing the car door. Going round to the driver's side, he slipped behind the steering wheel and turned on the ignition.

"Where are you taking me?"

"Where I'm taking you, and where I would like to take you, are two completely different places."

When she didn't comment and just sat staring straight ahead, Willie continued.

"I'm taking you back to Auntie's because the roads are too treacherous to attempt the long journey up North."

"What have you told them?"

"Told them?" Willie puckered his brow but never took his eyes off the road. It had started to snow again and the wipers were having difficulty coping. The heater wasn't providing much comfort either.

"About me? About what was wrong with me."

"The truth," Willie replied.

Victoria took a long intake of breath, and then slowly let it out again.

"Did you have to?"

"Yes, because I've never deceived them before, and I'm not about to start now. Elsie and Sean have been good to me –they don't deserve to be lied to, and anyhow, it was obvious I was hiding something. OK? Does that answer your question?"

The silence that accompanied the rest of their journey was only broken by the swish of the wipers and the hum of the engine.

Willie stole an occasional glance in Victoria's direction as he manoeuvred the small car along the narrow snow-covered road. Her face was ashen, emphasized by the bright colours of the tartan rug that she had drawn up to her chin, and, in spite of his anger, he started to feel the first stirrings of pity.

A blazing fire in the private sitting room greeted their arrival, and the chicken soup that Elsie said would take the chill out of their bones until dinner was ready portrayed a semblance of normality. Victoria thanked her profusely – a huge contrast in attitude compared to their initial meeting, and although the rest of the evening passed in a pleasant enough manner (all thanks to Sean and his anecdotes about some of their previous guests) there was, however, a sense of tension – a careful selection of topics and comments.

Shortly after 9. 30. pm Victoria yawned and Elsie suggested that she should have an early night – better to get as much rest as possible – it would help to build up her strength. Victoria agreed, and as she rose to leave the sitting room Willie called after her, "Room 5."

She stopped and stared at him, her eyes full of questions. It was obvious that she thought she had been abandoned to a room of her own.

Willie felt that pang of pity again, as she was standing in the middle of the large room like a lost child.

"See you later," was all he said.

She closed the door behind her without replying.

Elsie reached across and touched Willie's arm.

"What are you going to do?" she asked.

"I don't know," Willie said, rubbing his hands up and down his cheeks.

"To-morrow's another day," Sean said, "and for what it's worth, I think she's sorry."

"Of course she's sorry!" Willie retorted. "She got found out, and that wasn't in her plans. Victoria always got what she wanted," he continued. "Ever since she was a child, everything had to be her way, so this must be quite a shock to her system."

"Maybe she has grown up a little in the last few days," Elsie said.

"Go on up to her," Sean suggested, "for I have a strong notion that she won't be asleep."

Willie shrugged his shoulders and Sean continued, "Sure you know you have to talk to her without anybody else around. You can't avoid the inevitable for ever."

Willie's gentle knock on the bedroom door was answered with a low "Come in."

He tossed his jacket on the chair by the window then pulled back the curtain and gazed out at the white world. Bathed in moonlight, it was like a picture from a Christmas card, or even a scene from a film where the hero would rescue a damsel in distress from an avalanche, and they would fall in love and live happily ever after. How ironic that such a thought could enter his head, considering the present circumstances.

This shouldn't be happening, he mused. Victoria shouldn't be here – it should be Martha and we would just have returned from a walk in the moonlight and a snowball fight and Martha would be laughing and arguing that her aim was better than mine and that was why my hair was wetter than hers and then I would take her in my arms and we would kiss and then chase each other back to the house where Aunt Elsie would tut tut about how I had never grown up.

Then he turned and looked across at the big sad eyes staring at him from above the quilt on the narrow bed in the corner.

What was he going to do with this spiteful, devious, pathetic piece of humanity that he had married? What a mess. What a complicated, unbelievable mess.

"Willie, what are you going to do?" she asked, as if reading his thoughts.

"I'm going to sleep over there," he said, pointing to the other bed. "What did you think I was going to do?"

"I didn't mean that. I meant, what are you going to do about us?"

"What do you expect me to do?" he demanded. "You deceived me. You made a complete fool of me. So the best thing for both of us is to get this sham of a marriage annulled as soon as possible and then try and put it all behind us."

She started to cry. "Please, Willie no, no, don't do that. Just give me a chance and some day you might be able to forgive me and we could be happy together."

He didn't speak – just looked at her in amazement. How could she even imagine such a thing?

Suddenly she sat up and shouted. "It's her, isn't it; it has always been her, but you can't have her, you'll never have her, because she doesn't want you and she has only been stringing you along. She's Sammy's woman, she'll always be Sammy's woman, so you might as well get used to it. I know I deceived you, but at least I love you and I would have loved my baby too if I had got the chance."

She reached across and switched out the light on the bedside table, then lay down and turned her face towards the wall. Willie couldn't think of a suitable reply to her unexpected outburst, so he copied her actions as he lay down on the other bed, switched off the light and turned *his* face towards the wall.

Next morning a thaw was starting to set in, but only with the weather – Willie's attitude towards Victoria was as icy as ever. He realized his attitude was making Elsie and Sean uncomfortable, and the fact that Victoria was doing her best to be friendly and sociable towards them was making him feel as though he was the big bad wolf in the whole situation. So as the day wore on and Sean was his usual jovial self, Willie made an effort to be included in the conversations and even managed to keep smiling when Victoria got involved.

It was interesting, Willie thought, watching how nice Victoria could be when it suited her, but he was not deceived by her behaviour. As far as Willie was concerned she was doing what she had always done, she was manipulating the situation to her own advantage. If she could get Elsie on her side then she would assume she was half way to winning Willie over. However, Willie wasn't going to be fooled again; nevertheless, a pleasant, friendly Victoria would be easier to spend time with than the self-centred creature he knew she really was.

Later that evening Willie said he was going for a walk – just to get a breath of fresh air and leave the women to their blethering, he declared. He made the comment in a joking way for he didn't want to offend his Aunt, although he had to admit that he was quite amazed at how well the two women were getting along. He had frequently overheard them discussing current affairs. Although, on second thoughts, he shouldn't be surprised, since Victoria always had the ability to hold court when there was anyone around who was prepared to listen to her.

On his way back Willie met Molly coming along the path.

"Don't tell me you intend to ride that thing in these conditions," he said, pointing to her old rusty bicycle. "The roads are still pretty slippery."

"Ah, sure, it's no bother to me," came the cheery reply. "The worst I can do is fall off."

Willie couldn't help smiling - that girl was a ray of sunshine no matter what the weather was like.

"Well, be careful anyway," Willie warned as she attempted to place her foot on the pedal.

"You too," she said, "and, by the way, that young wife of yours.."

"Yes?" Willie encouraged when she hesitated.

"She loves you. It's in the eyes; it's always in the eyes."

Then her other foot was on the second pedal and she waved goodbye as she headed for the roadway. Willie watched as she disappeared around the corner. He waited, listening for the crash, but there was nothing to disturb the silence except the drip, drip of the melting snow.

Back on Daisy Farm it had been a day like any other in Martha's mundane life, except that it was a Friday. Martha liked Fridays for that was the day Nancy Shaw always called in to visit her mother and bring the latest news of the village. Being a midwife, she was in contact with a lot of different people so she always had something interesting to pass on and today had been no exception. First on the list was the report that Miss Hardy, the school teacher, had died – the funeral was scheduled for the next day at 2.p.m. Miss Hardy had been Martha's teacher in Primary school, so the three women agreed that Henry would need to go to the funeral. Martha assumed her father would think he had better things to do, but would probably go anyway out of what he would call 'decency's sake'. Then Nancy went on to relate how Bobby Birch had been apprehended by the police for having no tail light on his bicycle, but apparently they had let him off with a caution. Martha listened to all this as she set about making tea for their visitor – she made extra knowing that Sammy was about the yard helping her father with something, and seeing Nancy's bicycle propped against the wall they would know the kettle would be on and wouldn't hesitate to join them. Martha was right. The two men came in bringing a rush of frosty wind in their wake.

"For goodness sake, close that door at once," Martha ordered, "or we'll be blown away."

"Well Nancy," Henry said, when they were seated around the kitchen table. "What's the latest from the big city the day?"

"Some city," she laughed. "Down the main street and up the same street, but.."

There was a long pause. She took another sip of tea then cleared her throat, "I was keeping the best till last."

"Go on," Sammy urged. Normally he wasn't interested in the goings on of the village, but there was something in Nancy's voice that implied that whatever she had to relate might be worth listening to.

"I was in the post office this morning," she began, "and Bella was telling me – oh, by the way, she's thinking about retiring, she was saying that she has been postmistress there for over thirty years."

"Is that all?" Sammy asked. "I thought something exciting or unusual had happened."

"Well, actually, it has," she told him and went on to relate the story Bella had told her. Martha listened as if she had suddenly been transported into some huge sphere where everything outside it was muffled, yet still easy to understand. According to Nancy, Mrs Burnside had always kept in touch with Bella since they moved to Lisburn and she had phoned her the other day to tell her that their Victoria had got married to a young man she was at Queens' with. He was coming out a doctor and they were spending their honeymoon with friends of his in County Cavan.

Martha dropped the plate she didn't realize she was holding, as Nancy continued. "She said his name was Willie Rossborough and I was thinking, was that not what you called the wee fellow that stayed here during the war?"

"It was," Ruby said, "but we haven't been in touch with him lately."

Sammy let out a loud whistle and said, "I'm not one bit surprised. Victoria always had a notion of him; even when we were weans she clung to him like a cleg to a blanket."

"We would need to write and congratulate him," Ruby said, subconsciously rubbing her wrist. Martha knew the break had caused a lot of stiffness in the joint and automatically offered to write on her behalf without stopping to think about how hard it was going to be.

"Be sure and include me when you're writing," Sammy said, "for God help him, he'll need all the best wishes he can get when he's tied to that wee madam – he'll just be like a langled goat."

Later that evening Martha wrote

Dear Willie and Victoria,
I'm writing on behalf of my mother and father and of course myself, plus Sammy, to congratulate you on your recent marriage. We wish you all the best and hope you will have many long years of happiness.

Kind Regards and Best Wishes,

Martha Sloan

She addressed the envelope
Mr & Mrs William Rossborough
C/o Queens' University

Martha closed her bedroom door – it was good to finally be alone. She pondered over the last few hours of the evening. She had placed the letter in the window for the postman to collect the next morning and she had completed all the tasks that were necessary, including seeing her mother safely into bed.

Then she reflected on Sammy's behaviour. He had been unusually nice to her. It wasn't that he was ever not nice, but, as a rule, he always found something to pull her leg about. She was glad that he wasn't in his usual teasing frame of mind for she wasn't in the mood to return his good-natured banter.

He didn't even taunt her about stepping in the wrong place when they went into the pig sty to check on the sow that was due. Normally, that would have been her father's responsibility, but he had decided it was necessary to attend Miss Hardy's wake. A wake was always a good place to catch up with neighbouring farmers and chat about the good old days.

Martha lay in the stillness of the room – she heard her father entering the house and then the familiar sounds that followed. The noise of the clock being wound up, his footsteps on the stairs, then the opening and closing of the bedroom door and the muffled voices that slowly grew fainter. Now the night was hers – no one would be calling her – no one would need her until the morning when the routine would start all over again as if nothing had changed – as if nothing had happened to break her heart. Martha cried until there were no tears left, and then she made a solemn promise to herself that no man would ever make her cry again. Afterwards in a symbolic gesture she reached up, knocked on the wall above her bed and said, "Good Bye, Willie."

"You will stay – won't you?"

Willie looked at the thin pathetic face of the girl he had married, and didn't know how to answer her question. His original plan had been to drop her off at her parents' and then go straight to Queens' where he would try to get a good night's sleep in preparation for the tasks he had to carry out the next day - an appointment with a solicitor being the main thing on his list. But pity was starting to affect him again when he thought about the coolness in Mrs Burnside's greeting upon their arrival. There was no friendly welcome like they received in Cavan – just details about how space had been made in Victoria's wardrobe to accommodate whatever clothes he intended bringing with him, and there was no need for them to look for a place to live because the bungalow was big enough for them all and, of course, they probably wouldn't see that much of them anyhow as they would be spending so much time at the University. Willie had made no comment as she went on to inform them that there was salad in the fridge if they were hungry, and now she and Daddy were going out for the evening. Daddy was standing by, seemingly waiting for his instructions, when a slight nod of his wife's head indicated that it was time for him to put on his coat and they would be on their way. At the door *daddy* turned back, winked at Victoria and whispered, "Welcome home, both of you."

Then the door closed, the car drove away and Willie and Victoria were alone.

There had been no time and no opportunity to tell her parents that he wouldn't be staying. He had rehearsed his speech repeatedly in his head, all he had to do was say it – let them know what a scheming little madam they had produced and how he intended to end the marriage as quickly as possible. But Mrs Burnside appeared to have her speech ready too, and there was no opportunity to interrupt her. But had he been given the chance to say all that he intended to say, he had to admit that he probably wouldn't have been callous enough to do it at that particular time. It was the pity thing again and it was really giving him a lot of problems.

"Do you want some salad?"

"Not really," Willie replied. "Do you?"

"In the middle of January?"

Willie was certain that his Aunt Elsie's Irish stew would have been much more welcome, but refrained from making any comment. Victoria broke the awkward silence that followed.

"Are you going to bring your case in?"

When Willie didn't answer she pleaded, "Please Willie, don't do this to me, don't leave me. You know I'm sorry for everything I've done and if you would only talk to me."

"What is there to say that hasn't already been said?"

"I don't know, but you weren't being unkind to me on our journey and you did stop and buy me lunch and you even smiled once or twice so I thought that maybe...."

"Maybe what?"

"I don't know, I just don't know." She flopped onto the nearest chair and looked up at him with tears in her eyes.

"I better get over to the Uni. There are things I need to do."

"But you will come back, won't you?"

He didn't know how to answer, so he walked out, gently closing the door behind him.

The letter was there, staring up at him – the letter addressed to Mr & Mrs Rossborough. He recognized the handwriting, and he felt as though a band of steel was wrapped around his chest, getting tighter and tighter. With shaking fingers he slid open the flap and read the short note. Martha had chosen her words so carefully that he was sure her best wishes were sincere, which confirmed that she had never had any feelings for him apart from friendship, and the special moment they had shared had been nothing more than a moment of madness. The way Sammy's greeting was included with hers only added to his belief that they were romantically involved, and it would only be a matter of time before he would be hearing about *their* wedding. That thought did nothing to make him feel any better, but at least he knew the truth, he also knew that Martha Sloan would always hold a place in his heart that no one else could ever enter.

He placed the rest of his clothes in a bag and put it on top of the case that was still sitting on the back seat of the car. Then he drove to the outskirts of Lisburn, to a posh bungalow that he knew he could never think of as home. It seemed his future was sealed, and he no longer had the energy to fight the inevitable.

The slim figure of his young wife was standing in the open doorway as he pulled up in front of the house. She ran down the steps to meet him. "Oh Willie, you *have* come back."

"Take that inside before it gets cold," he said, reaching her a roughly wrapped parcel.

"What is it? she asked.

"Two fish suppers," he replied.

1958 CHANGES

They had only been gone fifteen minutes and already the house was strangely quiet without Martha and her mother, although Henry would never have admitted to anyone that he missed them. In fact, he even loathed having to admit it to himself. But it was something he would just have to endure for the next fortnight as the women had gone on their annual holiday to Portrush.

Henry didn't really approve of holidays; he thought they were the height of nonsense and a waste of money. Why pay to lie in a strange bed and eat food that somebody else cooked when there were perfectly good beds at home and plenty of food in the cupboard? The fact seemed to escape him that a holiday meant no cooking, no bed-making, no responsibility. Being able to please themselves was a rare treat for both wife and daughter.

Had it not been for the advice of Doctor McGoldrick, the first holiday would probably never have taken place. It was after Ruby's unfortunate fall that the good medic had suggested a couple of weeks at the seaside would be beneficial to the lady's health and would no doubt speed up her recovery, and of course it was necessary for Martha to go with her. The Doc. had been right. Ruby returned home with a bloom on her cheeks that had been sadly missing for quite some time, and Martha had also taken on a suntanned healthy glow. Much to Henry's surprise at his own generosity, that had set the precedent for the next six years.

Tam Logan was, as usual, their means of transport to the much needed and eagerly looked forward to time of relaxation in Mrs Lockhart's comfortable hotel, and the journey there was always enjoyable too, as Tam kept them entertained with his regular supply of jokes and witty replies. Today seemed different though, for Martha got the impression that Tam was a man with something on

144

his mind. Ruby didn't appear to notice anything unusual as she viewed the passing countryside, while sharing opinions with Tam about current affairs and how quickly time passes. But Martha had become aware of the taxi man looking at her in the rear view mirror. She smiled at him, but as she could only see his eyes she wasn't sure if he had responded, as he immediately looked away. Maybe where she was sitting was blocking his view and he was trying to see past her, she assumed, so she moved nearer the edge of the seat and out of the way.

Tam had glanced in the mirror at the pretty girl who spent her life practically shut away from the outside world as she went about her duties both inside the house and on the land, always there for whichever parent needed her the most at any given time. She should be having a life of her own, and a family of her own, but her single status must be from choice Tam decided, for he knew there had been several young men who would have been proud to call Martha Sloan their wife. But time had passed and it seemed that the single life was what she wanted. Or was she single because she couldn't have the *one* she wanted? If that was the reason, then perhaps this was a good time for her to be away from home.

It was Nancy Shaw who had given him the news earlier in the day just as he was getting into the car to drive to Daisy Farm to collect Ruby and Martha.

"Did you hear about yer man Burnside?" she called from the other side of the street.

"No, why, what has happened?"

Nancy came over with all the details according to the morning paper. Leonard Burnside, suddenly at his home etc.etc. and the funeral was taking place in the village at 2 pm on Monday. Nancy went on to conclude that it had probably been a heart attack when it was sudden and there would likely be a big crowd on account of him being so well known, and wouldn't it be interesting to see what Victoria looked like now, and of course, her husband too, for he was the wee boy who had been an evacuee up at Daisy Farm during

145

the war and it was a pity that Martha and Ruby would be away and miss him.

Tam didn't comment, for he couldn't be sure which would be the lesser of the two evils.

Tam glanced in the mirror again. At first Martha didn't seem to be aware of his scrutiny as she appeared to be concentrating on winding up her wrist watch, but suddenly she lifted her head and looked him straight in the eye. He instantly looked away. What would she think of him? But what he was thinking was much more complicated as he pondered the possibilities. If he didn't inform them of the death, then it would be all over before their return and there would be no opportunity for Martha to feel it was her duty to offer her condolences to Victoria, which would obviously mean meeting Willie again, and Tam had a notion that such an encounter could be uncomfortable, perhaps even painful, for the young woman sitting in the back of his car. But if he did tell them, would it spoil Martha's holiday knowing that Willie was back in the village, even if it was only for a short time? Tam was certain that Martha had, at one time, feelings for Willie – perhaps still had. He was equally sure that the feelings were mutual, so how or why did that fellow ever get himself tied to Victoria Burnside?

By the time they reached the hotel, Tam still hadn't decided what would be for the best until, quite suddenly, Martha asked, "Are you all right Tam? You don't seem to be your usual self."

"I'm fine," he replied, and as he looked at her kind, caring face his mind was made up. What she doesn't know won't hurt her.

"Just a bit tired," he continued. "Too many late nights."

"Well now, you take care of yourself, and don't be overdoing it," she warned.

"Don't worry; I'll take your advice," he agreed, and then laughed and said, "You know me; I always do what I'm told."

"I believe you," Martha replied in a tone of voice that implied she didn't believe a word he said.

"See you in a fortnight," he said, getting into the car, wondering if he had made the right decision.

Mother and daughter waved good bye from the hotel door then turned to accept Mrs Lockhart's friendly welcome.

"I suppose I would need to go to the funeral," Arthur said, placing a large dollop of champ on Henry's plate. Arthur was being neighbourly to Henry – thought it was the right thing to do - asking him over for his dinner on the Sunday on account of Ruby and Martha being away. Sammy had washed and cut up the scallions while Arthur had washed the spuds, but all this preparation had only taken place after they had come home from church. Henry's stomach was rumbling with hunger because he was used to eating much earlier on the Sabbath day. His women folk did all the preparing of the food the previous night and he followed their instructions as to the cooking time the next day, so they were able to sit down at the table as soon as the ladies had removed their hats and exchanged their high heels for their comfortable slippers.

"I suppose I would need to go too," Henry said.

"Of course you would," Sammy agreed, "for, after all, he's Willie's father-in-law and I suppose I should go too on account of us all being friends when we were young."

Henry nodded his head and reached for another piece of butter, but his thoughts were on a previous event when Willie had left the farm in the early hours of the morning leaving a note that Henry still thought conveyed more between the lines than the hastily scribbled words could ever express.

"What about the women folk?" Arthur inquired. "They'll not have heard. Will you ring the woman they're staying with and let them know?"

"I suppose I should," Henry mused, "but, on second thoughts I don't think I will. Knowing Ruby she would likely decide it was her duty to offer her sympathy to the family and she would be telling me to send Tam Logan to bring her home."

"You're probably right," Arthur agreed, "and it would be a pity to spoil their wee holiday."

The decision was made and nothing more was said on the subject as the three men tucked into their meal.

"Sorry for your trouble," Henry said.

"Thanks," Willie replied, reaching for Henry's outstretched hand.

Arthur and Sammy followed Henry's gesture, and then wee Davy, as everyone still referred to him, although he had grown to a respectable five foot nine, made his way through the crowd to inquire about Victoria's whereabouts.

"She didn't come," Willie informed him. "It would have been too much for her. You know how much of a daddy's girl she was."

Sammy was amused by the explanation, but couldn't be sure in what context Willie meant it. If he had been asked to decide he would probably have opted for the possibility that it was more tongue in cheek than with any deep understanding of his wife's grief.

"And how is Mrs Burnside coping?" Henry asked.

"She's very upset," Willie replied. "So she decided to stay with Victoria."

The three men nodded as if to say they understood.

"And how are things up at the farm?" Willie directed the question to Henry.

"Same as usual," Henry said.

"And Ruby? Did she make a complete recovery?"

"She's doing all right."

"That's good. Give her my best wishes."

Henry could sense the tension in Willie's voice – knew he was remembering his last visit to Daisy Farm, knew he was aware that Henry was remembering it too, and the fact that he didn't mention Martha confirmed Henry's suspicions that there had been something going on between them – something that had gone terribly wrong. Hence his hasty marriage to Victoria Burnside.

Sammy was also aware that Willie seemed to be uptight, but he had no sympathy for the young man who had, in his opinion, in some way upset Martha, so just to prove that whatever it was then it no longer mattered, he announced, "And Martha is fine too. I think her only problem is deciding which fellow to go out with, and she'll probably add a few more strings to her bow this fortnight when she's in Portrush."

Willie's face paled as he pictured Martha in somebody else's arms, but at least it proved that she and Sammy hadn't married. That discovery resulted in mixed feelings – relief that she was still single, but hurt at the knowledge that although she was free, he wasn't, and it was entirely his own fault. Eventually he managed to stammer, "Is her mother with her? Is she OK?"

The questions were directed to Henry, but Henry never got a chance to reply as Sammy continued, "OK? I'd say she's more than OK. Staying in Mrs Lockhart's hotel with a lovely sea view - plenty of good food and nothing to do all day, sure she's having the time of her life."

Sammy smiled with satisfaction. That would let him see that he wasn't needed; Martha was fine and had plenty going on in her life without him.

The rest of the mourners started to gather round wanting to speak to Willie, allowing Henry the opportunity to move away without any further conversation.

Sammy and his father followed close behind.

Martha was returning from the shop after purchasing a couple of her mother's favourite magazines.

"Martha, wait."

Martha felt her whole body tensing, but she kept walking while resisting the temptation to stop and turn around. It couldn't be him, she told herself, not after all this time and not here in Portrush. It would be too much of a coincidence that they would both be in the same place at the same time. It must be her imagination playing tricks on her – maybe it was just wishful thinking. Then she heard it again.

"Martha."

But this time the sound was accompanied by a hand on her shoulder.

"Please Martha, wait, I must talk to you."

Slowly she turned and their eyes met and it was as if the intervening years had never been, but the only thing that she could think of to say was, "What are you doing here?"

"I'm here to see you."

"Why?"

"Because I want to."

"How did you know…?"

"Someone told me – someone who didn't realize just how much information they were giving me."

By this time people were crowding around them trying to get past.

"We can't talk here." Willie said. "Meet me on Ramore Hill in half an hour."

"Will Victoria be there too?" Martha asked. "Are we having a school reunion?"

"Please Martha; don't be like that," Willie pleaded. "Sarcasm doesn't suit you. We have to talk. I need to explain."

"No explanation necessary," she said, as she reached up and pushed his hand off her shoulder.

"I'll go to Ramore now," he said. "I'll wait for you."

She didn't reply as she walked away without a backward glance. Yet she was conscious of his eyes following her as she made her way through the hordes of holiday makers who were lining the street – made her way back to the hotel where she knew her mother would be patiently waiting for her magazines - one of the little luxuries the elderly lady enjoyed during those two weeks in the year when she could relax in the knowledge that there would be no one to moan about the rubbish that is printed nowadays.

Martha wrestled with her sense of right and wrong as she listened to her mother explaining how tired she was and suggesting she should have a wee lie down instead of sitting outside in the sun. Martha needn't stay in, she insisted. She should go for a walk and get some fresh air.

It was as if fate was decreeing that she should do as Willie asked, but almost an hour had passed since they had met, so it was unlikely that he would still be waiting. However, some inner voice told her he would still be there.

Martha left the hotel and took the winding pathway that led past the churning surf of the Devil's Washtub, then further along and round a slight bend where she saw him, sitting on a rough bench that was secured into the side of the rocks. He was resting his elbows on his knees – his chin cupped in his hands, and then, as if sensing her presence, he rose and walked towards her.

His arm slid around her waist, and slowly, gently, he pulled her towards him.

Her thoughts were in turmoil. She knew she shouldn't have come; this was a big mistake. This wasn't right; he was a married man and he should be at home with his wife and she should be in the hotel with her mother. Her conscience told her to move away but her heart told her to stay. No one would get hurt, she argued with her feeling of guilt, because there would never be another pre arranged meeting – never be another time when they would be alone together. That was something she had decided before leaving the hotel, and it was a decision she knew she would have to abide by. Anything else would be wrong, so very wrong.

He tried to tell her about his life and the terrible mistake he had made and all because he had been too weak to fight for what he really wanted. She didn't want to listen or be reminded about how close they had come to the happiness they could have shared. It was too late, the clock couldn't be turned back, and there was only now, the present, these few stolen moments – moments that she would treasure for the rest of her life.

As the waves crashed against the rocks Martha put up no resistance as Willie pulled her closer into his arms.
"I love you," he said. "I'll always love you."
"I love you too," she whispered, as their lips met.

Some time later!

"I've got to get back to the hotel," she said, reluctantly releasing herself from the comfort of his arms, "or my mother will be organizing a search party."
"I'll walk with you," he offered.
"No," she told him. "I'd rather go alone."
His gaze followed her as she retraced her steps back along the narrow path until the tears blurred his vision. He sighed and sat down on the hillside as he relived every precious minute they had spent together. He knew he would never forget her, or the aroma of her perfume, the silkiness of her hair, the sweetness of her smile or the love that shone from her sad, green eyes. But most of all he would remember her integrity and the will-power that gave her the strength to walk away. A will-power that would forever keep them apart.

Now he must drive back to Lisburn where his grief-stricken wife would be waiting, probably in a foul mood because he'd been away for so long. He could lie and tell her that so many people wanted to talk to him and send her their condolences that he found it difficult to get away any sooner, or he could tell the truth and say he went to Portrush to meet another woman. Either way it wouldn't make any difference because she wouldn't believe him anyhow, so why bother giving an explanation. Willie had become immune to Victoria's unreasonable attitude. She constantly complained about the long hours he spent at the Royal, and her nagging had become nothing more than an irritating background noise that he frequently ignored. The fact that he was now a qualified doctor and took his chosen career very seriously seemed to escape her. Perhaps if she hadn't dropped out of University and had followed the career in law that she used to be so passionate about, then she would have had something to fill her days and her mind instead of lounging around the house all morning in her dressing gown.

"I was starting to get worried about you," Ruby said. "Where have you been all this time?"
"I went for a walk up over Ramore Head."
"But it's dark."
"Not really," Martha told her mother. "There's a full moon and it's shining on the waves and it's beautiful, really beautiful up there. I wish I could have stayed longer."
Martha told the truth, she just didn't tell it all. It was her secret, hers and Willie's.

Tam Logan put the cases into the boot, making the usual remark about how it didn't seem like a fortnight since he had brought them to the Port.
On the journey home he mentioned the fact that Leonard Burnside had passed away. Ruby was immediately concerned and wanted all the details, and wondered why Henry hadn't phoned to let them know. Tam said he assumed Henry didn't want to spoil their holiday. Ruby agreed with that possibility, but was so caught up in the unexpected piece of news that she didn't notice how quiet Martha had become. Apart from commenting that it was very sad, she had contributed nothing else to the discussion. There was something about her reaction to the information that gave Tam a sneaking suspicion that she already knew. But how could she? Unless? But no, that wouldn't be possible. Or would it? Of course

it was none of his business; he just hoped that someone special would come along some day and make Martha happy.

1965

Only four hours left of 1964, only four hours of what Martha considered had been the worst year of her life. It had started all right, just the same way as every other New Year that she could remember. A blazing log fire in the parlour, her father in a good mood and Arthur and Sammy invited over to drink a toast to the new beginning. Then before 8.am Nancy Shaw was the inevitable first footer with her traditional piece of coal for good luck. The fact that Nancy's black hair, which was considered the necessary qualification to be the first caller, was now a steely shade of grey didn't seem to occur to her, but the colour of her bun made no difference to the welcome she always received.

"Happy 1964," she had said, placing the black shiny nugget on the hearth.

"And to you too," came the usual reply.

"Ruby not up yet?"

"She's feeling a bit tired this morning," Martha informed her. "In fact, she has been complaining a lot about tiredness these last few weeks and she even refused her wee annual glass of sherry last night."

Martha pondered over that conversation she had had with Nancy as she sat alone in the kitchen with only the ticking of the clock for company, and realized how all the signs had been there but she just hadn't seen them; maybe didn't want to see them; or maybe it was because the changes were so subtle and gradual that they were only obvious with hindsight. When, six months later, the doctor had shook his head and said it was just a matter of time, Martha refused to believe him. It just couldn't be - it was unthinkable that her mother was going to die. Her mother had always been there, her

155

mother would always be there - she just had to be. But her bed had been brought downstairs to the parlour.

"Just to be more convenient for you," Henry assured Martha. "It'll mean you won't have to keep running up and down the stairs every time your mother needs you."

It was only then that Martha accepted the fact that her mother was going to die.

The bed had been brought down before her grandmother died and it had been brought down again before her Grandfather had passed away. As far as Martha was concerned that was all the parlour was for. A place to die and a place for the wake. In spite of all the cleaning and the amount of Mansion polish she used on the rich dark furniture, the room always retained a faint aroma of lilies. The fact that every New Year was welcomed in by its cosy fireside, and anyone considered too important to drink tea in the kitchen, ie. Rev. Murdock, was entertained there, did nothing to dispel Martha's phobia about its function. Happily on his last two visits the minister had stated that he would prefer to drink his tea in the kitchen because he found it much more informal and homely. Times were changing, and, in that respect, Martha thought it a good thing. She often wondered why some folk considered it necessary to have a parlour or 'a good room' as it was often referred to. She knew quite a few people whose houses weren't big enough to have such a room and they managed quite well without it. But for those who had the space she supposed that because it was considered the best room in the house the family always felt that their dear departing relative should get the benefit of whatever luxury it afforded. But why wait until they weren't in a position to enjoy it?

Martha recalled how, during one of her all night vigils when she thought her mother was asleep, she had suddenly opened her eyes, reached for Martha's hand and whispered, "I don't want to leave you, but I'm going to have to go." She passed away peacefully a short time later.

It was then Martha made up her mind that once her mother was carried from that room, she would never enter it again – she would close the door and pretend it wasn't there.

Easier said than done, for three months later friends and neighbours were gathering once again for the occasion of her father's wake.

It'll be my turn next, Martha thought, for there's no other use for it. It's only for wakes, so there would be no logs burning in the big black grate tonight to welcome in another new year. A cup of tea and an early night, and try to forget the past seemed the only practical option.

Suddenly the door opened, startling Martha out of her reverie, and Sammy walked in, his arms laden with logs.

"What…?"

"We're going to light a fire in the parlour."

"But…"

"No buts," Sammy announced. "And my Da agrees with me," he said, nodding towards his father who was now standing in the middle of the kitchen holding a bottle of sherry.

Both men walked past her while ordering her to put the kettle on and set out four cups for now, and four glasses for the New Year.

"Four?" Martha exclaimed.

"Aye," Sammy said. "Nancy's coming too. She'll be here any minute, so then she won't need to come in the morning and that'll mean you can have a lie-in, for you'll need time to recover from your hangover."

A vision of that brought a smile to Martha's face; it also brought tears to her eyes when she looked at her two good friends who were doing their best to cheer her up in the only way they knew how.

"Only me," Nancy announced, bustling in carrying a biscuit tin containing what Martha was sure would be a selection of the pastry that Nancy was famous for.

"Why all this?" Martha asked.

"Because we know you," Sammy declared, "and the fool notions that you have got into your head about that room, so we're here to prove that it is for more than wakes. So stop asking questions and get that kettle on."

Martha was about to protest, but Sammy silenced her with a look and continued, "Time is marching on and I have to get a good roaring fire going in there as soon as possible for we don't want to greet the New Year with chattering teeth."

Friends, Martha thought. What could be more precious? Their company that New Year's Eve had seen her through what would have been the most lonely night of her life, and, although a few sentimental tears had been shed for the folk no longer with them, 1965 was greeted with hope and determination to carry on and face whatever the new year had in store for them. A marriage proposal from Sammy was definitely not something that had been anticipated.

Now, here she was again, watching the clock, only four hours left until midnight, but not four hours until a new year; it was four hours until a new day. The day she had promised to give Sammy an answer to his all important question. "Tomorrow," she had said when he sat her down on the back of the trailer and announced that she would have to give him an answer one way or another for the suspense was killing him. What he didn't tell her was that his father was constantly asking him what was going to happen and he was tired explaining to him that Martha needed more time. Day by day it was becoming clearer to Sammy that his father was more anxious about the outcome than he was. Surely that couldn't be right? Nevertheless, Martha was a good woman and he would be proud to call her his wife. So tomorrow he would know what the future held, for Martha was the reliable sort and never known to go back on her word. Maybe this was going to be his last night of real freedom, he thought, for if her answer was yes, then she might expect him to change his ways and the Saturday night trips to Murphy's might be frowned upon, so maybe it would be a good idea to bring Saturday forward a few evenings just in case.

Monday nights were usually quiet in Murphy's pub, with only a few elderly locals sitting around the turf fire discussing the state of the country, the price of fags and who could be the best long-distance spitter. The winner was usually judged according to the capacity of the hiss. Occasionally a few strains of 'Danny Boy' could be heard and sometimes an old poem would be recited with everyone contributing when a line was forgotten or maybe even a verse missed.

"You're knocking them back the night," Hughie commented as he slid another glass of Guinness across the counter to Sammy.
"I'm not right started," came the abrupt reply. "Give me a haffin' when you're at it."
Hughie did as he was asked without further comment. It was obvious Sammy wasn't his usual self, he was a man with something on his mind, and experience had taught Hughie that this wasn't the time for small talk. Better to keep quiet and let him work it out in his own way, and although alcohol was not the most sensible route to take, Hughie had, on several occasions, seen its effects giving a chap the courage to tackle problems that he would never have been brave enough to handle in a more clear-thinking state of mind. He just hoped that would be the case with Sammy, for, although the man liked his pint of stout, with two being his usual tipple, he wasn't a whiskey drinker, so the outcome of tonight's spree could go either way.
"Suppose you think I'm a right oul' fool," Sammy said, waving the glass in a circular motion, the amber liquid threatening to spill.
"Why would I think that?" Hughie said, continuing to polish a beer glass.

159

"Thinking about getting married at my age – I'm pushing forty, and anyway, I don't even know if she wants me. Can't make up her mind, says she needs more time, although she did promise to tell me tomorrow, but maybe she won't, maybe she'll still need more time. How much more time *could* she need? She's known me all her blooming life." He started to laugh and waved the glass at his reflection in the mirror behind the bar. "See how I checked myself there - said blooming, I could have said something else, but she wouldn't like it, no no, my Martha wouldn't like it if I said bad words. She's a good woman, you know, there's nothing wrong with my Martha, but she just can't make up her mind."

Sammy swallowed the whiskey in one huge gulp, and then shook his head as the spirits stung the back of his throat. He drew the back of his hand across his mouth and said, "Here, Hughie, give us another."

"Maybe you've had enough," Hughie ventured. "Especially if you're driving."

"But I'm not driving," Sammy announced. "Oh no, I'm here on the bicycle. She can't hear the bicycle going down the lane, so she'll not know I'm out. I'm not as green as I'm cabbage looking. There's no flies on Sammy McCracken!"

"Well, Sammy, how's the world treating you now?" asked the familiar figure that had just occupied the adjacent stool.

"Ah Tam, me oul friend, good to see you," said Sammy, giving the newcomer a hearty slap on the back.

"Any word of you going home?" Tam inquired. "I'm here to collect the Dunlop brothers so I could drop you off on the way past."

"The Dunlop Brothers," said Sammy, waving the glass at his reflection once again. "Now, they're the boys," he continued. "They've no women to bother them – no women to keep them wondering."

Tam didn't reply – it was one of those times that the prudent taxi man knew a reply wasn't necessary. A time to let the talker do the talking, which Sammy continued to do, outlining the advantages of the single life the two elderly brothers had led. It was the classic country tale – the sisters had married and escaped the never-ending round of chores that befall the farming community, while the two brothers had stayed behind and consequently inherited the property when the parents died. According to Sammy, the men hadn't time to look for women, and even if they had, sure no right thinking female would have took either of them, because they were too set in their ways.

Tam and Hughie exchanged knowing looks, for who could be more set in their ways than Sammy McCracken? Even his 'Give us the usual' was as predictable as the next full moon, although tonight's whiskey spree was a huge break with tradition.

Sammy awoke with a headache because he had a hangover. Martha awoke with a headache because she had tossed and turned until after 3 am. and was awake again before seven, and in spite of the long hours of pondering she was no nearer to a decision now than she had been three weeks earlier when she had been shocked by the unexpected proposal.

Perhaps a walk in the crisp morning air and a chat with old Ned would help to untangle her jumbled thoughts. As she made her way along the lane she wondered why she hadn't thought of discussing her dilemma with the old donkey earlier. She realized that a normal, sane individual would consider it the utmost of folly to think that talking to a donkey could, in any way, help to reach a satisfactory conclusion to any problem. But Ned wasn't just any donkey. Ned was special. Ned had patiently listened to her tales of woe and tales of happiness since the first day he had arrived on Daisy Farm, and, although admittedly, his reactions to her stories had never shown any indication that he had formed an opinion about anything she told him, his quiet unassuming company and unconditional love had, at all times, been a great comfort. The way he always made his way through the long grass to greet her when she opened the gate was a sure indication that he was glad to see her.

But today was different. At first she didn't see him, then in the corner of the field......

It was another time to cry on Sammy's shoulder.

"What am I going to do now?" she sobbed.

"You don't need to do anything," Sammy assured her. "I'll take care of what has to be done."

Dear reliable, loveable, Sammy. What would she do without him? Then, suddenly, without one shadow of a doubt, she knew the answer to the question that had occupied her every waking thought since it had first been asked.

Looking up into Sammy's kind, hazel eyes she said, "Sammy, I'm sorry, but I can't marry you – I just can't."

For in that moment she realized she was in the arms of a friend, not in the arms of a lover. Maybe Ned had helped her to reach a decision after all.

LATER THAT WEEK

Willie Rossborough paced the floor, fraught with indecision. Sometimes he regretted ever having applied for the position, and now that he had been successful, he had to decide if he was going to accept it or turn it down.

Another cup of tea and twice more round the coffee table. He finally sat down on the couch, having decided to make a decision. With that thought he smiled. How ludicrous to decide to make a decision. It wasn't exactly what could be called rational thinking. But he knew that some clear thinking and a final decision was the only way he was going to get any closure on his dilemma. Let's start at the beginning, he told himself, and with that thought he recalled the last time he had talked to Martha – the last time he had held her in his arms – seven long years ago. But that was to be the very last time they would be together. He had promised, but only because she had pleaded with him to make that promise. He had kept his word, but it hadn't been easy. So many times he had wanted to ring Daisy Farm just to hear her voice, but he dare not, and all because of the promise he had made. There was to be no contact whatsoever, which he found really difficult, especially when he saw the notice in the paper about her mother's passing. He knew how distressed Martha would be. He also knew that Sammy would be there with his endless supply of comfort and help. How he envied that fellow, always by Martha's side through every event in her life. Then, when he saw the next announcement about her father's death so soon afterwards, he was doubly distraught by the fact that he couldn't contact her. He wanted to be there with her, he wanted to be the one she would turn to for consolation. But he knew it would just be another mistake in the long line of mistakes he had already made. Martha would never forgive him for breaking the agreement they had made. That night on Ramore Hill she had been adamant that they must never meet again. It was against her moral outlook on life to get involved with a married man and she felt the only way she could avoid the temptation was to stay apart. He must never contact her again and if they ever did meet it would only be by coincidence. Willie often wondered if there was any way he could meet her and make it look like a coincidence, but always discarded the idea every time it occurred to him, for Martha was shrewd; she would know he had orchestrated it. It would also be unfair to put her in that situation.

But things had changed now. He was no longer a married man; he was free. Had been free for almost a year. Perhaps he should have contacted Martha sooner, but he hesitated, for although she had never been particularly fond of Victoria even when they were children, she would still expect him to show some respect for his wife's memory. But maybe he had left it too long; maybe by now the love she once had for him would have diminished. He knew she hadn't married Sammy – occasional discreet inquiries had reassured him on that matter, but there was always the possibility that there was someone else in her life that he didn't know about. If he went back to the village and had to see her with another guy, he knew he would regret ever taking over from Dr. McGoldrick.

When he first knew the position was going to become available he couldn't wait to apply. If he was accepted it would be like a gift from heaven. He could picture it all, he would be back to the place he always thought of as home, and with Martha by his side his life would be complete. The dream was nice, but now that it was possible to achieve one part of it, the doubts about the rest of it had arrived with a vengeance.

If only! But life is full of ifs and buts and if it hadn't been for Victoria, but…

Victoria, the cause of all his problems. Or was she? He could have walked away when he discovered she had deceived him. He could have left her in that hospital in County Cavan and returned to Belfast. He could have got the marriage annulled and regained his freedom. He had wanted that freedom; the freedom to drive back to Daisy Farm and tell Martha he loved her, and fight Sammy McCracken for her love if necessary. But he hadn't been able to walk away; he wasn't callous enough to hurt Victoria as much as she had hurt him with her deceit. Then, of course, there was his stupid pride. That senseless, stupid pride that always got in the way. He often wondered about that evening when he and Martha had been alone in the field with old Ned and she had rushed away the second Sammy called her. That unforgettable evening before his hasty departure in the early hours of the next morning. Had he been right in thinking that Martha and Sammy were really intending to marry and that was why she had run off so fast when she heard him calling her name? Or was there a possibility that she thought something had happened to her mother? But he hadn't waited to find out. He had given in, run away and left the way clear for Sammy to win her love. Now, all this time later, they still hadn't married. He had been wrong; he had made the mistake that had changed his life so dramatically. He had no one to blame except himself.

Victoria hadn't been the easiest person to live with, but Willie had tried to make her happy. He didn't love her; he pitied her and he grew fond of her, he even cared about her. He just couldn't love her. She was vulnerable and spoilt, showered with material things from her parents to compensate for the love she craved, the love they didn't seem capable of giving her. She idolized her father, but any slight show of affection on his part was very fleeting, and never in front of Mrs Burnside. His death had devastated Victoria and resulted in her developing a severe bout of depression. In spite of all the treatment and care that Willie provided for her, she never

165

fully recovered. Then she did the unthinkable – she read her mother's diary and discovered that she had been having an affair with the man her Dad had considered his best friend.

It was then she took the tablets – her mother's sleeping tablets. Willie found her when he came back from a late shift; the diary was on the bed beside her, open at the incriminating page and the pen was still in her hand. "Don't put me in the cold hard ground," was all she wrote. The distraught husband did everything he could to revive her, but it was too late. Mrs Burnside was playing bridge with friends in Cushendall.
Victoria's ashes were scattered in Belfast harbour.

Willie collected his belongings from the house that had never been home, then drove away from the woman he considered to be the cause of his wife's death.
He took some time off work and went south to Cavan where the warmth and affection he received from both his Aunt Elsie and Uncle Sean contributed greatly to the way he coped with the trauma he had just been through.

Now, ten months later, he was contemplating another major event in his life. It was a case of, should he or shouldn't he? It was a decision that only he could make - a decision that had to be made within a certain time scale, but there was someone he needed to talk to first, someone he had wanted to talk to for a long time. Another cup of tea and then he would ring her.

"Have you heard the latest?" Nancy Shaw said as she sat down at the end of the table while Martha poured the tea. "No, of course you won't," she continued before Martha got time to reply. "You probably haven't been in the village this morning."

Martha agreed that she hadn't been anywhere all week and sat down opposite the retired midwife to listen to whatever it was that had got her so excited.

"Well," Nancy continued. "Apparently it was only the chosen few who were privy to the information and it seems those chosen few have known for quite some time, but it's common knowledge now so there's no harm in passing on the news."

Martha waited while Nancy took another bite of her pancake and washed it down with a leisurely drink of tea. Martha knew the older woman's tactics – the long pause was for effect and to build suspense, making the story more exciting, but as it was unlikely that there would be anything happening in the village that would be of any special interest to Martha, she was neither excited nor particularly interested. However, it was comforting to have the regular visits from the good friend that Nancy Shaw was, for so much had happened in so short a time and although she had no regrets about refusing Sammy's proposal of marriage, she had become very aware that she was alone in the world. She had plenty of distant relatives but that was all they were, just relatives, not friends. Not friends like Nancy and Arthur and of course Sammy. Martha was pleased that he had taken her refusal so well and sometimes mystified about how they were able to continue with their easy friendship almost as if the possibility of marriage had never taken place.

"Dr. McGoldrick is retiring," Nancy announced, jolting Martha back to the present.

Martha said she supposed he was that age now and remarked that Dr. Regan would probably get the position of senior doctor now.

Nancy agreed that would be the most likely outcome, but according to her source of information it would appear that Dr. McGoldrick was being replaced by someone with similar qualifications, so promotion for the junior doctor seemed unlikely in the foreseeable future.

The shrill ringing of the phone prevented any further discussion on the topic of the doctor's retirement.

"Help yourself to more tea," Martha said, rushing through to the hall.

"Heth I will," Nancy said, as she reached for the teapot. There was nothing Nancy liked better than a nice strong brew, especially if it was in the company of someone she was fond of.

Martha lifted the receiver and quoted the number.

"Hello," the male voice said.

"Hello," Martha repeated. "Who is this?"

There was a long pause during which time Martha began to feel uneasy. Sammy had warned her that she would need to be careful about who she spoke to on the phone now that she was on her own. Martha thought his warning was a lot of nonsense. After all, what harm could anyone do to you when you were in your own home and the caller was obviously out there somewhere else? But Sammy had concerns about unsavoury characters who might ring to find out if there was anyone at home with the intention of breaking in. He had also heard about a spate of anonymous calls that were being made to some of the women in the village and had told Martha to put the receiver down if the caller didn't identify themselves immediately. She was about to take Sammy's advice when...

"Martha, it's me. Please don't hang up."

Martha couldn't speak; she couldn't find the words, but her mind seemed to be working over time. It was as if she had been suspended in some sort of an alien place where she knew everything but nothing made sense. It was Willie; there was no doubt about that. But why? Why now? Why, after all this time, had he broken his promise and thrown her dull mundane world into disarray?

"Martha, are you still there?"

"Yes," was all she could say.

"I've got to talk to you. I've got to see you."

"You promised."

"I know I did, and I kept that promise, but things are different now. Please Martha, I must see you."

"There's someone here. You can't come here." Common sense was returning and although she realized there had to be a genuine reason for Willie to phone and make such an urgent request, she still couldn't agree to let him come to the house without knowing what his reason was.

"OK," he said, "I understand. Or at least I think I do. But please, meet me tonight. I'll wait at the end of your lane. I'll be there at 9 o'clock."

Martha didn't reply as she gently replaced the receiver. This was so reminiscent of their last meeting when he had said he would wait for her on Ramore Hill. She hadn't replied that time either, but he had waited and she had gone to him. She knew he would wait this time too, but what would she do?

"I hope that wasn't one of those funny phone calls that I've been hearing about," Nancy said when Martha returned and sat down at the table.

"No," Martha assured her, "it was just a friend wanting to chat."

"That's all right then," the older woman said. "But you've gone very pale."

"That's probably the result of being indoors so much," Martha said. "I'll really have to make an effort and get that vegetable patch sorted out."

"You're missing that old nag, aren't you?" A sympathetic hand was placed on Martha's arm.

Martha nodded in agreement, a tear threatening to spill.

"Cheer up," came the light-hearted comment, "sure you've still got Sammy."

"Suppose."

"What do you mean by 'suppose'?"

"We're not getting married."

"Oh! Not a big fall out, I hope."

"Oh no, nothing like that." Martha said, "We're still friends. We've always been friends and I suppose that was the problem. I just couldn't be anything else except his friend so that's the end of that quandary."

Martha was relieved when Nancy said she would have to be heading home. It wasn't that Martha didn't enjoy her visits; it was just that she had a lot of thinking to do and she needed to be alone with no distractions. There were so many unanswered questions crowding her mind. The main one being – why now? But there had to be some reason for Willie to get in touch so unexpectedly after seven years. If it had been when either of her parents had died she would have understood. No, that was wrong; she wouldn't have understood, she would have thought he was using the situation as an excuse. Then she chided herself for having such an unkind thought, for she knew Willie was genuinely fond of both her mother and father, and especially her mother. So why didn't he contact her then when she would have needed him? Now she knew she was being unreasonable. She was the one who made him promise to never get in touch, and maybe he didn't even know that either of them had passed away. But what did he mean when he said things are different now? How different could they be? Was it possible that he had left Victoria? Had divorced her? Or maybe Victoria had grown tired of him. Victoria had a history of wanting what she couldn't have and then, as soon as it became available, she lost interest. Neither of these possibilities gave Martha any pleasure, for although she loved Willie she had hoped that he would find some degree of happiness with the girl he had married.

Seven o'clock. Another two hours and Willie would be there, waiting for her. Would she go to him? And if she didn't, would he come to the house? What if Sammy saw him? What would Sammy think? Would he assume that they had been secretly meeting all along and that was why she had turned down his proposal of marriage? She was glad it was lodge night. He and his father always left before eight, so they would be long gone before Willie would arrive. But how long would Willie wait if she didn't go out? He might still be there when they came home. Martha reached the conclusion that there was nothing else she could do except walk down the lane at 9 o'clock and let fate take its course.

"That's us away now," Sammy said, poking his head round the side of the door. "Be sure to lock up."
"OK," Martha replied. "See you tomorrow."
"Aye, see you tomorrow," he agreed, then added, "Why don't you have an early night? You're as white as a sheet."
"Oh, thank you, kind sir. It's not often I get such a beautiful compliment," she replied with mock sincerity.
Sammy made a funny face, and then he was gone.

Martha was watching from an upstairs window when she saw the car pull up at the bottom of the lane. Then, with just the glimmer of the sidelights to indicate his presence, she felt a great wave of compassion for the man who had kept the promise not to contact her, and was now keeping his promise to come here and wait, although she had never agreed to see him. What had happened in his life to bring about this meeting after all this time?
Martha put on her coat and took what she considered to be a step into the unknown, as she closed the door behind her, turning up the collar of her coat to protect her from the chilly autumn night. Why should she keep him waiting, when she knew she would go to him regardless of the outcome?

She was still some distance from the car when the driver's door opened and Willie ran towards her.
"Oh Martha, you are here, really here."
Martha didn't reply as she went willingly into his outstretched arms.

She didn't know why he was here. She didn't know why he wanted to talk to her. She didn't know anything except that with him she felt safe, she felt complete and she felt she belonged.

All the years they had been apart seemed to disappear and only the present mattered. Regardless of the right or the wrong of the moment, her lips met his without hesitation.

Martha didn't question his intentions about where they were going when he held open the passenger's door for her. She was content to go wherever he had decided to take her, but she was pleased when they stopped in the old familiar place, close to where they had gone to school and to church. In the glow from the few street lights she was able to see his face more clearly now.

The village was quiet with only the occasional straggler making their way from one house to the next where it would be tea all round and a good night's chat. Willie had parked the car across the street from Dr. Murdock's surgery. He wanted to take in the atmosphere of the area once again, although he had never completely forgotten it. He also wanted to tell Martha about all the possibilities that lay ahead.

Bit by bit the story unfolded – his knowledge of her parents' passing and how much he had wanted to contact her, his life with Victoria and her tragic death, his moving from his mother - in-law's house in Lisburn to his small apartment in Belfast and eventually his opportunity to become a family doctor in the practice on the other side of the street.

Martha listened with a mixture of surprise, shock and sadness, and apart from her facial expressions she had made no comment. Words had failed her.

"Well, now," Willie said, "I suppose you could say that's me in a nutshell, so what about you?"

172

Eventually Martha found her voice. "Other than the death of my Ma and Da, which you say you already know about, there's nothing else to tell."

"What about Sammy?"

"Sammy's fine," she replied, and then wondered why she hadn't remembered about the important question he had asked her a few weeks previously.

Willie was satisfied with her answer. It seemed obvious that the fellow he had always thought was the barrier between himself and Martha had been, and still was, nothing more than just a good neighbour and a good friend.

Then Martha remembered and was about to let Willie know that Sammy's feelings had changed towards her and he had asked her to be his wife. But somehow she couldn't find the right words to explain the unusual way it had all come about. There had been no indication beforehand to raise her suspicions that Sammy was harbouring such thoughts, and the way he had accepted her refusal was definitely not the reaction of a spurned lover. Although Martha was delighted that they were still friends she still found his reaction very strange. She decided to leave that short episode of her life for another time, especially as Willie appeared to have dismissed Sammy's existence from his mind as he proceeded to talk about his possible new appointment and how he wanted Martha to be part of it.

Martha didn't consider it the appropriate time to discuss such matters. It was too soon after just having learned that his wife had died – it seemed disrespectful. In the few minutes of silence that followed, her thoughts were in as big a tangle now as they had been earlier in the day when she had got his unexpected phone call.

"Penny for them," Willie said, reaching across and gently touching her cheek.

"I was just thinking, I would need to be heading home."

"Why, what's the rush?"

"Sammy's at a lodge meeting and when he gets back and doesn't see a light in my window, he'll be over to see what's wrong."

Too late! She had said the wrong thing and the deep, long sigh from Willie confirmed her mistake.

"You know what he's like," Martha said, trying to undo her blunder. "He thinks he has to be responsible for everything and everybody, and especially since Da died. I do believe he thinks I'm a prime target for murder – that I'll be strangled for my money." She giggled to emphasize how ridiculous that idea was, but Willie didn't appear to be amused.

"Oh well, we mustn't cause Sammy any distress."

Willie started the engine and the short drive back to Daisy Farm was travelled in silence until they were approaching the end of the lane.

"Will I drop you off here in case Sammy sees me, or can I take you on up to the house?"

"Here will be fine," Martha said, reaching for the door handle before the car had come to a complete standstill.

"Nice to have seen you again," she said, and before he could reply she had jumped out and slammed the door shut behind her and was hurrying up the lane. Her emotions were all over the place and she just couldn't cope with anything more.

She rushed upstairs and switched on her bedroom light. Sammy would think she had taken his advice about an early night, so he wouldn't call round to check if she was OK. She would have the rest of the night for tears and regrets. Why, oh why, did she mention Sammy in that way when she knew it would give the wrong impression? Stupidity, she decided, plain silly stupidity. Then, refusing to accept all the blame, she decided that Willie had behaved like a spoiled child. A few seconds later she was regretting her hasty departure from his car. That had been childish behaviour too. Why did it all have to go so wrong? It was all Sammy's fault, was her next line of reasoning.

Sammy had spoiled the special moments she had been sharing with Willie all those years ago when he had called her name for no particular reason, and now he had spoiled them again tonight, and he didn't even know he was responsible. Now Willie had gone out of her life another time, and probably for the last time. There had been no arrangements to meet again, but of course there had been no time to make any plans. Willie was irritated because Sammy had invaded their time together as he had always done and she had let it happen. Now Willie was gone and although she knew he worked in the Royal she couldn't remember what part of the city he had told her his apartment was in. But it didn't matter anyhow because she wouldn't try to contact him. She may have lost the man she loved, but she still had her pride.

Willie clenched and unclenched his hands around the steering wheel a few times then banged it with his fist. He was glad no one could see him – it wasn't the accepted type of behaviour for a professional person who, to all who knew him or had ever met him, was considered a young man with extraordinary self-control. He was a man who, in all situations, coped with dignity and patience, and could bring a sense of calm and acceptance to a distressed patient or a recently bereaved family. This was a completely different situation. He was the person in distress and he had no one to turn to for help or understanding. The fact that he had parked his car in a laneway just round the corner from Daisy Farm and was able to occasionally see the light in Martha's window as the trees swayed in the wind, only added to his sense of aggravation at the way the evening had turned out when it had obviously started off so well. What had gone wrong? Silly question. He knew the answer. It was Sammy. It had always been Sammy and there wasn't a thing he could do about it. They may not have married but somehow it seemed as though it was Sammy's life time ambition to be her guardian, her protector, and to keep her away from everyone else. Was he one of these nasty people who, although they may not want something, they can't bear the thought of someone else getting it? Maybe that was the situation and Martha didn't realize it. Maybe she had been waiting all these years hoping Sammy would eventually pop the question. Selfish, arrogant, possessive – Willie thought of several other words he could use to describe his tormentor, but resisted speaking them aloud, even in the privacy of the car.

It was getting late and a thick mist was starting to fall. Willie pulled the starter and drove off in the direction of Belfast.

TWO DAYS LATER

Two days was long enough to wonder about the 'what ifs' and the 'maybe buts'. Willie had made his mind up – he was going to Daisy Farm and he was going to sort out the confusion one way or another, but first he would stop in the village and buy a box of chocolates. He knew Martha was partial to Cadbury's Milk Tray, so, hopefully, armed with the familiar blue box, she would be more tolerant of his past juvenile sulk. But now that he was ready to get into the car after making his purchase and was about to travel the last part of his journey, he didn't feel as confident of the outcome as he had done when he left the city earlier that morning.

"Hello Willie. What are you doing here?"

It was Bobby Birch who had pulled up beside him, trailing his foot along the ground to bring the rusty piece of metal to a standstill. It was a well known fact that Bobby's bicycle didn't have a brake, and even if it had, it was unlikely that he would have used it. Bobby had his own way of coping with everything and the bike was no exception.

If it hadn't been for Bobby's behaviour and his two-wheeled horse as he often referred to it, Willie probably wouldn't have noticed him as his thoughts were else where. But Bobby, although not the sharpest tool in the box, never forgot a face or any bit of conversation he happened to overhear.

Willie acknowledged the other fellow's greeting with a polite, "Hello, nice to see you again," and was about to get into the car when Bobby dropped the bombshell.

"I suppose you're going up to Daisy Farm."

"Probably," Willie replied.

"Isn't it exciting," Bobby said, lifting his shoulders up until they were almost touching his ears, and with a big cheesy grin on his face he continued, "Everybody is delighted; but of course, we always knew Sammy and Martha would get married, but some folk are saying that she's keeping him guessing, but sure that's the height of nonsense when she's going to take him anyway. My Ma says she has likely been waiting for him to ask her for years and now he's done it. Isn't it great?"

Bobby didn't wait for an answer as he put his foot on the pedal and rode off down the street waving his right hand above his head in a cheery farewell.

Willie stared after the retreating figure as if in a trance, then his attention was drawn to the other side of the street where Sammy McCracken was climbing down from the tractor. Oh no, Willie thought, this is just too much.

"I just thought it was you," Sammy said, walking towards him. "Are you going up to Daisy Farm?"

Willie looked at his watch to give the impression that he might have been considering a visit but had probably decided he didn't have time.

"Never worry about the time," Sammy said, "for if Martha finds out you were here and didn't call in, she'll be raging."

"How is she these days?" Willie inquired as if he hadn't seen her in years.

Sammy informed him that she seemed to be OK and had coped reasonably well with the death of both parents in so short a time. Then he inquired if Willie knew about their passing and when Willie said he did, Sammy commented that he thought he'd maybe have seen him at some of the funerals. Willie thought he was being sarcastic but couldn't be sure, so decided to give him the benefit of the doubt. Sammy went on to say that although Martha was looking a bit pale these last few days, she seemed to have got a sudden burst of extra energy for she was gardening and washing windows and sweeping the yard like something demented. Willie just wished that Sammy would stop talking so as he could make his excuses and escape from this unexpected encounter. But escaping from Sammy wasn't going to be easy as he continued to chat about Martha, so Willie decided he would have to mention the forthcoming wedding, just to get the subject out of the way.

"I hear wedding bells are not too far off."

Sammy shook his head and laughed. "I'll say one thing for this village, if you leave it for a while, you'll not be back very long until somebody fills in the gaps for you. But as usual they always get it wrong."

Then Sammy related the true version of how he had proposed to Martha, but she hadn't agreed with the idea.

"Turned me down flat, so she did."

Needless to say, Willie was delighted and had great difficulty keeping the pleasure from showing on his face. Further conversation led Willie to the belief that Sammy didn't seem to care either way, and that it had really been his father's idea in the first place – he had put the notion into Sammy's head.

"You were only going to marry her because your father thought it was a good idea?" Willie exclaimed. "Do you not love her?"

"Love her? Of course I love her. I worship the ground she walks on, but I don't fancy her, if you know what I mean." He nudged Willie's arm with his elbow and gave a sly wink. "But if she'd said yes then I definitely would have married her, for she's a good woman and I wouldn't have let her down. But how's things with you?"

"Fine," Willie replied. "I'm working in the Royal."

"Very good," Sammy said. "And what about Victoria?"

"Victoria is no longer with us."

Sammy wasn't sure how to react to this bit of information or even how he was expected to react. *No longer with us* could mean a lot of things. Fortunately, Willie was conscious of Sammy's confusion and added, "Victoria passed away ten months ago."

Sammy was shocked and hoped he had made the right responses by saying how sorry he was and commenting on how uncertain life can be, but he didn't ask any questions. He got the impression that

Willie didn't want to talk about it. Meanwhile, his mind was racing to the conclusion that Willie was definitely here because of Martha, and, in spite of his casual air, he had every intention of going to Daisy Farm. Sammy couldn't let the matter drop.

"Will you have time to call up with Martha or will I tell her you said 'Hello'?"

Willie checked his watch again.

"I think I *will* take the time and pay her a visit."

"Aye surely, why not? Sure you might as well now when you're so near, and if you don't rush away I'll maybe see you up there. I only came down to the village to leave off a bag or two of spuds at the grocers."

The two men said their farewells, then Sammy made his way across to the tractor, narrowly missing Bobby Birch who was doing another lap of the village.

"Are you going up to the farm now?" Bobby called to Willie.

"Of course I am, but I have to make a phone call first," Willie said, walking towards the red box on the corner.

Martha was still in a state of irritation at the way things had turned out. Angry at Sammy, angry at Willie and angry with herself. As she couldn't accuse Sammy of anything for he wouldn't know what she was talking about, and she couldn't challenge Willie about his attitude because he wasn't there, there was no one left to take her fury out on except the weeds, the windows, and the yard. In due course they had all endured the force of her vehemence and now the range was next. Anything that was moveable was removed, including the front grate and the ash pan. She was on her knees removing the ashes, she had a smudge of soot on her nose, and her hair was a massive frizz because she had been out in the rain earlier in the day. Her skirt had a smearing of ash and her big toe had escaped through a hole in her bedroom slippers.

She heard the door opening but she didn't look round.

"Unless you're here to make yourself useful you needn't stay."

180

"What do you want me to do?"

Martha froze, then slowly stood up – trying to run her fingers through her hair while her other hand made a vain attempt at removing the ashes from her clothes. He stood in front of her looking like a model in Burton's window – grey flannels, checked sports coat, open-neck white shirt and his fair hair neat and tidy. A faint aroma of after shave completed the handsome man who had just entered Martha's kitchen.

Willie put his hands on Martha's shoulder and announced, "No more misunderstandings. I'm here to tell you that you are never going to get away from me again and tomorrow we are going to County Cavan to visit my Aunt Elsie and Uncle Sean. I rang them before I came here and naturally they want to meet the girl I am going to marry."

"But,"

"No buts," he said. "We have wasted enough time and we need a few days away from here to sort out all our plans. The peace and quiet of that part of the country will be the ideal place to do it."

Martha couldn't grasp the enormity of all that was happening, so in a state of shock and confusion she produced a long list of questions and as many excuses, most of which she could only think about but not speak. This was all too sudden. Did Willie really mean what he was saying? Then, of course, there was the small matter of Sammy's proposal which she hadn't mentioned and now wasn't the time to bring up the subject when the mere mention of his name had caused so much trouble such a short time ago.

"What about your work?" she asked. "Are you not needed at the hospital?"

He was already on leave, he informed her, so a few days down South wouldn't be a problem.

"I'll put the kettle on," Martha said, not knowing what else to say.

"Forget about the kettle," Willie said pulling her into his arms, "You haven't answered my question."

"I didn't hear any question – I only heard instructions."

Typical Martha, she could never make things easy for a fellow, so Willie dropped on one knee and announced, "Martha Sloan, will you marry me?"

A sound in the open doorway drew Martha's attention and there was Sammy, wide-eyed with his mouth gaping open. Sammy may have had his suspicions, but, nevertheless, this was a shock.

Martha held her breath. In that split second she was sure this was the end – the end of any chance she had of spending the rest of her life with Willie, and probably the end of her friendship with Sammy because of the inevitable conclusion he would reach.

Sammy broke the silence. "For pity sake woman, give the man an answer and don't keep him in suspense the way you did with me."

The situation was getting worse by the second and Martha was sure she was going to faint. Her legs were feeling weak and the colour had drained from her face.

"It's all right," Willie assured her. "I know all about it. I was speaking to Sammy before I came here."

"You'll have to start again at the beginning," Sammy told Willie. "In the meantime, I'm away over home and when she makes up her mind would you let me know?"

Sammy closed the door behind him and remembered something his father had a habit of saying when any situation finally got sorted. 'All's well that ends well'. Surely this was something that was meant to be and would end well. He had always felt that there was something special between Willie and Martha. Even when they were children they seemed to belong together and Sammy often wondered why they didn't eventually become a couple. Martha had done a good job of concealing her feelings when she heard Willie had married Victoria Burnside but she hadn't fooled Sammy. He knew her too well. But with time Sammy assumed she had got over the hurt and, although he would have been quite happy to marry her, he had to admit it would only have been a marriage of convenience. Two people who couldn't have the person they really wanted had seemed like a sensible solution at the time, but now, having seen Willie and Martha together again he realized it would have been a disaster and was thankful that Martha had had the good sense to refuse his proposal.

"Martha Sloan, will you marry me? And please answer me before there are any more interruptions."

"Yes."

"You will?"

"Of course I will."

INDECISIONS

So much had happened in the last twenty four hours that Martha had to pinch herself to make sure she wasn't dreaming. Willie Rossborough had proposed and she had accepted -she had been to the hairdressers and the frizzy mop had been trimmed leaving her hair in its own natural wavy state. A small brown case was sitting inside the kitchen door and Nancy Shaw had arrived to oversee the departure. Sammy was also there to reassure Martha that he would look after the hens or anything else that might need attended to in her absence.

Then Willie arrived in the yard, tooting the horn to announce his arrival as if his appearance would go unnoticed, and, within minutes, Martha was on her way to meet her future in-laws leaving Sammy and Nancy standing together, each with their own private thoughts. Nancy, smiling with pleasure, knowing that Martha had found true love at last, the sort of love she had known with her Charlie, the sort of love that would endure the test of time. It was plain to see that this romance hadn't just happened overnight – there had to have been something there all along or Martha wouldn't be sailing off with this young man after little more than a moment's notice. To the best of Nancy's knowledge, Willie had only paid a couple of visits to Daisy Farm since the time he had left there as a young boy during the war, and soon after his last visit she had heard that he had married Victoria Burnside. Nancy sighed and wondered how they had missed their way somewhere in the past, but they had found each other now, and that was all that mattered. She was glad that Martha had had the good sense to refuse Sammy McCracken's proposal, for if she hadn't, then wouldn't that have been a handling now with the reappearance of the handsome young doctor?

"Well, I suppose I better be heading home," Nancy informed Sammy. "You'll make sure the door is locked and so forth."
"Aye, no problem," Sammy assured her, turning back towards the house.

Willie stopped at a small café on the Southern side of the border, but Martha didn't feel like eating anything. Of course, she would have to have something, Willie insisted, adding that it was doctor's orders.
"OK," she said. "Will it be two teaspoons three times a day or four?"
They were giggling like teenagers as they went inside and selected a corner table by the window where they could look out over the rambling hills and be separated from the other diners. Martha felt as if she had stepped into another world or even another life where the last thirty five years had been lived by someone else that she only vaguely knew. This was reality, this was the way it was meant to be, this was where she belonged, here with Willie. The way he was looking at her confirmed that he was feeling the same. It was all so perfect, exactly how she had dreamed it would be, so what was the cause of the slight feeling of uneasiness that she couldn't evade? Was it excitement, she wondered? After all, it wasn't every day that a girl got an unexpected proposal of marriage. With this thought she had to smile, for hadn't she got two in less than a month. Maybe it was just the speed at which her life was changing that was taking her by surprise and the practical side of her nature hadn't been able to keep up.

"Wake up, sweetheart," Willie said, reaching across and touching Martha's cheek.
She opened her eyes and gazed at the beautiful building before her. It had wide steps leading up to the front entrance where columns adorned each side of the large door that had suddenly swung open

and a very attractive middle-aged lady came slowly down the steps to greet them.

"My Aunt Elsie," Willie said, "and that's Sean in close pursuit."

Martha went willingly into Elsie's outstretched arms.

"I'm so very glad to meet you again," Elsie said. "I can still recall your wee sad face the day we collected Willie from your home."

"And I can still recall how sad I felt," Martha informed her.

Both women laughed at the memory as Sean approached with his big friendly hand held out in greeting.

"Ah, sure, isn't it great to have you here – both of you."

"And I'm delighted to be here," Martha told him.

Then Elsie ushered everyone inside where a delicious meal was served and the conversation flowed as freely as the contents of the bottle of wine that Sean said had to be finished because it wouldn't keep once it had been opened. He winked at Willie and nodded towards the ladies as much as to say 'don't make them any the wiser'. Elsie and Martha pretended to believe him, which resulted in a lot of laughter as they declared that the men folk would have to drink the rest because one wee glass was all each of them could manage.

The rest of the evening passed in a friendly, relaxed manner.

Elsie and Sean sympathised with Martha on the loss of her parents and inquired how things were on the farm and in the local village. Martha complimented them on the standard and luxury of the hotel and commented on how fortunate Willie was to have such a caring family.

"He's just the son we never had," Elsie said, reaching across and placing her hand on Willie's shoulder.

"Ah, shucks, Aunt Elsie," was the reply, "you'll be making me blush."

Willie placed his hands on either side of his face in mock embarrassment.

The light-hearted banter continued for some time until Willie suggested showing Martha around the grounds.

"Good to see you again," Willie exclaimed as they met Molly cycling up the drive to start her evening shift. "How's things?"

"Ah, you know, just the usual," she replied, getting off her bicycle.

"I'd like you to meet Martha," Willie said, then added, "the girl I'm going to marry."

Molly extended her hand, taking Martha's in a firm grip.

"It's very pleased I am to meet you; for sure doesn't this fellow deserve a wee bit o' happiness."

Martha smiled in response and felt the same warm glow of acceptance that she had experienced earlier when introduced to Elsie and Sean.

Willie and Mollie continued chatting about the hotel and Mollie's family. Martha was highly amused at the other woman's response to the query about how many children she had now and how did she find the time to help with the work here at the hotel.

"Ah, sure I only live up the road a bit from me Ma and when me oul' man finds the odd bit o work here and there I leave them off way her."

"All seven of them?"

"If it's through the week some of them are at school, but if it's during the holidays, then she has them all. Sure she never notices for she was always used with wee ones running around her feet and my oldest is only a year younger than me brother Pat, and anyway, sure we're all the one family."

"It must be a lot of fun being part of such a large extended family," Martha said, thinking of her own childhood when the company she loved so much could only stay for a certain length of time, and as they weren't welcome in the house the winter evenings were often long and boring.

"Ah now, to be sure, it has its moments," Molly chuckled, "but that's life. You just have to accept whatever the good Lord throws at ye."

The dark clouds that had been threatening a downpour for the last half hour finally fulfilled their promise as the first heavy drops of rain started to fall. Martha excused herself from the conversation and started back the way they had come, while Willie continued speaking to Molly about her family. As she walked away she caught a snatch of something Molly said – 'this is the right one now'.

It was then she realized what had been troubling her all day. How could she have been so stupid? Suddenly, the few raindrops became a cloudburst and Martha rushed to the nearest place for shelter. She pushed open a tall ornate iron gate that led into a walled garden and quickly made her way to the summerhouse. She sat down on one of the bamboo chairs and listened to the noise of the rain pelting off the roof. She was relieved that Willie hadn't followed her, for she needed time to collect her thoughts. Then in the distance, she heard him calling her name. She didn't answer – didn't want to see him now or talk to him either. She hoped that he would think she had gone indoors and would continue his search there. She huddled into the corner of the seat, wrapping her arms around herself. The mild autumn evening had suddenly turned cold and she started to shiver as the pink cotton blouse she was wearing was no match for the sudden change of temperature. She felt wretched and lonely and the only thing she wanted to do was wake up in her bed on Daisy Farm to discover that the last few days had only been a dream; that life was still simple and boring, and she didn't have to make life-changing decisions and Sammy would be there to cope with anything that went wrong. However, this wasn't Daisy Farm with all its draughts and blue striped mugs on the kitchen table and Sammy wandering in and out causing muddy footprints on the tiled floor. This was the private garden of a luxury hotel in County Cavan and the man she had loved for years was searching the grounds trying to find her. If she needed proof to confirm that she *wasn't* dreaming, it was standing there in front of her - rain dripping from his fair hair and the previously immaculate white shirt clinging to his body.

"Why didn't you answer when I called you?"

Martha didn't reply. How could she tell him that she didn't want to talk to him?

How could she tell him that she wanted to go home? How could she explain that she didn't want to walk in someone else's footsteps?

"Martha, why didn't you answer me?" Willie asked again.

"I, I, don't know."

Then realizing she was upset about something, he rushed across and gathered her into his arms.

"You poor darling, you're trembling, I'm sorry. I didn't mean to be abrupt with you."

It felt good to be so close to him, safe and warm and loved, yet seconds earlier, she was sure she would never want to speak to him again. Then, remembering those moments of turmoil, she pulled away from him.

"What's wrong?"

"You wouldn't understand," she replied.

"You're not making any sense," he accused.

A long silence followed as Willie paced backwards and forwards, hands in his pockets and a grim expression on his face. He couldn't think of anything that could have upset her. Elsie and Sean had been pleasant and welcoming and Martha appeared to be happy and at ease in their company and it was obvious that she had enjoyed chatting to Molly. As far as Willie was concerned, whatever was troubling Martha had to be some unreasonable flight of imagination. As he had never been aware of her ever being afflicted in such a manner, he was completely mystified by the whole situation. In fact, even as a child, he could never recall a

189

time when she had huffed or given anyone the silent treatment when something didn't please her. No, that wasn't Martha's way of dealing with situations. Martha was always what he would have described as 'up front'. What you saw was what you got.

Martha had returned to the chair and taken up her earlier position of huddling in the corner trying to keep warm.

"What is wrong?" he asked again. It was obvious it had to be something serious for Martha to be behaving in such a way.

"I shouldn't be here."

"What?"

"You heard me."

"I heard you, but I don't understand you."

Then it all came tumbling forth. He shouldn't have brought her here, brought her to the place where he had brought Victoria for their honeymoon. She wasn't Victoria and she never would or could be Victoria and she should have had more sense than to agree to come with him. He hadn't given her time to think clearly so it was all his fault, and anyhow, it was disrespectful to his wife's memory. She wasn't even dead a year.

Willie was completely flabbergasted. How could she have reached this ludicrous conclusion? He had told her all about their first night here and the miscarriage. How could she compare that with a honeymoon? To even imagine that he was in any way comparing her to Victoria was ridiculous. Martha was Martha, the girl he loved, the girl he had always loved and if he hadn't been so stupid she would have been his wife a long, long time ago.

"I knew you wouldn't understand," Martha said, "so there's no point in talking about it. I'm cold and it has stopped raining, so I would like to go inside now, please."

"Of course," Willie said.

Elsie fussed about the state they were in and recommended a hot bath to take the chill out of Martha's bones, but added that a drop of rain wouldn't do Willie a bit of harm, for where there was no sense,

190

there was no feeling. Willie retaliated by pretending he was going to strangle her - his actions incurring a lot more good natured banter, and although Martha appeared to be joining in, Elsie got the distinct impression that all was not well between the two people who had arrived earlier in the day brimming with happiness and a great love for each other.

Martha lay awake staring at the ceiling. The few items she had unpacked earlier in the evening were now back in her case and the note was on the bedside table. The leaflets she had lifted earlier in reception, detailing the timetables of buses and trains to various parts of the country, plus the telephone number of a local taxi firm, were in her handbag.

"Sammy, can you come and get me?"
"Why? Where are you? What has happened? Are you hurt?"
"No,no, nothing like that. I'm all right. I'm in Belfast. I'm at the train station and I just want to go home, and I don't want to take the bus to the village after everyone knowing I was going away."
"OK, no problem, I'm leaving right now. But where's lover boy?"
Before Martha could answer Sammy continued, "Oh never mind, it doesn't matter where he is. I'm coming to get you now. Just stay put."
Sammy replaced the receiver, grabbed the car keys and rushed out of the door almost colliding with his father who was coming in carrying a creel of turf.
"Where's the fire?" the older man asked.
"I'm going to bring Martha home."
Arthur shook his head as he watched the old Ford disappear round the corner of the house.
"What is going to be the outcome of those two?" he asked, and then smiled at his foolishness, for there was no one there to answer his question.

"Ah well," he conversed with the stillness again, "I'll keep a good fire on for it's not the warmest of days, and only the Man above knows what state the poor girl will be in when she gets here. Something terrible must have happened."

If only she had married Sammy, he thought, as he went about his chores, then she would have been here, safe and loved and among the people she knew, instead of gallivanting round the South of Ireland with a stranger. As far as Arthur was concerned Willie Rossborough was only the wee boy from the city who had lodged with Martha's people during the war. Why he had come back into their lives after all these years was something he could not understand. They were all happy and content the way things were, and although Martha had refused Sammy's proposal before Willie came back on the scene, Arthur still thought that, given enough time, she might have changed her mind again and everything would have eventually turned out the way he had planned. The return of the tall, fair-haired man had dashed all hopes of that ever happening. Although in the light of today's events, whatever they were, he assumed something hadn't gone too well with the big romance or Sammy wouldn't be on his way to dear knows where to bring Martha home. So there might still be hope, Arthur decided as he set the table for three. Whatever had taken place, the girl would need a bite of food when she arrived, something that would stick to her ribs, and a good Ulster fry was always acceptable at any time of the day.

Having left the city behind and driving along the quieter country roads, both occupants of the car were lost in their own private thoughts.

Sammy was recalling the pathetic sight that Martha had presented when he first saw her - sitting alone with her head bowed and her wee case at her feet. She had insisted she was fine and everyone had made her welcome, but Sammy wasn't entirely satisfied with her story. If everything had been so good, then surely she would still be with Willie instead of returning home in a little over twenty four hours. It just didn't make any sense. He didn't want to force her into telling him anything that she preferred to keep to herself, but without all the details he couldn't plan how he would deal with the big fella if he had upset Martha in any way.

While Sammy struggled with his tangled thoughts Martha was picturing the scene back at the hotel; she knew that by now, both her disappearance and her scribbled note would have been discovered.

Had she been too hasty? she wondered. In the cold light of day she realized that her fears of being compared to Victoria had been unfounded. Her behaviour towards Willie, plus her tip-toeing out of the house like a guilty criminal in the early hours of the morning were both childish and unreasonable. However, like everything else that had ever happened in her life, there was no turning back. Now she was going home to where she belonged, amongst the people who knew her, the people who had been her friends and would always be there for her no matter what the world threw at her. The possibility that she had ruined what was probably her last chance of happiness with the man she loved cast a dark shadow over everything else that was safe and comforting in her life.

"Keep calm, there's nothing you can do just now," Sean advised.
"I have to do something," Willie insisted. "I just can't sit here while Martha is out there all alone. I have to follow her."
Sean advised against that course of action, stating that by now she may have decided to return. Anyhow, she was a sensible young woman and if she had decided to go home, there was no doubt she would have made her way there without any problems.
"Her reason for leaving would be my biggest concern," Elsie remarked.
Apart from disclosing the contents of the note which merely stated that Martha felt she had to leave and to please give Elsie and Sean

her heartfelt thanks for all their kindness and hospitality, Willie had not disclosed the events of the previous evening and the cause of Martha's distress. Now, looking at the anxiety on his Aunt's face he couldn't hold back the details any longer. As usual, Elsie could see both sides of the situation – Willie's eagerness to introduce the girl he loved to his family and Martha's unease at being brought to the place where her predecessor had been.

"We can't be sure how long she's been gone, so have some breakfast," Elsie advised, "then ring Daisy Farm and, by then, she'll probably be home."

Willie had always loved his Aunt's capable, sensible, reassuring way of coping with unforeseen situations, but this morning she only irritated him. He didn't want to be sensible or practical, he just wanted to find Martha and take her in his arms and never let her go and the fact that his Aunt was probably right only added to his sense of frustration.

Willie had no appetite for the cooked meal that he was presented with, but did his best to appear as though he was enjoying it, although every bite seemed to be sticking in his throat.

If only they had been sharing a room, he was certain that this situation would never have arisen. He would have had the opportunity to talk to her - reassure her that the past was not important. It was gone. It was the present that mattered and that she, Martha, had been, and always would be, the only woman he could ever love. He recalled his Aunt's reaction when he telephoned to say that he was bringing his future wife to meet them. She had been delighted – said she couldn't wait to meet her again after so many years, but had added, "It will be single rooms for the pair of you."

"Auntie," Willie had exclaimed in mock horror. "Do you not realize this is the swinging sixties?"

Elsie had replied, "And do you not realize this is still Catholic Ireland?"

194

They had laughed at the comments, and on reflection, Willie noted that no final decision had been taken. Martha had said Good Night and gone off to her single room without comment or any show of either relief or disappointment. Considering her hasty departure the following morning, the situation had suited her plans perfectly. If only things had been different, if the memory of Victoria hadn't come between them... his thoughts drifted back to a moonlit night on Ramore Hill.

Willie dialled the number and held his breath while he listened to the shrill ringing tone, but no one answered its command. At first Willie felt panic. Had she lost her way? He knew she had never been down South before and wasn't familiar with the area. Had she been hitching a lift and the wrong person had obliged? There were many nasty people out there – being a doctor, he had seen the results of their behaviour on several occasions. Then another possibility – she was with Sammy, and, although that wasn't a pleasant thought, it was preferable to the other possibilities.
He hated the idea of having to contact the person he had, for so long, considered his rival, but there was no other option open to him that he could think of.

Sammy lifted the receiver and quoted the number.
"Willie here," the voice on the other end of the line said, and then continued, doing his best to sound casual. "I was trying to ring Martha but she doesn't seem to be at home. Is there any chance she has popped over for a wee chat with you and your dad?"
"No," Sammy replied, "She didn't pop over for a wee chat, but she *is* here - safe and well. I met her at the station. I don't know what happened to make her come home so soon, but if I find out that you have upset her in any way then you and I will have to have a little talk."
Sammy replaced the receiver before Willie had time to reply.

"She's with Sammy," was all Willie said as he slumped down on the nearest seat.

"Give her time," Elsie said. "Just give her some space and everything will sort itself out."

"That was Willie on the phone," Sammy said, coming through from the hall and sitting down at the table beside Martha. "I told him you were here with us."

"Thanks," Martha replied. Her voice was no more than a faint whisper as she thought, the cat is really amongst the pigeons this time.

"More tea?" Arthur offered, refilling her cup. "There's nothing to beat a wee drap o' tay," he continued with a broad smile on his face. Things had really taken a turn for the better in his opinion. Martha was here where he felt she belonged, and if the expression on Sammy's face was anything to go by, the new boy had got his comeuppence and would hopefully take the hint that he wasn't needed. With a bit of luck he would stay away and let things get back to normal.

Martha got through the next three days in a state of disbelief. How could she have been so stupid? She never used to be like that, she argued with herself. She had always been so organized, so capable in all situations, and now here she was, aged thirty five and acting like a confused, out of control teenager. She really would have to get a grip. What had changed her? Silly question, she chided herself – she knew exactly what had brought about this new set of emotions she had to deal with – Willie Rossborough! There was no denying the fact that life had been a lot simpler before he re emerged.

"Three days," Willie said, "Three days and she hasn't tried to contact me. I think it's all over."

"Don't be such a gosoon," Sean declared. "The girl loves you, although I would be pretty certain she won't be the first to get in touch."

"Why not?"

"Because she's not the type of girl who would chase after a man – she has too much pride – too much dignity."

"How can you be so sure? She was only here for a few hours."

"When you've spent as many years as I have in the hotel business you learn to read people fairly quickly. She's a fine girl and if I was twenty years younger I would give you a run for your money – but don't tell your Aunt Elsie."

He gave Willie a playful punch on the shoulder and both men started to laugh.

"What's you pair up to?"

"Oops!" said Sean. "We were nearly caught!"

Willie liked the early morning, especially here at the hotel. It was that special time of day he remembered, when, as a boy, he loved the freedom it gave him to run around, lost in his own world of memories and big dreams for the future before any of the guests emerged from breakfast to take advantage of the view and the beauty of the garden. For Willie, the early dawn seemed to have a stillness that seeped into the soul and created a sense of peace. If only Martha had stayed long enough, he mused, perhaps she would have found that peace too, a peace that was so obviously missing or she wouldn't have run away. If only he had been given the opportunity and the time, he was sure he could have made her realize that she was the one he loved and that there were no visions of Victoria invading his thoughts. He could have shown her around the garden – shown her this path he was strolling along now – the path where he had walked alone on his wedding night, wishing she was the one waiting for him in the Honeymoon suite, instead of the girl he had married a few hours earlier. He could have shown her the room with the two single beds where he had lain with his face to the wall, while Victoria did the same at the other side of the room. Then he could have pointed to the chair he had sat on when he admitted to Sean that the baby she had lost belonged to someone else. If only, if only! Willie had encountered many *if onlys* in his life, but this one was a whopper. How was he ever going to put things right? Would Martha ever forgive him for the thoughtless way he had brought her to this place of memories? However, they were memories that he would gladly have erased if it were possible, for no one likes to be made a fool of, no one likes to be lied to. Admittedly, Victoria didn't actually lie, she just didn't bother to tell him that she was pregnant with another man's child.

With hindsight, Willie realized that, although he had explained to Martha how all the past events had come about, he hadn't actually put into words how he had felt back then, especially the string of emotions that had led to his hasty marriage, and how much he had regretted the outcome. He hadn't told her about how many times he had dreamed that he was free again, back on Daisy Farm, holding her in his arms, and how he had sometimes woken up whispering her name. No, he hadn't told her any of these things. He hadn't taken the time to think about how Martha would be affected by the suddenness of it all, rushing her into an unexpected trip to County Cavan before she even got time to think about what she was doing. His only excuse was that he had found her after so many wasted years and he didn't want to run the risk of losing her again. Sammy was still close by, and in spite of the fact that Martha had refused his proposal of marriage and Sammy didn't appear to be offended or feel rejected by it, Willie was thinking perhaps the guy was playing the waiting game by giving Martha more time to reconsider and perhaps change her mind. Remembering how many times he had overheard remarks about how well suited Sammy and Martha were, it was natural for him to be apprehensive. Willie always felt *the boy next door* was a threat to his future happiness with the girl he loved.

Reluctantly he had to admit that folk were right. Sammy and Martha *were* well suited – too well suited for Willie's peace of mind. They had so much in common; they had shared a childhood, they had grown up together, they had worked in the fields together and were obviously at ease in each other's company. They had what Willie could only describe as, a comfortable togetherness. Willie wanted to believe that it was born out of habit, but those niggling doubts wouldn't go away and he grudgingly considered the possibility that there on the farm with Sammy was where Martha belonged. Perhaps she had been born to be a farmer's wife after all, and maybe she wouldn't be happy any other way. These thoughts plagued Willie as he made his way back through the garden and up the steps to the back entrance. "Ah, there you are. Breakfast is ready, and I want no excuses about it being too early to eat. You have a long journey ahead of you this morning – that's if you still intend going back today."

MORE CONFUSION

"What's keeping you?" Sammy poked his head round the side of the door as Martha stepped into her shoes. That was her routine when going anywhere – get ready and leave the shoes until last. She loved her high heels, but her slippers were more practical for the speed they allowed her as she rushed around doing the last minute chores she considered necessary before leaving the house. Making sure the taps were properly turned off at the sink and closing the windows were high on her list of 'must dos'.

"Where's your Da?" Martha queried as she approached Sammy's car.

"He's still sneezing and coughing and he said nobody would want to sit beside him in church for fear of catching his germs."

"Tell him I said he's an oul bluffer, he just wants a lie in," Martha replied with her familiar giggle.

Sammy smiled. It was good to hear her making a joke again. He had been starting to think that the Martha he had known so well had disappeared and perhaps would never return. It was obvious to Sammy that Willie Rossborough was the love of Martha's life, but something had gone terribly wrong, and as he still wasn't privy to the cause, there was nothing he could do or say to make things any better.

"Where are you going?"

"I'm going to church with you," Sammy said, getting out of the car.

"What?"

"I said, I'm going to church with you."

"I know. I heard you. But why?"

"Because I want to."

200

"You're not making any sense," Martha declared. "You've never come to church with me before. Why now?"

"I've already told you, it's because I want to."

"But it's just an ordinary Sunday. There isn't a special service for any special occasion or anything, special."

Sammy told her that she was starting to ramble and declared that he thought every Sunday service was special. Martha accused him of splitting hairs and trying to confuse her. Sammy said it was time they went inside because people were starting to stare. Martha looked around and discovered he was telling the truth. The usual gathering of folk who always arrived early to give themselves time to catch up on the latest developments in the area before the service would start had made them the centre of interest. Sammy took Martha's arm and led her towards the church door.

"Good morning, Martha, Good morning, Sammy," greeted them from several spectators and the Minister shook Sammy's hand and announced how pleased he was to see him there. His announcement was loud enough for the bystanders to hear and several heads nodded in a knowing manner as if to say, 'the rumours were right, there's going to be a wedding – at last!"

Once inside and seated Martha whispered, "You won't enjoy this. It's too straight forward compared to what you're used to in the Church of Ireland."

"Don't be silly," he chided. "Do you think I've never been in a Presbyterian church before?"

"When?"

"The Orange parade," he informed her.

She couldn't argue with that.

'Red sky at night, Shepherd's delight.' Willie remembered Sean's accurate forecast on numerous evenings when, as a boy, he had been eagerly looking forward to the next day when something exciting had been planned for the free time that school holidays allowed.

So tomorrow will be fine, Willie decided, looking at the pink streaks that were still decorating the sky. A nice, sunny Sunday when he would travel to the outskirts of the village he knew so well, and then make his way up the bumpy lane to the farmhouse that held his future happiness. Yes, he had decided, 'come hail or high water' as his Auntie used to say when she had finally decided to do something that didn't seem possible or even sensible at the time, he was going to win Martha back and they were going to get married. The time had come for him to act like a man instead of an uncertain teenager who didn't know his own mind from one minute to the next.

With the fine weather and little traffic on the road, the journey from the city was pleasant and taking less time than Willie had expected. However, as each minute ticked away, Willie's anticipation and trepidation vied for superiority. How great it would be to see Martha again and get all the misunderstandings out of the way. Then, what if she didn't want to talk to him because she had decided that their love for each other was just too much to cope with. Regardless of the outcome, he knew he had to see this situation resolved one way or the other. He had made that decision; in fact, he had made it as a promise to himself. He checked his watch again and realized that Martha would still be in church. He hesitated between two courses of action. Either he could go on up to Daisy Farm and wait for her to come home, or he could stop at the church and wait for her coming out. He assumed Sammy would be waiting too as their service was usually over first but of course he could tell him he didn't need to wait. With a rush of courage and determination, he chose the latter.

Martha was relieved when the benediction was over for she felt that everyone was watching her. The fact that the minister had chosen Ephesians chapter 5 for his text, only heightened her imagination as to what folk were assuming.

Now she just wanted to get out of the door as quickly as possible and into the car without getting involved in conversation with anybody. What was Sammy thinking about or what sort of a silly prank was he trying to pull? she wondered. Did he not realize what people would think or did he want to give them the impression that they were an item? Was it possible he thought the rumours and the gossip would make her change her mind and decide to marry him just to keep tongues from wagging? Surely he couldn't be that silly? Anyway, he seemed happy enough when she turned him down, and his attitude towards her hadn't changed. In fact, he seemed pleased for her when Willie came on the scene.

"Is you two going to get married after all?" Bobby Birch asked. Bobby didn't go to church very often. He just went when he felt like it – it was Bobby's way, always had been. But why did he decide to come today? Martha mused. Nevertheless, she laughed heartily in response to his question and, fortunately, was rescued from having to reply as Nancy Shaw came forward and whispered, "Well pets? Does this mean something?"

"Absolutely nothing," the younger woman replied.

"Where's Willie?"

"I have no idea, and I don't want to hear his name mentioned again."

Nancy got the message and turned her attention to Sammy. "It's great to see you here," she told him. "Will you be making this a regular practice now?"

Then she realized the tactlessness of her comment and her face turned bright red. She started to stammer and tried to explain that her comment was only made as a joke, but with every word she appeared to be digging a deeper hole. Neither Sammy nor Martha had ever seen Nancy in such a state of embarrassment, and the rarity of the event caused both of them to dissolve into fits of uncontrollable laughter.

Martha didn't notice the car with the tall, fair-haired driver that rushed past the assembled crowd.

I have my answer, Willie decided, as he made his way back towards the city. Sammy had won and there wasn't a thing he could do about it. He had been right after all. Martha belonged to Sammy, but how was he going to cope with seeing them together on a regular basis? That was something else he couldn't do anything about, because he had accepted the post of village doctor. That announcement was going to be the highlight of their visit to County Cavan. He had it all planned – in the twilight and with the twitter of the birds for added effect they would walk in the garden and he would tell her his news. Instead there had been torrential rain and she didn't want to be with him.

To-morrow he would be back on duty in a busy hospital that demanded his undivided attention and commitment.
To-morrow was the beginning of another chapter in his life – a life without Martha.

After reassuring Nancy that she hadn't done any permanent damage, and apologizing for laughing at her discomfort, Sammy and Martha were finally on their way. At first, the atmosphere was tense with Sammy not knowing how his passenger was going to react to the events he had orchestrated. Her silence was an indication that something hadn't pleased her but if the past was any indication of what was about to happen next, then he wouldn't have to wait too long.
"What sort of a trick was that to play on a good Sunday morning?"
The fact that the day of the week or the condition of the weather had nothing to do with the present situation amused Sammy's sense of humour.
"Don't know what you mean," he replied.
"Do you think I was born yesterday?"

"Nope."

"Sammy, you are really starting to irritate me. I don't know what sort of a carmudgen you're turning into. Now wipe that silly grin off your face and answer me."

He didn't respond immediately, and as they reached the fork in the lane Martha announced, "Don't bother answering me because it probably wouldn't make any sense anyway, so just let me out here." Sammy did as she asked. Sammy knew the score. Martha was angry, but her anger wouldn't last long. He would let her cool down for an hour or so and then call over, and they would have a cup of tea and laugh about the confusion they had caused.

Martha was washing the dishes and thinking about how few items there were in the sink compared to the way things used to be when the farm was in full production and the men were coming in hungry from their labour in the fields.

Things change, and times change, it is just the way life is, she reflected. However, the speed at which the changes in Martha's life had taken place was hard to comprehend. Now, with all hope of a future with Willie apparently gone forever, and with only herself to blame, it would seem that there was nothing else likely to change again. Life was back to normal, or at least the normal she had settled into when she had come to terms with the fact that both parents were gone and she was alone. Martha's father, in spite of his apparent lack of interest in his daughter, had, nevertheless ensured that her future was financially secure. Comforting and reassuring as that was, it couldn't take away the loneliness that she saw stretching ahead of her. Admittedly, she had friends, especially Nancy Shaw and, of course, Sammy and his father. They were her specials, but the years were passing. Nancy wasn't getting any younger and neither was Arthur, and if anything happened to him there was always the possibility that Sammy would sell up and move away. He had left before, and Martha often wondered if he would ever have come back if it hadn't been for the letter she sent to inform him of his father's accident.

The sound of the door closing jolted her out of her reverie.

"Put the kettle on. There's a good girl."

Martha turned and looked at the big lumbering friend standing there, his eyes twinkling with devilment, and the mop of auburn hair back to its usual untidy state in spite of the amount of Brylcream he had controlled it with earlier in the day. She shook her head with exasperation and threw the tea towel at him. He caught it, then feigned deep concentration as he folded it in two, then placed it on the plate rack above the range. Martha ignored his antics and demanded, "Have you any idea the stir you caused in that church today? Did you not realize that folk would put two and two together and get five? Have you no sense?"

"Does it matter what anybody thinks?" Sammy asked. "Do you really care?"

Martha considered the question for a moment then admitted, "To be perfectly honest, I suppose I don't, but I'm not used to being the centre of attention. Folk don't normally pay me any notice. I am just me – Martha Sloan - Henry Sloan's daughter. I was practically invisible until a while back when you started all this marrying talk and got everybody on a 'will she, won't she' escapade, and just when I thought they were starting to forget about me, you go and start them off again."

"Is that what you really believe? Do you honestly think that nobody was paying any attention to you? Oh Martha, Martha, what sort of a twilight world have you been living in? Did you never realize that, since you entered your teens, the folk in the village have been continually speculating about who was going to be the lucky boy that you would agree to marry?"

"Are you trying to make a cod of me?"

"Of course not," Sammy assured her, and went on to explain that he was usually tipped as the winner, except for the occasional time when some other chap came on the scene, but as those romances were always short-lived he quickly became favourite again.

Martha knew that although Sammy teased her occasionally, he wouldn't lie to her, so his revelations were both a shock and a source of amusement. She pondered this unexpected revelation for a few seconds then said, "I wonder what all these interested people would say or think if I let it be known that I was considering taking in another lodger – a young man this time."

"You wouldn't!"

The expression on Sammy's face was priceless. Whether it was the thought of a young man sharing her home, or the gossip the event would cause in the village that had widened Sammy's eyes, she couldn't be sure. Either way, she found his reaction highly amusing.

"Have an early night," Sammy advised before leaving. "You're as pale as a ghost."

"And how many ghosts have you encountered lately?" Martha demanded.

"Only joking," Sammy replied, "but seriously though, you would need to take more care of yourself. Why don't you make a wee drop of punch? It would help to put you over – give you a good night's sleep - you would snore till the morning. The windows would be rattling with the noise."

"Oh aye," Martha replied, "Rise with a sore head – a great cure."

"Don't knock it till you've tried it," he replied as he stepped out into the night.

Martha called him back. "Sammy, why *did* you go to church with me today?"

Sammy shrugged his shoulders and replied, "I thought you might want a bit of company on account of it being the first Sunday since…"

He didn't finish the sentence as he raised his hand in a farewell gesture, then made his way across the yard to where the two lanes

207

joined and led to the house beyond where his father would be waiting for his night time cocoa.

Martha closed the door, sighed and sat down beside the fire. Sammy was so kind, so thoughtful and so dependable. If she hadn't already refused his offer of marriage there was a strong possibility that tonight, she would have accepted it, for he knew her so well – was tuned into her every mood and he would have done everything in his power to make her happy. Had she been a fool to reject him? With Sammy, there would have been no misunderstandings, no past to cloud the present. It all seemed so right, but in her heart, she knew it would also be wrong. She loved Willie Rossborough and there wasn't a single thing she could do to alter the way she felt. Sammy deserved better – Sammy deserved someone who would love him in the way she knew she never could.

The house seemed strangely quiet and lonely now with only the ticking of the clock to break the silence. Nine o'clock. It was too late to think about housework and too early to go to bed in spite of Sammy's good advice. Then she noticed the letters the post man had given her the previous day. She had been busy at the time, and seeing the brown envelope on the top she had assumed it was just the usual mail that arrived with predictable regularity – a bill for something, a few leaflets and the largest envelope at the bottom would be her seed catalogue. She slipped the rubber band off the bundle and everything was as she expected, except for a small white envelope tucked in among the others. She didn't recognize the handwriting, and with great speed and curiosity she tore open the flap. It contained one sheet of neat, tidy writing and Martha immediately scanned the bottom line to discover it was from Lorna.

Dear Martha,
Just a few lines to thank you so much for your hospitality and your kindness to me during my stay in your lovely farmhouse. And of course, the use of your trusty bicycle was an added bonus.

Without it, I would have missed so much of the beautiful scenery and I wouldn't have got the opportunity to meet so many interesting people.

I think Mum was lonely without me, so it is nice to be back home again. I had so much to tell her – we have talked for hours.

Thanks again for everything and I hope you and Sammy will be very happy together. Tell him I said 'Hello'.

Love

  Lorna

Martha was pleased that the young girl had taken the time to write. It was nice to hear from her, and to know that she had enjoyed her stay. Nice of her to mention Sammy too – she would tell him tomorrow – tease him that he must have created quite an impression.

Martha felt the letter deserved a reply and fetched the notepad from the kitchen drawer.

Dear Lorna,

Thank you very much for taking the time to write to me. I was delighted to hear from you and to know you enjoyed your stay here.

I'm sure your Mum missed you terribly and is glad to have you back. In fact, I am missing you too and all our little chats – it can get quite lonely here in the evening, so if you ever decide to take another wee trip in this direction you will be a very welcome guest.

I'll pass your 'Hello' to Sammy tomorrow morning – I'm sure he will be pleased to know that you haven't forgotten him.

Do keep in touch.   Love.   Martha.

Martha read what she had written and wondered if she should have mentioned the 'together' Lorna had referred to.   Should she have explained that, regardless of village gossip, there was no 'together' between herself and Sammy? Or was it better to avoid any comment on the matter in case Lorna would be embarrassed by the fact that she had been wrong? After a lot of consideration Martha decided to leave the letter as it was, so she popped it into the envelope, copied the address from the top of Lorna's page and placed it in the window. She thought of the times her father used to chat to Paddy McGrath for ages when he was on his rounds, but this younger man wasn't interested in idle chatter. If you didn't see him the minute he arrived, when you looked again he was gone, although he always did take the time to glance at the window just in case.

Martha checked the time on the mantle clock, 9.45pm. Perhaps an early night would be a good idea after all. However, sleep evaded her for hours. It was the letter – something concerning the letter, but she couldn't decide whether it was Lorna's letter or the reply she had written that was the problem. Lorna's had been complimentary and cheerful, so that was Ok, she decided, and she was sure her reply was quite acceptable, so that was fine too. However, there was still something puzzling her that she couldn't quite understand.

Martha finally drifted off to sleep without reaching any satisfactory conclusion to her quandary.

Next morning the postman was earlier than usual, so Martha didn't get time to reconsider checking over what she had written as he shouted, "Do you want me to take that?" pointing to the envelope that was propped against the window pane.

"Aye, please. Thank you. That'll save me a trip to the village."

Martha continued mixing the food for the hens, her thoughts still on the letters. Had she overlooked something that she should have told Lorna, or was there something in Lorna's letter that she hadn't taken on board?

Her outside chores completed, Martha decided to read Lorna's letter again. Apart from the mistaken idea that she and Sammy were a couple, there was nothing unusual about its contents. Then, suddenly, she realized what it was that had been niggling at the back of her mind – it was the address. There was something familiar about the address. She was certain that she had seen it somewhere before – but where? Then, with a sharp intake of breath, she remembered. She rushed to what had always been referred to as 'the odd drawer' - the drawer that held everything imaginable – scissors, tube of glue, box of dominoes, her father's silver arm bands that he always wore on his shirt sleeves on special occasions. She had forgotten about them as they were so seldom seen. His only special outings were funerals or the 'twelfth day.'' She searched further into the drawer. She knew what she was looking for, but time and the addition of other miscellaneous items had pushed it to the back. Finally, she found the brown paper bag that contained the letters Sammy had written - letters with a Liverpool postmark. She opened the first one and read the following.

Dear Martha, Sorry for not writing sooner but I was waiting until I got a permanent address. I've got a job on a building site and lodgings with a nice family that love anybody who comes from anywhere in Ireland. Apparently, the woman of the house is a great great granddaughter of a man who was born in County Down. So how's that for a bit of good fortune.

The address was the same as Lorna's. But it didn't make sense. Why had she come here? She couldn't have known Sammy when he was in Liverpool because she was too young. Much, much too young. Too young! There was another sharp intake of breath. Martha started to make calculations as she remembered - 1946 - her sixteenth birthday, she and Sammy had been to a dance in the village hall, and next morning there was the awful discovery that

211

Sammy had left home and no one knew where he was for quite a while until Martha received the letter with the Liverpool postmark. Forty-six from sixty-five equalled nineteen, and she had assumed Lorna's age to be around eighteen. Could she be...? No! Martha argued with herself. She had to be wrong. She shouldn't be thinking along those lines. Sammy wasn't the callous type. He wouldn't just walk away if what she was thinking was right. Still, it all added up. Lorna might be Sammy's daughter – but no, she couldn't be – she would have told Martha why she was here, or if she didn't want to disclose her true identity to someone she had just met then at least she would have introduced herself to Sammy. Maybe she had and Sammy had refused to believe her. Maybe that was why she left sooner than Martha had expected. No! There had to be some other explanation. Perhaps she was the granddaughter of the people he had lodged with. Maybe they had told her about the chap from Ireland who had stayed with them all those years ago, and with the natural curiosity of youth, she decided to seek him out while she was in the area. But why didn't she say who she was? Martha was sure Sammy would have been delighted to meet someone connected to the family he had known. All these theories, possibilities, ifs, maybes and buts, when really there seemed to be only one logical explanation – Lorna had to be Sammy's daughter. But if she was, then why did he never admit that he had a child? Perhaps he didn't know. But if that were the case then wouldn't he have guessed when he heard her name. At this stage, Martha realized that Lorna's surname had never been mentioned except for the evening Tam Lorimer had brought her to Daisy Farm and introduced her as Miss Webster, whereupon the young girl had laughed and said, "Oh please, no Miss Webster. You make me sound like a cranky old school teacher. I'm Lorna," she continued, reaching to accept Martha's outstretched hand.

"Queueee... it's only me," Nancy Shaw announced, popping her head round the side of the open kitchen door.

Martha hastily placed the letters into the bag and pushed it to the back of the table.

"Busy?" Nancy queried.

"You know how it is," Martha replied. "There's always paper work to sort out – what has to be kept and what goes in the fire."

Then another face appeared at the door. "Can I borrow your rake? I'm just after breaking the shaft of mine?"

"Of course you can," Martha said. "Take whatever you need."

She turned towards the range and pulled the kettle onto the ring. Anything to avoid looking at him, but her efforts were in vain as he announced, "Ah, I see there's tea a making."

He said it in a joking way implying that he was going to stay, whereupon Martha would usually have retaliated saying something about him being like a bloodhound on the scent of a rabbit. When she didn't respond immediately Sammy realized there was tension in the air, and as he wasn't sure why, he made a hasty retreat saying, "See you later."

"Are you all right?" Nancy asked.

"Just a bit tired."

Nancy assumed the lack of humour was because of whatever had happened concerning Willie Rossborough. She didn't make any comment on the subject. Better to leave that topic out of the visit. If Martha felt the need to confide in anyone then she was there for her, but if she wanted to keep the matter to herself then Nancy would respect her wishes and wouldn't try to force her into discussing it. She just hoped everything would work out all right for the girl she had helped bring into the world.

Martha always enjoyed Nancy's company, but today she was secretly glad when the older woman said she would have to be heading home.

Alone at last, Martha opened the brown paper bag and drew out the letters once more.

For almost an hour Martha sat with her elbows on the table, her chin resting in her cupped hands as she stared at the two letters

213

lying side by side, written nineteen years apart, yet somehow connected. She pondered over the earlier possibilities she had considered and concluded that the only possible explanation had to be the fact that Lorna was indeed Sammy's daughter. How ironic if that was true, when the previous evening she had been thinking how simple life could have been if she had married Sammy because there would have been nothing in the past to cloud the present. It was another of those times when Martha wished she could turn back the clock to the time when her life was straightforward and uncomplicated – a time when she didn't have to make important decisions – a time when her life was ruled by routine and duty. Now, with the freedom to live her life as she chose, she felt she hadn't really made much of a success of anything she had done. Considering the way she had ruined her chance of happiness with Willie, what was the likely outcome of how she would deal with the mystery of the two letters? Should she give Lorna's letter to Sammy to read and then be guided by his reaction? Or should she burn it and never mention the girl's name again? However, if she is his daughter, then he has a right to know. But was she, Martha, the person who should be telling him? Then another possibility – it was all just one big coincidence and she had let her imagination run riot. Perhaps she should start writing fiction stories for one of the magazines her mother used to read. So lost in thought, and with a smile on her face at having such a flight of fancy, she didn't notice Sammy passing the window until it was too late.

"What are you up to?" he asked.

"What do you mean?" Martha hastily folded up the letters.

"You have a guilty look about you," Sammy replied, "and you were acting strange when I was here earlier."

Martha didn't speak.

"Is that from lover boy?" Sammy nodded towards Martha's hand, still clutching the information that, unknown to him, could dramatically change his life. She knew he wouldn't let the matter drop. Martha felt a wave of relief wash over her. The decision was made, and it was Sammy who had made it. She told him to sit down, gave him the two letters, then walked away to prepare a pot of tea – the comforting solution in all situations.

"Imagine you still having this," he said, holding up his scribbled note – a satisfied grin on his face.
Martha didn't comment. Then he looked at the second piece of paper. It was obvious he wasn't making any connection between the two.
"That was very nice of her to write to you," he commented. "A lot of young people nowadays wouldn't bother."
Martha still didn't speak. It was then he realized there was something happening that he didn't understand. He looked at the letter again. "Nice of her to mention me too," he said, assuming that was what Martha was waiting for him to comment on.
More silence, then…
Martha watched as Sammy's face displayed a variety of emotions, the most obvious being disbelief.

Martha sat quietly at Sammy's side when he didn't speak, she listened when he talked, she held his hand when he cried and she put whiskey in his tea when he asked her to. They talked long into the night as the story unfolded.
Her name was Nora, the daughter of the couple who owned the boarding house where Sammy had stayed. They fell in love and they talked about getting married. Location was a problem. Her parents needed her to help with the business and his father, unaware of his son's romance, assumed he would return home when he got over his wee sulk. But Sammy had considered staying in England if that was the only way he could be with Nora. Then Nora discovered he was writing to a girl called Martha and that resulted in jealousy and mistrust, and when Sammy immediately packed his bags after receiving a letter from this girl, all Nora's suspicions rose

to the surface, resulting in a disagreement that hadn't been resolved before his hasty departure.

"Why didn't you get in touch with her later on when your father had recovered?"

It was the first question Martha had asked.

"Why didn't she get in touch with me?" he replied. "I left her my address. She was the one who caused the row because she didn't trust me."

"Oh Sammy, Sammy, you stupid man! Could you not have seen the situation from her point of view? Talking about getting married while you were writing to a girl back home. She had no way of knowing that we were just friends, and then rushing back here as soon as you got a letter from me. What was she supposed to think?"

Sammy shrugged his shoulders and took another sip from his cup.

"I know what *you're* thinking," he suddenly declared. "You think this Lorna girl is my daughter and she came here to find me and when she did, she didn't like what she saw so then she just went home again."

"What I think isn't important," Martha said. "What do you think?"

"I don't know what to think, but if there was a baby on the way Nora should have let me know – I had every right to know – I loved her – I would have loved it too…. oh, what's the use…" Sammy didn't finish the sentence and Martha didn't comment as he got up to pace the floor, running his fingers through his hair and repeating, 'This can't be happening, I must be dreaming. No, it's not a dream, it's a nightmare.'

Then he started to consider other possible explanations. Perhaps Nora had married some other fellow and Lorna was *their* daughter, and when she decided to do a bit of sight seeing in County Antrim, Nora had told her about the boy she used to know from that area and Lorna just wanted to see what he looked like. Martha had toyed with that possibility too, but it still didn't explain why Lorna's surname was the same as Nora's had been when Sammy knew her.

It was a lot to grasp in such a short time – a lot to come to terms with. The ordinary farmer boy who led the ordinary farming life, suddenly at the age of thirty nine discovers the young girl he met and talked to, and had described as 'a nice wee buddy' could in all probability be his daughter and she had left without telling him who she was.

"If she *is* my daughter why would she leave without telling me?"

"Read her letter again," Martha advised. "Can't you see she had got the impression that we were together, so she probably thought it best not to disrupt your life or even mine. There's also the possibility that she was hoping to reunite you and her mother and then came to the conclusion it wasn't possible because of me – Martha, the girl you had kept in touch with."

Sammy rubbed the back of his neck with his big calloused hand as if trying to separate his head from the rest of his body.

"This is one….," He hesitated, searching for the right words, but the right words wouldn't come as he sat down again, burying his face in his hands.

"This really isn't a problem." The absurdity of Martha's statement got Sammy's full attention.

"What! What did you say?"

"This really isn't a problem," Martha repeated.

He watched, enthralled, as she calmly poured herself another cup of tea, then holding up the pot and nodding towards *his* cup she asked, "Another wee drop to warm that up?"

He shook his head, preferring to top up with another wee drop of something stronger. Then, turning towards her as she took the seat beside him, he said, "O K, now tell me all about this problem that isn't a problem."

"The way I see it," Martha explained, "is – assuming that it isn't a coincidence, there are only two ways it can be."

She took another sip of tea.

"Go on," Sammy encouraged.

"It could either be what you suggested earlier. Lorna is not your daughter and she was curious to see what her mother's old boyfriend looked like, or else she *is* your daughter, and for reasons that we can only guess at, she chose not to disclose who she really was."

Martha gave him time to mull this over, but his only reaction was to shake his head in disbelief at the unexpected situation he found himself in.

Martha continued, "If she is your daughter, then you should consider yourself a very lucky man."

Sammy stared at her, unable to understand her logic.

"Lucky?" he exclaimed.

"Aye," she said. "Lucky – very lucky. If she *is* yours, then you have someone you can call your own. Sometimes I wish I had been foolish."

Sammy didn't know how to react to that remark, for this was a Martha he didn't recognize - a vulnerable, lonely woman in spite of all the people she knew and all the people who cared about her.

He gathered her into his arms and cried, "What am I going to do?"

"When you get more time to think about it," she told him, "you'll know what to do. Your heart will tell you what to do."

Martha sat by the fireside long after Sammy had gone home. How ironic that she had unknowingly been the cause of Sammy losing the woman he loved and Sammy unknowingly had been the cause of *her* losing the man *she* loved. There were many, who, if they ever became aware of all the facts, would be certain that all their assumptions over the years had been right - Sammy and Martha were meant for each other.

Next morning the ringing of the phone awakened Martha out of her tangle of dreams where it seemed everyone she knew, including her father, was telling her what to do, but they were all talking at once so she couldn't hear them clearly. She squinted at the clock on her bedside table and was surprised she had slept so late. She rushed down stairs, grabbed the receiver and quoted the number.

"Morning, Martha."

"Who..?" before she could finish the question the caller identified himself.

"Johnny here, Johnny Connery. I was just wondering if you had given any more thought to what we talked about a wee while back – about the land and you maybe thinking about selling."

"No, Johnny, not really," Martha told him. "I have been busy and I'm uncertain about what I want to do. You know how it is. I was born here, I've lived here all my life and the place holds a lot of memories."

"I understand," Johnny agreed, "and I don't want you to think I'm trying to force you into making any decision that you might regret later on. But, as you know, I've been depending on con acre for a good number of years, and now with the young boy growing up I'd like to extend the land – give him a wee bit of extra security for the future."

Martha said she understood his situation and promised to keep him in mind. He thanked her and added that, even if she decided to stay put, he would still be interested in the land even without the house.

Sell Daisy Farm – what a thought! Admittedly, the idea had crossed her mind some time back, but other more important issues had taken over. If she did decide to sell, what about Sammy and his father? They had already taken the land this season, so in all fairness, she couldn't sell to somebody else if they wanted it. Then, of course, there was the possibility that they couldn't afford to buy it. Their farm was quite small by neighbouring standards, but it had supported them well over the years and perhaps they were financially better off than some who had more to show. Decisions – decisions! This brought to mind something Nancy Shaw had said, 'The more you have, the more bother you have.' She had been referring to the bicycle Bobby Birch had found one day when he was plouterin' about at the dump, believing that there was always treasure to be found if you kept looking. He found the old bike instead and eventually got it sorted to almost an acceptable state of roadworthiness, and then couldn't make up his mind which bike to ride. Apparently this dilemma had caused him many sleepless nights until, eventually, he solved the problem by returning his treasure to the dump where he had found it and retrieving his 'old faithful' from the back of the house. Martha wished she could solve her problems as easily as the fortunate Bobby, for although Willie Rossborough would continue to be the biggest problem in her life, she now had the added concern about Sammy, and how he would cope with his unexpected discovery. The selling of her land or house was way down on her list of priorities.

It was one of those days that seemed to stretch on forever in spite of the extra two hours Martha had slept. She couldn't get the events of the previous evening out of her head as she pondered on how so little can make such a difference. It was the 'throw a pebble into a stream and the ripples keep going out' scenario.

If Arthur hadn't fallen, Sammy would have married Nora, and, in all probability, stayed in England. If Martha hadn't written to Sammy he wouldn't have known about his father's accident, so he wouldn't have come rushing back causing the break-up between him and the girl he loved. So was it Arthur's fault, or was it hers? Had she been too hasty? Perhaps she should have left the decision to Arthur. If he had wanted Sammy to come home at that particular time, then perhaps he was the one who should have written the letter. But Martha had been angry at that time – angry at the way he had left his father in the same devious and callous way his mother had done sixteen years previously. She was also angry about the fact that he had left without telling *her*. She had to admit that she *had* penned the letter with a certain degree of satisfaction and an attitude of 'that will put the gallivanting out of his head and give him something more to think about other than himself.'

How impulsive youth can be. Would she do the same if it was happening now? Probably, so there was nothing to be gained by regretting her actions. If regretting could change anything, she wouldn't be sitting alone wondering where Willie was, what he was doing, and whether he ever thought about her.

Thirty miles away Willie was drinking tea as if it was going out of fashion with the letter of confirmation in his hand. There was no turning back. The decision was final, he was going to be the village doctor, and he was going to have to live with the unhappy situation of seeing Martha and Sammy as a couple. His only consolation – he would be close to her – he would know if she was well and he would be there for her if she ever needed him.

THREE WEEKS LATER

It seemed there was nothing else to talk about except Dr. McGoldrick's retirement. It had been common knowledge for quite some time that he was reaching that age, but now, suddenly it had become the main topic of conversation at every possible opportunity. The reason? Who was going to replace him? Bobby Birch was the first with the answer.

"That Willie fellow that used to play with us when we were weans," he informed the wee gathering of ladies in the Post Office on pension day. No one doubted Bobby's announcement, as he was always accurate with any titbit of news he ever related. Bobby's ability to be ahead of the most well informed in the community was a mystery to everyone, and even under the most thorough probing, Bobby never revealed the source of his information, his only reply being, "I just keep within earshot."

His good memory for all the details he attributed to his neighbour Nancy Shaw, who insisted on giving him Cod liver Oil and Malt every Saturday night because she thought his mother wasn't looking after him properly.

The only other person in the area who was likely to be in possession of any information concerning forthcoming events was the taxi man, Tam Lorimer. Unlike Bobby, he never repeated anything he overheard, and even when the news became public knowledge he still refused to be drawn into making any comment or admitting to any prior knowledge. Tam's reputation for discretion was legendary and he intended to keep it that way.

By the time Martha entered the Post Office for a packet of envelopes everyone was agog with the news, and assumed she could add something more to what they already knew. Martha said

222

she couldn't, and gave Bobby the credit for being so well informed. Then with her purchase secured and paid for, she escaped from their disbelieving stares as quickly as possible. It was obvious they thought she was concealing some vital piece of news that Bobby had missed, which would be a rarity, or else there was some other reason for not wanting to be involved in the matter. What that could be they couldn't imagine, so decided to go with the first option – she knew more than she was prepared to disclose.

So it really was happening, Martha accepted. Willie was coming to the village, and she would have to get used to having him close by, but not close to her. So engrossed was she in her thoughts, Sammy had to call her name twice before she heard him.

"Where's the bike?" he asked, when he finally got her attention.

"I didn't bring it," she told him. "It's a nice day, so I decided to walk."

"Hop on," he said. "I'm heading home now, so you may as well come with me."

"I suppose you're right," she agreed, climbing into the link box as she had done many times before.

She didn't know Willie Rossborough was watching from the other side of the street.

Willie sighed as he watched them drive away – so comfortable and at ease in each other's company, he felt like a complete outsider. However, he had made a commitment, and he would have to see it through he decided, as he turned towards the home of Dr. McGoldrick, where he would finalize the plans to purchase the older man's property. The house was ideally situated in the centre of the village, with only the newsagents and the cobblers between it and the surgery. It was the place he had hoped would be the home he would eventually share with Martha. A new beginning for both of them – he, back to the area he loved, and Martha still within the area she grew up in, and most importantly for Willie, not next door to Sammy. Now the possibility of his hopes and dreams ever becoming a reality were rapidly disappearing. However, Willie wouldn't go back on his word – he had agreed to buy, and the good doctor, having complete trust in Willie's pledge had put a deposit on a bungalow in Cushendall – Willie wouldn't let him down.

"I'll be over later," Sammy said, as Martha thanked him for the lift, glad that the noise of the tractor had prevented any conversation during their journey.

"I have something to tell you," he added.

"Something important?" she queried.

"Very important," he replied, and winked. "See you later."

Martha knew he had written to Nora, so if his broad smile and cheery attitude were an indication of the outcome, then everything must be going his way.

Martha stepped inside, closed the door, and wished she could lock it, pull the curtains and be alone with her thoughts. No such luxury - Sammy would be arriving shortly, and she didn't want to overshadow *his* news by telling him hers.

"Are you all right?" were his first words as he walked into Martha's kitchen.

"Of course I'm all right," she replied. "Why would I not be all right?"

"I was also in the post office earlier today."

"Soooo…."

"You can't fool me," he said. "You've heard about the Prodigal's forthcoming return. You couldn't have missed it, for they were gathered in there like chickens in a coop, only making twice as much noise."

"You have a very interesting way of describing people," Martha said, then imagining the ladies of the village looking like chickens she started to laugh.

"That's better," he said. "Forget about that long string of misery, you don't need him."

"Of course I don't."

"You'll be fine without him."

"Of course I will."

Life goes on, she decided, and she would survive without Willie Rossborough. After all, she had done it before. Tomorrow she would go into town on the bus and buy a new dress and matching shoes, and maybe a nice wee bit of cretonne to run up a pair of curtains for the kitchen window.

Nora's reply had been encouraging, but, according to Sammy, not actually telling him anything.

"You read it and tell me what you think." Sammy pulled the crumpled envelope from his pocket.

Martha hesitated, not wanting to intrude.

"Go on," he insisted. "There's not much to see."

Martha unfolded the pale pink sheet of scented paper and read.

'Dear Sammy, it was quite a surprise hearing from you after all these years. I think we need to talk, so if you phone me then perhaps we will be able to sort something out.'

She included her phone number and signed her name.

"Doesn't tell me much," Sammy said. "Does it?"

"Not really; so, did you make the call?"

"Not yet."

"Why not?"

"I don't know."

Then being aware of Martha's expression – eyebrows raised and head tilted to one side - he continued, "You think I'm scared. You do. You think I'm scared of hearing what she might tell me."

"Are you scared?"

"Probably."

They sat in companionable silence for some time, each with their own private thoughts. Martha, concerned for Sammy and the outcome of the belated correspondence, coupled with the peculiarity of how they could be having such a conversation when, a few weeks previously they had been considering the possibility of marrying each other.

Sammy's thoughts were running along similar lines. Strange that he should be here with Martha discussing the possible outcome of his past romance when he had recently asked her to marry him. He would have been happy if she had accepted, but what a complicated mess it would be now when maybe, just maybe, he might have a future with the girl he had never forgotten, plus the possibility of a daughter. Martha had been shrewd when she turned him down, he realized. She had understood the situation for what it really was – a marriage of convenience, whereas he had been carried along with his father's suggestion, plus a great fondness for the girl he had grown up with. He had always wanted what was best for her and at one stage he thought Willie Rossborough was the answer. It was obvious they loved each other, but something had gone wrong – something had prevented the happy ending that Martha would have deserved.

Sammy broke the silence. "I meant it when I asked you to marry me – I do care about you."

"I know you do," Martha said, smiling as she reached across and took Sammy's hand. "And I care about you, but the truth is, we were never in love with each other and never could be, because you still had a special someone on your mind and so did I."

Sammy felt the time was right to ask. "What happened? Why did you come back from Cavan so soon?"

Sammy waited, giving her time to either explain or change the conversation.

"I was stupid," she admitted. "I blamed Willie for comparing me to Victoria. I know I was just being silly and childish, but I acted on impulse and then there was no turning back and I haven't seen or heard from him since. End of story!"

"And when he rang our house and I told him you were there with me that probably made matters worse, and it's all my fault."

"It's nobody's fault," Martha assured him. "It just happened, so I suppose you could say it makes us even, for, after all, it was my letter that caused the problem in Liverpool."

Sammy started to laugh and declared, "It's a pity we didn't marry, for we would have made a right pair of ejjits – a perfect match!"

"As well matched as a couple of book ends," she giggled. "But now to more serious matters. Are you going to make that phone call?"

"I think I will."

"I think you should."

She wondered what Willie would say or think if he could see them now, for it was so obvious that they were, what they had always been, and what they always would be - just good friends.

A WEEK LATER

"Are you there, Martha? Where are you?"

"Over here," Martha replied, coming round the side of the stack, her arms laden with dark brown peats. Arthur followed her into the house where she tipped the bundle into the big basket that sat beside the range.

"Have you any idea what our Sammy's up to?"

Arthur's sudden, unexpected question took Martha by surprise.

"Why?" she stammered. "What has he done?"

"This sudden notion he has took about going to England to visit the folks he lodged with the time he was over there – that time years ago when he took off in a huff because I wouldn't buy a tractor."

"What makes you think it's a sudden notion?"

"I suppose you know all about his plans," Arthur stated, without answering her question.

"Aye," Martha admitted. "He said he was going on Friday night. I was listening to the weather forecast and they give it good for the next week, so hopefully he'll have a smooth crossing."

"I suppose you also know that he has Bobby Birch and a couple of other boys from the village hired to work at the spuds in the meantime."

"He did mention something about that."

There was a long awkward pause.

"Do you think he will come back?"

"Back? What do you mean?"

"Sammy. Do you think he will come back?"

"Of course, he'll come back. Why wouldn't he?"

"I don't know. Do you know?"

The question was so direct and so obviously needing an answer.

"Arthur dear," Martha said, indicating for him to sit down. "How would I know what goes on in that silly big fool's head? Sure didn't he throw me into a state of confusion a while back with his notion that we should get married, and me not having the slightest idea that he was thinking along those lines."

Maybe that wasn't the best answer, she mused, but it was the best she could come up with in view of the circumstances, and to give her more time to think of something that would reassure him without actually telling either truth or lies. She hadn't previously considered the possibility that Sammy wouldn't return, but now that Arthur had voiced his concern it put doubt in her mind too. Surely he wouldn't pull a trick like that again, she hoped. Or would he? She recalled how he had admitted that staying in Liverpool in 1946 had been a strong possibility, so who knows what notion he would take once he got there and met his long lost love?

"I wish you two could have settled down together," Arthur declared, "for you're so well suited. It's just a shame, a crying shame that the pair of you couldn't have a bit of sense and do the wise thing."

"That's life," Martha replied. "You never know what it has in store for you."

Bad choice of words, another time, but it was too late to take them back.

"That's the problem," Arthur agreed. "I don't know what's going to happen once he gets away. I'm just not sure that he'll ever come back, and you're not sure either. Are you?"

"Is it ever possible to be a hundred per cent sure of anything these days?"

"Has he given you any hint that he might not come back."

"Of course not, so stop worrying. Didn't he say he'd be back on Monday, and he knows the rest of the spuds have to be gathered before the weather turns nasty."

Martha didn't feel as confident as she sounded, but she hoped she had allayed his fears for the time being, although her own suspicions were growing by the second.

"Do you really believe that? Do you really believe he will come back?"

"What I believe isn't important," she replied.

Arthur was quiet for a few seconds, then, rising from the chair and putting his hand on her shoulder he said, "You're a good woman Martha Sloan – a good woman, but you have a powerful way of answering questions without saying anything."

A movement outside the window caught Martha's attention – it was Nancy Shaw propping her bicycle against the windowsill. Martha was delighted to see her. She couldn't have arrived at a better time.

"Only me," Nancy announced, rushing in the door, and flopping down on the chair Arthur had just vacated. "I do declare, that wee hill is getting steeper by the day." Then not waiting for a reply to her comment she continued. "And how are you keeping these days Arthur?"

"Just the same as usual," he told her. "You know how it is – you just have to keep going."

"Well now," replied Nancy, "the work can't be doing you any harm, for I've never seen you looking better. It must be all that time you spend outside in God's good fresh air."

"A bit of fresh air never does any harm," Arthur agreed.

"Indeed it doesn't," said Nancy, "and isn't it great weather for getting the rest of the crops in."

"Couldn't be better," Arthur replied.

"But you can start to feel that wee bit of a nip in the air now," Nancy said. "You still need a wee gleed of a fire after the sun goes down."

"Aye, it gets cool enough later on in the evening."

Martha listened to the exchange of conversation, noticed the bloom on Nancy's cheeks, and wondered, not for the first time, if maybe, just maybe, Nancy might have a wee liking for the silver-haired farmer. Of course, it might have been the exertion of pedalling up the hill that had caused the rosy glow, but then, perhaps not.

Transferring her attention to Martha, Nancy asked, "And what about you pet? I hope you are taking care of yourself."

"Of course," was the reassuring reply.

"New curtains?"

Martha said they were, and mentioned that she still hadn't got around to putting up the frill.

"All in good time," Nancy reassured her. "So long as the old treadle didn't let you down, that's the main thing."

Not being interested in either curtains or sewing machines, Arthur consulted his pocket watch and declared he would have to be on his way for there was still work to do. Then turning towards Martha, as if about to say something, and then apparently changing his mind, he shrugged his shoulders and walked out closing the door firmly behind him.

"What was that all about?" Nancy inquired.

"Good question," Martha replied, then holding up the teapot to distract the older woman's attention from Arthur's strange exit she asked, "A wee cuppa and a slice of apple cake?"

"Aye, go on then, although I can't stay very long. I have a lot of wee errands to do, but I thought I had better come up and let you know the latest."

Martha waited – it would be the usual procedure -long pauses between sentences for added effect. Finally, after sucking her lips against her teeth several times she made the big announcement.

"Willie Rossborough is in the village."

"Whereabouts?"

Martha's thoughts were racing ahead – was it possible he was on his way up to the farm.

"He's at the doctor's," Nancy interrupted her train of thought. "Apparently he's staying there for the time being."

Martha felt the colour drain from her face. Silly way to behave, she silently chided herself. After all, she shouldn't be surprised. She knew it was going to happen and she had prepared herself to accept his nearness. Now that he was actually in such close proximity, she discovered she wasn't as well prepared as she thought.

"According to Bobby Birch," Nancy continued, "Willie has bought the doctor's house and the doctor is moving to the seaside."

"Really?"

"What seaside he is actually going to, Bobby still doesn't know, but I'm sure it won't be too long until he finds out."

"I knew Willie was taking over the practice," Martha said. "I heard all about it when I was in the Post Office last week, but I didn't know he had actually arrived."

"I only heard it today," Nancy said. "I have been away all week visiting my cousin in Cookstown, and I only got back late last night."

"I thought Dr. McGoldrick wasn't retiring until the end of next month," Martha said.

"He isn't," Nancy informed her, "but apparently, or at least according to he who knows everything, and we know he's never wrong, the good doctor decided it would be a good idea for Willie to accompany him on some of his rounds to give him a chance to get to know a few of the patients who need house calls."

Martha nodded her head to indicate that she could see the benefit of the arrangement, as Nancy continued. "And I suppose it will give them a chance to get to know him too, for it's not easy, especially for older folk, to accept a new doctor when they've known the old one for so long."

"I suppose you're right," Martha agreed.

There were no further comments made on the matter as the conversation turned to more mundane topics – the weather, the price of spuds, and how well Arthur McCracken stood the years, etc. etc.

Alone again, Martha was pondering over these latest developments. Willie being back in the village sooner than expected and Sammy off to Liverpool in a couple of day's time, was a lot to take on board. She was especially concerned about Sammy. Although he was excited about the outcome of the telephone conversation he had with Nora, he was still none the wiser about Lorna. 'We'll sort it all out when you get here' she had told him, and now he was like an excited teenager anticipating a first date. Martha weighed up all the possibilities. If the young girl was his daughter, the invitation to visit could be Nora's way of giving them a chance to spend time together as a family and really get to know each other in privacy. Martha hoped that was the reason, since she could see that the idea of being a dad was swiftly growing on Sammy, though how he would ever explain the situation to his father would be another matter. Taking into account Arthur's past experience of the fairer sex, he would naturally be hesitant about accepting such an unexpected turn of events. All women, with the exception of Martha Sloan, were unreliable as far as Arthur McCracken was concerned. And of course there would be the gossip to contend with too, and he'd had enough of that when Sammy's mother deserted them. However, the worst scenario, in Martha's opinion, would be, if inviting Sammy over to Liverpool was only a ploy to make him look and feel foolish in retaliation for his previous sudden and insensitive desertion. *The 'hell hath no fury' etc*. quote came to mind. Then of course, there was the other possibility that troubled Martha – the doubts that Arthur had planted in her head earlier in the day –Sammy might not come back. Martha felt so sorry for him. It was obvious he was worried – worried that his son would walk out of his life the way his wife had done. Although he had given up hope of ever seeing the auburn haired woman again, and he had learned to live with the situation, he had never forgotten her, and the feelings of betrayal and rejection were still as painful as they had been the morning he had found her note on the table. The note now crumpled from frequent handling and stained with tears.

Martha decided to have a few firm words in Sammy's ear before his departure. His father didn't need any more hurt to add to the wounds he already carried.

In the meantime, Martha had her own wounds to think about, the sort of wounds that a few stitches or a piece of sticking plaster wouldn't mend, plus the decisions she knew she would have to make.

Johnny Connery had been on the phone again - said he had got first refusal on other land, and although he preferred Martha's, he couldn't run the risk of losing the other twenty five acres that he so desperately needed, but if she ever did decide to sell he would still be interested in buying hers too. Martha was glad he had the opportunity to increase his property. She knew how much the extra ground meant to him. On reflection, she realized how much her land meant to her too. The memories of all the years she had worked in those fields with her father were precious to her, and all those times Sammy and Arthur had shared in that work. Then she thought about the times when it became their turn to return the favour, and she and her father had progressed beyond the March hedge as if they belonged there too. Her decision was made –she wasn't going to sell her land. The house was a different matter. She knew she could walk away from it without a backward glance. It held many happy memories, but quite often, the sad times overshadowed them.

She looked around the familiar kitchen – nothing had changed since her grandparents' day. The same tiled floor, the same faded wallpaper, the same green gloss paint that had stood the test of time behind and above the scorching heat of the old range that faithfully produced a down - blow every time the wind turned. It was the way her father liked it. Then, without giving the matter any further thought, she knew she wanted a fresh start somewhere else. Suddenly everything seemed old and jaded – everything except the curtains she had made with the five yards of floral material she had purchased on her trip into town. Now she just needed to put up the frill to complete the task.

She fetched the length of plastic coated spring wire from the kitchen drawer and carefully eased it through the channel. Then having decided it wouldn't be worthwhile bringing in the stepladder another time for such a small job, she climbed onto a chair. With the eyelet hooked on a nail at the one side of the window, she stretched across to attach the other end. All of a sudden she was on the floor, trapped between the table and the wall, with her ankle caught between the bars of the chair.

"Sorry boys, but you have to go out again," Mrs McGoldrick announced as her husband and Willie got out of the car.
"Who's in trouble this time?" the older doctor asked.
"Martha Sloan," she replied. "Sammy McCracken rang. Apparently Martha has had a fall and he doesn't want to move her about too much by putting her into the car in case she has broken something."
Willie's mind was a blur of jumbled thoughts. Was Martha seriously injured? What would she say when he arrived? What would he say to her? Then of course there was the green-eyed monster to contend with. Why did Sammy always have to be there when she was in trouble? Why was he always the one who came to her rescue? Why was he always the ever dependable, ever reliable, ever comforting hero? Yes, the green-eyed monster was clearly in evidence.
"Home ground for you here, Willie," Dr. McGoldrick said as he turned into the lane that led to Daisy Farm. "There'll be no need to introduce you on this call."

"No, I think they should remember me," Willie replied.

At first, Martha wasn't aware of Willie's presence as the chair Sammy had lifted her onto was partially turned away from the door. "Well now, young lady, what have you been doing to yourself?"
"Not much really," Martha insisted. "I'm fine, honest, I just slipped off the chair."
Without giving Martha a chance to belittle her calamity any further, Sammy delved into his account of how, by good luck, he just happened to come over at that time to return the rake he had borrowed, and found her lying behind the table with her face screwed up in pain and unable to disentangle herself from the chair.
"Not to worry," the kindly doctor assured her, "we will soon have you sorted out and good as new."
It was the 'we will' that caught Martha's attention and caused her to look round.

"Hello Martha, good to see you again."
Martha didn't reply – just held his gaze. Unanswered questions and unspoken words hung between them like an invisible bridge that neither knew how to cross.
Then through the blackness that descended upon her, she heard someone saying, "She'll be all right, she has only fainted – it's just delayed shock."
The mist slowly cleared. Willie's face came back into focus and Martha was reassured that the injury to her ankle was just a sprain, so rest was the best cure and the various bruises on her arms would disappear in a few days.
"Take these two pain killers now," the doctor advised.
Sammy immediately fetched a glass of water.
"And two more before going to bed," he continued, "but be careful because they're quite strong. They'll make you sleepy and they can cause dizziness, and we don't want you to take another tumble."

While Martha was expressing her gratitude for his visit and apologizing for causing so much fuss and bother and insisting that it hadn't been her idea to call them out, she noticed Sammy indicating to Willie that he wanted to speak to him outside.

"What are your intentions towards Martha?" Sammy demanded as he closed the door allowing them the essential privacy for the delicate matter that, in Sammy's opinion, needed to be sorted out for everyone's sake.

"I could ask you the same question," Willie replied.

"You could," Sammy agreed, "but seeing as I asked first I think I deserve an answer first."

"OK," Willie replied. "I want to marry her. I love her, and I thought she loved me, but as you are the one she turns to, the one who is always there for her, I have to accept the fact that I don't stand a chance of taking her from you."

"You're right there, Willie," Sammy agreed. "You can't take her from me, because she never was mine in the first place."

Willie didn't speak so Sammy continued. "Didn't I tell you that day I met you in the village that I had asked her to marry me, and she had refused, and very wise she was, for it wouldn't have worked."

"Why not?"

"Various reasons that we don't have time to discuss just now, but the most important thing is this - she loves *you*, always has done, and why you can't believe that is a mystery to me."

"But *you* are always with her. I was outside the church the Sunday after she came back from Cavan, and you were with her, and the other day in the village I saw her getting into the link box of your tractor."

Sammy erupted in fits of laughter. "She's a country girl, she's as much at home in that link box as she is in her own kitchen."

"And Church..?"

"I went with her that day for moral support. You know what it's like in a small village. She had left with you and suddenly she was back, so I thought she needed a bit of company, but according to her I only made matters worse, and she didn't hesitate in letting me know."

Willie started to pace backwards and forwards, running his fingers through his hair, loosening his tie, and then pulling it back into place.

"Would you stand at peace for a minute," Sammy said, "for you're making me dizzy."

"I'm a fool," Willie declared. "A ridiculous fool! "

"I agree with you, completely!" Sammy replied. "You really do take the biscuit for stupidity."

"You're right. I am stupid, and I've been stupid for years!"

"I won't argue with that. So, wise up and see what's staring you in the face. She doesn't want anybody else only you. So what are you going to do about it?"

Without hesitation Willie replied. "I'll go back to the village with Dr. McGoldrick and collect my own car, and then I'll come back."

"Good for you," Sammy said, giving Willie a hearty slap on the back. "Good for you."

THE RESOLUTION

"What did you say to him?" Martha asked, the minute Sammy came back in.

"Him? Who? Oh, aye, him. Ah, nothing much, we were just chatting, you know how it is. Just blethering about things. Is there anything I can do for you before I go over home?"

"You could put up that frill for me."

Sammy looked at the piece of gathered fabric hanging from one nail and declared, "What do I know about putting up frills?"

"Absolutely nothing," Martha said, "but you're never too old to learn. Of course, maybe you'd rather sit down and tell me what you and Willie were talking about outside."

"Show me what to do."

Sammy listened intently.

"Do you see that wee round open -headed shiny thing sticking out at the side of the hem – at the side of the frill?"

"I do."

"Then catch it before it runs back up inside that channel."

"Got it!"

"Now, stretch across and place it over that nail at the other side of the window."

Sammy hesitated.

"At the top of the curtain, the same nail that the curtain wire is on."

"Oh aye, I see it now."

Sammy completed the job and then made a good attempt at distributing the gathers evenly along the wire.

"Anything else, Madam?" he asked with mock sincerity.

She assured him that there was nothing else needed doing. The painkillers were starting to take effect and she was feeling lots better. So far she didn't feel dizzy, so she was confident that she could limp around and do anything else that she felt like doing. Sammy didn't like the idea of her being too confident in case some other disaster befell her, but his biggest concern was that she didn't pursue the subject of his talk with Willie. It just wasn't like her to let go so easily. Normally she would be like a dog with a bone if she had the slightest suspicion that he was up to anything. Maybe she had done herself more harm than the doctor realized. In spite of the fact that she might resent his interference, for he knew she would get the truth out of him eventually, he had to be sure that she was in her true senses.

"Are you worried about what I might have said to Willie when we went outside?"

"No."

"Are you not concerned that I might have made matters worse?"

"No."

"Martha, you are not making any sense. You are too calm. This is not like you."

"I am calm," Martha reassured him, "because I know everything is going to be all right."

"How do you know?"

"I saw it in his eyes, and I know he will be back. I just don't know when."

I do, Sammy thought, but decided to withhold the information – she would find out soon enough.

Doctor McGoldrick had been right when he said the painkillers would make her sleepy and could cause dizziness, although Martha wasn't sure if the light-headed feeling was caused by the tablets or the fact that she was sailing on a sea of happiness. Curled up on the couch with her head on Willie's shoulder and his arms wrapped around her, she had never known such contentment or sense of belonging.   But sleep was threatening to claim her, and she struggled to stay awake. Although they had talked a lot, they still had so much more to say to each other. Eventually the medication

240

won, and Martha drifted off into a deep contented sleep that lasted until morning. Willie knew the benefit of rest, so, although his arm was suffering from cramp, he didn't want to disturb her. The only respite from his discomfort was the few times he dozed off.

Martha thought she must be dreaming when she looked up into the smiling face of Willie Rossborough. As the haze of sleepiness cleared, she realized that what she was seeing was real – Willie was actually there, beside her, holding her in his arms.
"Good morning, sleepy head."
"Morning? Did you say morning?"
Willie pointed towards the clock on the shelf above the range.

When Sammy saw Willie's car still there at 6 am. he drew his own conclusion.
Sammy didn't know that 'sleeping together' had taken on a whole new meaning.

"How's the patient this bright sunny morning?" Sammy inquired.
"Still a bit sore, but the tablets have helped."
"You had better take things easy for a day or two."
"Of course I will."
Knowing her impatient ways, Sammy didn't believe her, and promptly told her so, then asked, "Any word from Willie?"
Martha gave him one of her looks that said 'who do you think you are trying to fool?'
"OK," Sammy said, holding up his hands in mock surrender. "I know he was here." Then making a great effort and great pretence of clearing his throat he added, "I saw him driving away a wee while ago."

Martha just smiled at the insinuation, then asked if he could come over later in the evening, and bring his father with him, because there were things she wanted to tell them and things she wanted to discuss.

"That sounds serious," Sammy commented.

"I've made a few decisions," Martha admitted. "So I suppose that is something serious, especially for me. But what about you?"

Sammy looked puzzled so Martha continued. "Are you coming back from Liverpool, or are you toying with some romantic notion of sailing off into the sunset with the lovely Nora?"

"Of course I'm coming back," he declared. "I don't know what's going to happen when I get there, or how I'll feel when I see her again, but one thing I am sure of, I won't desert my father again. I am coming back."

"Is that a promise?"

"That's a promise."

"Then let him know that you are coming back – don't leave him wondering."

"Why, has he been thinking that I might stay over there? Has he said something to you?"

"Just tell him that you will be back on Monday as arranged."

Setting off to Liverpool the next evening had been, and should still have been uppermost on Sammy's mind, but now the mystery of Martha's decisions was taking first place. He assumed that marrying Willie would be one piece of news she would tell them, but she had said decisions, not just decision.

It was a long day as far as Sammy was concerned, but his father had a different opinion on the passing of time. The quicker the minutes passed the sooner Sammy would leave, and the fear that he wouldn't come back still hung heavily on the older man's shoulders.

"Right Da, it's time we were getting over to Martha's, for I can't wait to hear about these decisions she has made."

"There's no rush," Arthur said. "We can hear about them some other time."

"But if I don't find out this evening, then I won't know what she's up to until I get back on Monday, and the suspense is killing me."

"You're coming back then?"

"Of course I'm coming back."

The two men listened intently as Martha outlined her plans. She and Willie had decided to get married (no surprise there) and after spending a few days away, they would return to the village, where she would move into the house Willie had bought from Doctor McGoldrick.

Then the inevitable question from Sammy. "What about this place? You can't leave here. This is your home."

"This is my home now," Martha replied, "but the house in the village will become my home when I get married."

"You might regret it when the novelty wears off," Sammy warned.

"No, I won't," she insisted. "I had already decided to move before Willie arrived – I wanted a fresh start."

"And where had you been thinking of going?"

"I had no idea."

Sammy was flabbergasted. This was so unlike the girl he knew. How could she have been planning something like that without telling him, he wondered?

Martha went on to explain how Johnny Connery was interested in buying her land, but at present she wasn't inclined to let it go, but if she ever did decide to sell, she assured Sammy and Arthur that they would get first refusal. Arthur said he appreciated her loyalty, but leasing the land suited them better.

"What about the house?" Sammy inquired. "You can't just walk out and leave it."

"Maybe I'll sell it, or maybe somebody will want to rent it. I don't know. I suppose I haven't thought that far ahead."

Back home both men were in a state of bewilderment at the speed with which everything was changing.

"It's hard to imagine," Sammy commented to his father, "that less than a year ago we sat in Martha's parlour welcoming in the New Year and expecting everything to continue as normal – just taking it for granted that Martha would always be there with the kettle always on the boil. And now she's going to leave, and the house will be empty – it's not natural – it's not right."

"She's not emigrating," Arthur consoled. "She's only going to live in the village."

"I know that," Sammy said, "but still, it's not the way things should be. Martha belongs over there where she has always been, and if she leaves, things will never be the same again."

"That's true," his father agreed. "But the worst thing about the whole situation is the fact that you have lost her for good. You'll never get her back now."

Going to Liverpool to try and rekindle what he thought he had lost forever was his real dilemma. Sammy sighed; a sigh that his father assumed was for the loss of Martha.

Sammy stood on the deck, as he had done nineteen years before, and watched the lights of Belfast harbour grow smaller and fainter. Back then, he was a young man with a sense of adventure, and a firm opinion that he was always right. His father's final refusal to 'move with the times' had been the last straw – hence his decision to go to England and do things his way. He would show the old guy that he could please himself and live his own life. His only regret was that he hadn't told Martha he was leaving, and he knew she would be as mad as a March hare.

This journey was different. This wasn't an act of defiance. This was the result of an impulsive decision but, now, with no opportunity of turning back, he started to doubt the wisdom of his judgment. Was he crazy to think that after all this time Nora would rush into his arms and they would both feel the same as they did in

244

1946? Even if Lorna was his daughter, would she be a bond between them or a reminder of his desertion? If only the girl had never come to the village, then the past wouldn't have invaded the present. He would never have known of her existence, so he would never have had to make this decision. Maybe with time and a little more persuading Martha would have eventually agreed to marry him, and then life could have continued in the nice, uncomplicated way that suited him so well. Had he been too hasty in trying to sort out the difficulties between her and Willie? As his father said, he had lost her for good, and the idea of her going to live in the village made matters worse. Life without Martha in the house across the lane was going to be very strange, very strange indeed.

Back at Daisy Farm, Martha and Willie were discussing their wedding plans.

"Where would you like to go for our honeymoon?" Willie asked.

"Portrush," was the immediate reply.

"Portrush?"

"Aye, Portrush."

"Why there? Why not somewhere further away?"

"If you're thinking what I think you're thinking, then you can forget it!" Martha announced. "I am definitely not going to Cavan."

Willie started to laugh. "My dear girl, the thought never crossed my mind."

"Just make sure it never does," she warned.

"So, you're really serious about going to the Port."

Martha nodded to confirm her decision.

"Why?"

"Because I have never forgotten that evening we met on Ramore Hill. We shouldn't have been there, it was wrong, but I still never regretted it. So now I want us to go there again, and sit on that same seat, and watch the moonlight on the waves and listen to them crashing against the rocks, and know that there is nothing and no one to keep us apart any more. I suppose you think I am talking a lot of silly, romantic dribble."

Willie pulled her closer. "No, darling, there's nothing silly about what you said. I have never forgotten that evening either, so Portrush it is. Now we just need to see the minister and get the earliest possible date for this wedding that should have taken place years ago."

"Better late than never."

"Better late than never," he repeated.

SAMMY'S RETURN

"They were both there waiting for me when I got off the boat," Sammy said. "Lorna was all smiles, but Nora was a bit more, sort of cautious, as if she didn't know what to say, and of course neither did I. Then Lorna reached for my case and said she would carry it, for she didn't want her old man to hurt himself."

"How did her mother react to that?"

"She just smiled and said, 'That's our Lorna. A girl of action.' So that told me everything I needed to know."

"Were you pleased?"

"I think I was more relieved than pleased. It took away the uncertainty. Not knowing either way had been driving me crazy. One minute I had myself convinced that she was mine, and the next minute I decided she wasn't. I didn't know what to think."

"So what happens now?"

"I'm not sure," Sammy admitted. "A weekend isn't really long enough to make plans of any sort, and there's still the problem of England versus Ireland."

"That is a problem," Martha agreed.

"It's all such a muddle," Sammy said. "If I had known about the baby I wouldn't have deserted her, but before she got the chance to tell me, I had shown her your letter, and told her I had to go home because my father needed me. Then she got a notion into her head that you were my girlfriend, and that I had only been passing the time with her, and she got very angry."

"Why would she think I was your girlfriend?"

"I suppose I had mentioned your name a time or two."

Did he not realize, Martha wondered, that it was foolish to mention one girl's name when in the company of another, or had he been trying to make Nora jealous? If that was the case, then obviously he had succeeded.

"Then I got angry too," Sammy continued, "and we had a whopper of a row. I said she was a jealous-minded… something, and she said I was a cheating, bad-tempered rat, and she wished she had never met me. So I gave her my address and told her to get in touch when she cooled down. Then I packed my bags and left."

"But why did she not let you know about the baby?" Martha asked. "No matter what disagreement you had, you were still entitled to know that you had a child."

"According to her, she was still feeling angry and betrayed, and vowed that she would *never* tell me. But then as the weeks went by she thought that maybe she was being unfair, and she was going to write to me, but then she changed her mind."

"Why would she do that?"

"She said she was scared of causing trouble between us, and it wouldn't have been fair on you, when none of it was your fault."

"She must be quite a girl," Martha said. "Most women in her position would have delighted in causing trouble."

"Nora's not like that – Nora's a very kind and thoughtful sort of person – you would like her."

"I'm sure I would," Martha agreed, "but why did Lorna come here and not let on who she was?"

"I wondered about that too," Sammy said. "It all started years ago when Lorna started to ask questions about why her friends at school had a daddy and she hadn't. And where was her daddy? And did he go away? And was he coming back? All that sort of thing. Nora had tried to explain everything to her as best she could, but the only way she could pacify her, was to promise that she would allow her to go to Ireland and look for me when she was eighteen."

"Poor wee thing," Martha sympathised. "It's not easy for a wean to understand these situations – everything's so black and white in their wee world."

"I suppose it is," Sammy agreed. "Nora thought that by the time she would reach her teens she would have lost interest in who I was, but she didn't – she was still as curious as ever, so Nora bought her the ticket and gave her my address, but only on the condition that she wouldn't make herself known."

"Quite an adventure for a young girl on her own," Martha commented.

"Her mother wasn't happy about it, but she knew it was something Lorna had to do. Then when she was getting off the bus in the village, she asked the driver if he knew where she could get lodgings. He pointed across the street to Tam Logan's and told her he would probably know about somewhere suitable."

"She must have been shocked," Martha declared, "when Tam arranged for her to stay with me."

"She was," Sammy said, "and when she realized we weren't married, she thought there might be a chance of her mother and me getting together again. But then she got talking to Bobby Birch, and he told her we were engaged, so she kept her promise to her mother and left without making me any the wiser."

"And if I hadn't shown you her letter…"

"That's right," Sammy said, "and Nora didn't even know she had sent it until I got in touch."

"It's quite a story," Martha declared.

"I suppose it is," Sammy agreed. After a long pause he said, "We were thinking it might be a good idea if she came over here for a week or two to give us more time together – a wee bit more time to see how we feel."

"That's a good idea," Martha agreed.

"So I was wondering…" Sammy hesitated, but Martha was ahead of his question.

"You were wondering if she could stay with me."

Sammy nodded.

"Of course she can," Martha assured him, "She'll be more than welcome. It'll keep the tongues from wagging, and, of course I'll enjoy telling her all about what you were like when you were a wee nipper with your wee knobbly knees and your front teeth missing."

"Those sorts of memories work both ways," he threatened, then in a more serious tone he added, "I told my Da that I enjoyed meeting the family again, and one or two of them might want to come over for a holiday some time."

"I suppose that's all he needs to know until you're sure about what you want to do," Martha said. "But don't consider leaving him again - he couldn't cope without you."

"Don't worry, I have no intention of leaving him. In fact I'm hoping that Nora might consider moving here."

Sammy went on to explain that Nora's parents had relatives in County Down and they came over to visit them every year in late autumn when things weren't so busy in the B&B. It had always been their plan that when they reached retirement age they would buy a place in that area. Nora had never been to Northern Ireland, but she had often toyed with the idea of moving with them when the time was right, and running her own business over here.

"County Down would be a lot closer than Liverpool," Martha remarked.

"It would," Sammy said, shrugging his shoulders. "So I suppose I'll just have to take it a day at a time and decide about everything as I go along."

ENLIGHTENMENT

The news that Martha Sloan and Willie Rossborough were engaged and planned to marry in the near future had circulated the area with lightning speed. *'But what about poor Sammy? What sort of a fool did she make of him?' 'What will he do now? He must be heartbroken.'* These were just some of the comments that were exchanged between the ladies of the village as they congregated in the corner shop, the Post Office or anywhere else they happened to meet. The men folk who frequented Murphy's bar were more inclined to agree that Sammy had only himself to blame. The farmer boy had been what they described as 'too backward about coming forward'. Others were closer to the truth when they insisted that *'the pair 'o them were too used to each other to ever be anything more than just friends.'* One gentleman, who had consumed the amount of whiskey that loosens the tongue, but still allows the memory to function, announced, "Martha Sloan is the only girl I ever loved, but she didn't want me. She wouldn't even go out with me on *one* date, but I loved her just the same."
"But you married somebody else," one of the men declared.
"I did," he admitted, "but I never forgot Martha - it was Martha that I really wanted - I would have married Martha, any day of the week. But, I wish her all the best." Then holding up his glass he said, "Here's to Martha."
His companions joined him in the toast - then they made a pact that they would never repeat what Johnny Connery had told them.

By the time the folk in the village had run out of comments about the forthcoming wedding, another matter had caught their attention – the stranger who had arrived from England and was staying with Martha Sloan. Was she one of Martha's distant relatives, they wondered, or maybe she was some relation of Willie's? They had never met any of his family or known very much about him, apart from the fact that he had an Aunt somewhere in the Free State. Maybe this *was* his Aunt, here to give Martha the 'once over'. But no, on second thoughts, this woman was too young. The speculation continued, and when Nora was seen in the car with Sammy on a few occasions, that added to the mystery. Nora had been introduced to Nancy Shaw as a friend of Sammy's that he had known when he was in England, and she was over in Ireland for a wee visit and decided to give him a call. Nancy assumed there was more to the story than the introduction implied, but she kept her suspicions to herself, and refused to be drawn into any of the local gossip. What went on at Daisy Farm, was Daisy Farm business, as far as Nancy was concerned.

However, the locals weren't the only ones speculating about the stranger in their midst. Arthur McCracken was drawing conclusions of his own. It was too much of a coincidence that Sammy should take the unexpected notion of visiting the people in England, and then suddenly one of them arrives over here and Sammy spends every free minute with her. It was all a bit suspicious – there had to be more to it than a simple desire to see the green fields of County Antrim. Martha was bound to know more than he was privy to, he decided. After all, the woman was staying in her house. He knew Martha was a hard nut to crack if she didn't want to tell you anything, but she was his only hope.

"What's going on between Sammy and this Dora, or Nora woman?"
"I think they were going to the Lough," Martha replied. "Nora was interested in seeing it on account of it being the largest in the British Isles."
"I didn't mean, *where* were they going. I meant *what's* going on?"
"How would I know?"

"But you do know. I know you know, and I admire your loyalty, but I'm troubled by it all."

Arthur continued with his catalogue of worries. Sammy heading off somewhere with this woman and not coming back, was his major concern. Although Arthur did admit that he could see why his son would like her. She was very nice, and he was sure that if he got to know her a bit better he would get to like her too. He just didn't want Sammy to like her too much. Martha knew it was already too late, for Nora had confided in her that she and Sammy still felt the same about each other as they had when they first met, and they had been discussing different ways they could be together. So now Martha was in the unenviable situation of trying to allay Arthur's fears without misleading him, while still staying discreet about Sammy's love life, and it was getting more difficult with every passing day. Sammy would have to be honest with his father, or at least tell him something that would reassure him and keep him from dreading the worst. She didn't know how much longer she could keep up this pretence of innocence.

"Leave that wee problem with me," she told Arthur. "I'll see what I can do about it."

Arthur was none the wiser for his visit, but he was confident that all would be well. Martha would sort it out. Martha would sort Sammy out too if she thought it necessary. Martha was a great woman – if only...

Sammy and Nora came back from their outing in high spirits – they'd obviously had a good time, and Sammy was making a great pretence of doing the gentlemanly thing by seeing the lady safely indoors before leaving. Nora was laughing – highly amused at his antics and loving every minute of it. Very gallant, Martha thought, but what about the elderly father who was distraught about the possible outcome the visitor could have on the future?

"I need to talk to you," Martha said, pointing her finger at Sammy, who immediately pulled out a chair and sat down.

Gosh, thought Nora, how does she do it? Just a few words and she gets his immediate attention!

"What have I done?"

"It's what you might do, is the problem."

"Go on then," he encouraged. "Tell me. What might I do that has you in such a tizzy?"

"I'll just go and freshen up," Nora said, and hastily made her way upstairs.

"I don't know *what* you might or might not do, and neither does your father. That's the problem."

"Has he been over here quizzing and poking his nose in?"

"He's worried, and it's no wonder. You're spending so much time with Nora he's assuming romance is in the air, and as she doesn't live within walking distance he's imagining all sorts of things."

Sammy was about to comment, but Martha put up her hand to indicate that she hadn't finished.

"I know what you're going to say," she continued. "*Nora is here to give you both a chance to see how you feel about each other,* and that's fine. But your father doesn't know your reasons and he's not stupid, and I don't want to lie to him. In fact, I *won't* lie to him, and I can't keep fobbing him off, so you're going to have to tell him something."

"But what can I tell him?"

"How about the truth?"

A slight tap on the door leading from the hall, and a small voice asking, "Is it OK to come in?" announced the return of Nora.

"Of course it is," Martha replied. "You didn't have to leave in the first place. I was only trying to talk some sense into this big clown who has no idea of the distress he's causing that poor soul across the lane."

"She thinks I should tell him the truth," Sammy announced, directing his remark to Nora. "Imagine what reaction that would get. Tell him the truth!"

Sammy started to pace the floor. "Why can't he just read the paper or listen to the wireless or whatever it is old boys of his age are supposed to do, and let me get on with my own life?"

"Most old boys of his age *would* be reading the paper or listening to the wireless," Martha informed him. "But your old boy is still working. Without him you would need more help than you get from the casual part-timers you only hire as and when you need them. So just take that thought on board before you dismiss your father's worth."

Sammy sat down, then he got up and repeated, 'The truth, the truth' as if it was a dirty word and completely ignored everything Martha had said.

In Martha's opinion, he was behaving like a spoilt child, so in a few more well chosen words she let him know what she thought of his attitude.

Nora put her hand on his arm and in a calm, clear voice she said, "Wasn't it the absence of truth that got us into this situation in the first place?"

Sammy just stared at her, apparently lost for words - a look of total bewilderment on his face. Sammy could cope with a disagreement, or argue until the cows came home, but Nora's cool logic had really surprised him.

"I have some chores to do outside," Martha said, a giggle threatening to escape. Sammy had met his match at last. Their future was sure to be interesting.

A short time later, the *lovers* came looking for Martha.

"Over here by the hens' pen," Martha called in reply to Sammy's "Where did you go?"

"We're going to own up," Nora said. "But we won't tell him everything – we won't mention Lorna – that might be too much too soon."

"It probably would," Martha agreed, "but he'll have to be told some time – when the time is right."

"Aye," Sammy sighed, "when the time is right. I wonder when that will be?"

"It'll come," Martha assured him. "And it'll all work out OK." Then turning to Nora and *pretending* Sammy couldn't hear her, she said, "I think once Arthur would get used to the idea of being a Granda he would be quite pleased, for I'm sure by now he has given up hope of this specimen of manhood ever producing an offspring."

"Martha Sloan," Sammy stated, "you have a cutting tongue in your mouth. Poor Willie – I wonder has he any idea what he's letting himself in for!"

The good-natured banter seemed to have lessened the tension, and Sammy appeared to have lost some of his earlier sour attitude.

Martha made a face in response to his teasing, which Nora found highly amusing.

Martha was still awake when she heard Nora's light footsteps on the stairs and the gentle closing of the bedroom door. It was past midnight, so whatever had taken place in the McCracken household, it hadn't been sorted or discussed in a matter of minutes. Hopefully all had gone well and Arthur had been reassured that he wasn't going to be abandoned.

Over breakfast, Nora related the events of the previous evening. She and Sammy had admitted to having been romantically involved during his time in Liverpool when he boarded with her parents, and although they were spending time together now, there was no possibility of Sammy ever going back to England on a permanent basis. Martha was relieved to learn that Arthur had been reassured. Now she could talk to him without the fear of letting the cat out of the bag.

Later that afternoon Martha was waiting for Willie to arrive when Arthur's cheery 'Hello there' gave a clear indication that he was feeling much more positive about the future.

"Come on in," Martha called, as she made her way through to answer the phone. "Make yourself at home - I'll be with you in a minute."

"Martha?" queried the male voice that she didn't recognize at first.

"Yes."

"Derek McGoldrick here."

Martha hesitated for a second.

Aware of her uncertainty he quickly added, "Doctor McGoldrick."

"Oh yes, yes of course – sorry, I was miles away - is Willie all right?"

"Very all right, I would say. In fact he has just left – I understand you and he are heading off to finalize some plans for the big day."

"That's right," Martha agreed. "Even with a small wedding, there are still arrangements to make."

"Of course, of course," the doctor replied, and wished her all the best, hoped the weather would be fine for the big occasion, and talked about Willie in glowing terms.

Why doesn't he just get on with it, Martha thought. She was sure he hadn't rung just to talk about the wedding, and she wanted to have time to speak to Arthur before going out for the day. She had something important to ask him, and time was marching on.

As if reading her thoughts, Doctor McGoldrick said, "I understand you are considering renting your house if you could find a suitable tenant."

"I am," Martha replied, "but *if* is the problem, for I wouldn't want somebody who would destroy the place or maybe even cause problems for Arthur and Sammy on that part of the lane that is shared."

"Very wise," the doctor replied. "So would you consider my good lady and me as responsible tenants?"

257

Martha was taken aback. She knew he had put a deposit on a bungalow and assumed the transaction had gone ahead, and of course the sale of his own house had been completed the previous day. Willie was now the proud owner of Seventeen, Main Street, but Mr and Mrs McGoldrick were welcome to stay on until removal arrangements were made.

"But I thought you had bought a place in Cushendall."

"We have," he replied, and went on to explain about the alterations he wanted to make – extend the kitchen, update the lounge and probably a few other things that they hadn't previously thought of, but would most likely occur as time passed. The original idea had been to live with the upheaval, but during a casual conversation with Willie the subject had come up about the house at Daisy Farm being available for rent, so Mrs McGoldrick thought staying there in the meantime would be a good idea, and less stressful than trying to live on a building site.

Martha was delighted, and they quickly came to an arrangement about finance and dates and all the other necessary details involved, especially the muddle they could get into with the contents of both dwellings. They would be taking all their furniture, but Martha would be leaving a few items behind, so they laughed and joked about ending up with too many chairs or maybe not a seat to sit on.

Things were really working out well, Martha decided; all their plans were coming together nicely, and today they would visit the Adair Arms to book a reception for the small gathering of close friends who would be attending their wedding.

Returning from the hall Martha found her elderly neighbour seated by the fire reading The Telegraph.

Martha took the seat opposite.

"I suppose there's nothing I can tell you that you don't already know," he said.

"I know that you are not going to be left alone, that's the main thing."

"It's all your doing - if it hadn't been for you I would still be wondering."

As Martha was about to protest Arthur continued, "Whatever you said to him it has made a difference, but I knew you would sort it, for you're the only one he listens too."

"But that could be about to change," Martha said. "He might be taking Nora's advice from now on."

The sound of Willie's car pulling up prevented any further comment on the outcome of Nora's influence on Sammy.

"Well, I better be heading over home," Arthur said, "and leave you young folk in peace, for I'm sure you still have a lot of planning to do."

"Most of it's sorted," Willie said, coming to stand beside Martha.

"Not quite," Martha said.

"I suppose the dress is going to be the biggest hassle," Arthur commented. "I suppose you can't make up your mind what you want."

"The dress is already here, and it's a secret," she giggled. "But what I do need is someone to give me away, and as my Da is no longer here, I was wondering if you would do that wee job on his behalf?"

Without hesitation Arthur replied, "I would be honoured to do that job for him. Henry and me were always good friends – aye, as good a friend as any man could ask for."

"Thanks," Martha exclaimed, throwing her arms around him. "You're a darling."

Arthur's face went bright crimson at the unexpected show of emotion.

"You can let me know what I have to wear and all that sort of thing some time again. I'm sure you're wanting to get away now before the town gets too busy."

Martha's eyes followed him as he made his way across the yard – a lonely figure, probably remembering another wedding - a marriage he thought would last forever.   But her assumption was wrong. Arthur's thoughts were on the finality of the situation. Yes, he felt honoured to be taking Henry Sloan's place at Martha's wedding – he just wished the groom could have been Sammy.

FINAL

Martha stood in the gathering dusk and with mixed emotions surveyed the contents of the over- crowded out-building. She recalled the numerous times, when as a child, she had tried to follow her father inside, but he had always chased her away saying it wasn't a safe place for a wee girl to be poking around in. Now she could come into the old zinc shed any time she wanted to, and no one could prevent her. But she derived no pleasure from the freedom this allowed, for it only emphasized the fact that her father was no longer there – no longer lord and master of the rusty out-dated implements that hung on equally rusty hooks from the cob-webbed walls. She viewed the numerous grimy tin boxes scattered over the workbench - some with their lids partly open – others *without* lids and displaying an assortment of nails and screws in various sizes and lengths, and other miscellaneous bits and bobs that she couldn't identify. But it was the biscuit tin that sat alone on the top shelf that held her interest. Why was it put in such a place that it could only be reached by using a stepladder? It didn't make any sense to Martha's logical mind, but it didn't matter now, for there was nothing in this musty old place that her father would ever need again. She sighed, sat down on an old wooden trunk and finally gave in to the tears that had threatened to spill since early morning. She had no regrets about the decisions she had made, yet she knew she'd miss the farmhouse with its draughty windows and doors, the way the smoke billowed out of the old range, and the crowing of the rooster to welcome the dawn.

She left the shed, locking the door behind her and returned to the house where she would spend her last night as Martha Sloan. She felt uneasy – as if there was something else she needed to do –

some unfinished business she needed to attend to. She knew everything on her list had been ticked off – she had checked it several times. Then, suddenly, she realized what had been niggling at the back of her mind for the last half hour. It was the box; the box that was out of reach, the box that didn't fit with the rest of the mishmash. Five minutes later she was standing on the top rung of the old rickety wooden ladder and had the box firmly clutched in her hand. It felt light. At first she thought it was empty and assumed that was why it had been abandoned to the top shelf, but when she shook it, it was obvious there was something inside. She decided to take it indoors before opening it.

An hour later, the box was sitting unopened on the table, and Martha was coping with a jumble of mixed emotions. Curiosity about what lay within its innocent portrayal of assorted biscuits, and guilt about wanting to find out. The fact that it had been placed out of reach indicated that whatever was inside was nobody's business. It was obviously something that her father wanted to keep concealed. But now that she had found it, what was she supposed to do with it? She couldn't put it back, because eventually someone else would discover it, and as it was private to her father then a stranger gaining access was unthinkable. Option two – she could put it, unopened, in the chest of keepsakes that she was taking to her new home. That seemed like a good idea, but, of course there was the possibility that her dad, being aware that some day she would be in possession of everything he owned, had set it aside from all the other boxes to make it more obvious, so *expecting* her to find it.

Was this what her father had been trying to tell her before he died? His speech had been slurred, but Martha had been able to understand enough of what he was saying to realize his distress was something to do with the old shed. She knew he had been working in there just before he had taken ill, so she assumed he was probably worried in case he had left the light on. Henry Sloan had an obsession about lights burning in empty places. Nevertheless, in spite of all her efforts to reassure him that everything in the shed was fine, he still appeared anxious and insisted on trying to talk. A short time later he passed away, and although Martha was heartbroken at the loss of her father, she was doubly saddened by the fact that the last thing he wanted to talk to her about was a dilapidated old building. Now it seemed that the dilapidated old building held something that he considered important to his daughter.

So many possibilities. Martha felt she couldn't cope with a final decision and considered ringing Sammy and asking him to come over. Finally she decided against that course of action. The box had been her father's —now, it belonged to her. So it was her responsibility to deal with whatever it contained.

She slowly removed the lid – the way a child would treat a jack-in-the-box. She gasped as she saw the tiny pair of shoes –her first pair of shoes, size 0, black patent, and badly scuffed. She felt a lump rise in her throat and her eyes filled with tears – her dad, who had been so practical, had kept her first wee shoes. She held them to her breast, thinking of the tall quiet man she had adored, and wishing she could tell him how pleased and happy it made her feel to discover that he had considered her shoes important enough to keep. Eventually she set them aside and lifted out the next item – an old sepia coloured photograph of a woman whom she didn't recognize. She knew it wasn't her mother and wondered if perhaps it was her Granny Sloan? Granny Sloan had been petite, whereas this woman appeared to be quite tall. She dismissed its importance, as something else much more intriguing took her interest – a brown envelope – a bulging brown envelope.

She turned the package over, but there was no writing or markings to indicate what was inside – the only clue to its contents was that it was light and obviously contained paper. Money, she assumed.

But why would he keep money in the shed? There was only one answer – he was cheating the Inland Revenue. What a dilemma! What would she do with it? If she declared it, then what sort of confusion and paperwork would that involve, and if she kept it, then was she becoming a tax dodger too? Of course, there was the possibility that it was just some savings he had accumulated, and was leaving it for her as a belated present. Yes, that was most likely the simple answer, and she chided herself for jumping to the wrong conclusion – her father wasn't the type to cheat.

Martha ran a knife below the gummed flap and found something more confusing than her previous assumption. She stared at the bundle of letters, tied together with a piece of rough string. The postmark on the first one was slightly blurred, but enough of the print was visible for Martha to see that it had been posted in Scotland in nineteen and fifty something. Who in Scotland could be writing to her father? was her first thought; followed by a series of others, each as puzzling as the last. Did he have relatives there? If he did, then why had he never mentioned them? And why should he keep their correspondence a secret? Had there been a black sheep in the family, and unknown to anyone else, her Dad had been keeping in touch with him or her? Still keeping the string in place she flicked up the corners and discovered that the dates were in rotation, the latest on the top, and had spanned almost twenty years. But why had the letters stopped? Then she remembered that they got the telephone installed during the fifties, so probably that was why. But she could never remember anyone, other than the folk she knew, ever ringing and asking to speak to him. Perhaps whoever it was had a regular time for getting in touch, she thought, and it had coincided with the times she was either at work or out somewhere. However, if they were a member of the family, then regardless of whatever misdemeanours they were guilty of, they were entitled to know that her father had died, so it was her duty to contact them and pass on the information.

She undid the string, opened the first letter in the pile and pulled out the single sheet of paper. There was no address and no name - just the words, *love as always* at the bottom of the page. Martha was bewildered and hurriedly scanned the rest of the small, neat writing, though not actually taking enough time to read it properly. Then suddenly, one sentence stood out from all the rest – **great to know you have got the phone, it's safer than running the risk of missing the postman. This is my number**. A row of digits followed. Her suspicions had been right. This was quite exciting; the intrigue, the suspense, the possibility of having a relative with a colourful past and the mystery of what they had done to be excluded from the fold was fascinating. This was as good as any novel she had ever read.

With hindsight, Martha was certain that her father's distress had not been *about* the shed, it had been about what was *inside* the shed, and he had wanted her to know about it. Therefore, with a clear conscience, Martha started to open a few more of the letters, and gradually the truth unfolded. There was no black sheep – no mysterious relative - the correspondence was from Sammy's mother. Page by page, Martha discovered that her father, the man Arthur McCracken considered his best friend, the man Sammy McCracken had always looked up to, had been keeping the runaway wife and mother informed about everything that was happening in their lives.

When Martha read the passage that stated, **'it's useful to have a friend who is an air hostess** she was especially outraged. She knew that every Christmas when the card arrived with a different postmark, Arthur was puzzled and concerned about where his wife was, and what sort of a life she was leading. In another letter, Martha discovered that the elusive Mrs McCracken had made an annual trip across from Scotland to attend the Ballyclare Fair.

Martha recalled that, regardless of the weather or any pressing concerns on the farm, her father never missed that occasion – he said it was the highlight of his year. Now Martha knew why. Her father and Peggy McCracken were romantically involved. Martha felt sick – unable to comprehend the enormity of what she had discovered. All the love and respect she had for him suddenly became worthless. He had betrayed everyone who cared about him. Christmas was just a few weeks away, and she knew that when another card arrived with a foreign stamp, Sammy would rant and rave about the woman who had deserted him as a child, and wonder once again why she couldn't tell them where she was, or else leave them in peace. Now Martha had the information that could end their years of wondering, but what was she supposed to do with it? Did her father want her to tell them, because he didn't have the courage, or was he simply being selfish, trying to ease his conscience before departing this life? But he had left Martha with the predicament, and she knew she couldn't be responsible for the hurt it would cause her friends.

If only she had found the box sooner, she thought, then she would have had time to talk it over with Willie and ask for his advice. But tomorrow was her wedding day, and she would be walking into the church on Arthur McCracken's arm. She recalled how pleased he had been when she had asked him to give her away, telling him that he was the perfect choice to fulfil the role that would have been her father's. How was she going to manage?

Martha sighed – two more envelopes to open – perhaps they would give some indication of Peggy's whereabouts. She opened the first one, but like all the others, no address. *My dearest Henry*, the letter commenced, ***I am so relieved that you got my other letter. He was the only person I could think of who would be discreet enough and please give him my heartfelt thanks. I understand why he refused to be involved again, but as you have promised to always meet the postman before Ruby gets a chance to take the mail, then hopefully we will be able to keep in touch. Please write to me***

266

soon and let me know how wee Sammy is coping without me. I miss you. Love always.

She had asked him to keep in touch, so she must have given him her address. It had to be in the one envelope that was still unopened – the one that had been at the bottom of the pile – the one with the oldest postmark – the one addressed to Mr Henry McCracken C/O Mr Tam Logan. Martha hurriedly tore open the envelope and there in capital letters at the top of the page was an address in Glasgow. In an instant, Martha's mind was made up. At the first opportunity she would go to Glasgow, and she would find that address, and even if she had moved on somewhere else it was still a starting place, and somehow, somewhere, she would find Peggy McCracken. Then she would tell her about the anguish she had caused and she would threaten to expose her dirty secrets if she didn't contact Arthur and Sammy of her own free will. Perhaps that seemed like blackmail – perhaps it *was* blackmail, but Martha didn't care, for now all her feelings of hurt and betrayal were replaced with a burning anger.

Martha looked at the address again, then decided to read the rest of the letter, for she had only skip- read the others in her rush for an explanation. However, as this was the first one that had been written, perhaps it would reveal more than all the rest.

My darling Henry, **Martha read,** *I'm writing this letter although I don't know if you will ever receive it. I realize it's too risky to send it to your address, so I will send it in care of Tam Logan. He's an honest good man and I know he won't be happy about being used in this way, for I'm sure he will guess who the sender is. But it's the only way I can think of to make contact with you and to ask you to forgive me for my hasty departure and for not letting you know of my intentions. Please believe me when I say I still love you, I will never stop loving you. What we have is too precious to let time or the miles destroy.*

Martha couldn't read any further. The tears were blinding her, and although she wasn't superstitious, the old tradition of the groom not seeing the bride after twelve o'clock on the night before the wedding, prevented her from ringing Willie and telling him that she needed him. She wanted to snuggle into the comfort of his strong arms and she wanted him to tell her everything would be all right. She desperately needed a shoulder to cry on, and this was one time she couldn't use Sammy's. Discovering that her father had been in contact with Peggy all along was bad enough, but finding out that there had been a romance between them was a bitter pill to swallow. She thought about her mother, dear, sweet, gentle person– how could he have betrayed her with a woman who was callous enough to desert her four-year-old boy? In that moment, Martha hated her father with a vengeance she never knew she was capable of.

The clock struck the half hour – thirty minutes past midnight. Martha knew she should be in bed and fast asleep if she wanted to look her best on the most important day of her life. But she wanted to read the rest of the letter, and then she would put them all back into the brown envelope and place it safely at the bottom of the chest until she was in a more clear thinking state of mind to decide what to do with them.

Martha picked up the page and started to read. *'I just couldn't cope any longer. Seeing you with Ruby, when all the time I wanted you for myself was hard enough, but with her baby about to be born, it was too much for me to bear, for I knew I would have to watch you being daddy to it, while you couldn't admit to being da...*

"No, oh no!" Martha screamed, "and we almost – we could have - we might have.."

It was the second time in Martha's life that she fainted.

THE END

GLOSSARY

Stout	Guinness.
Close to the chest	Won't disclose information.
Up with the lark	Get out of bed early in the morning.
Chinwag	Harmless gossip.
Wee buddy	Small person
Keep an eye out	Be observant.
Atal	At all.
Mitching	Avoiding school.
Two-piece	Skirt and matching jacket.
In the know	In possession of information.
Beating about the bush	Avoiding telling the whole story.
Put that in your pipe and smoke it	Consider all the facts.
Morellis'	Ice cream parlour in Portrush.
Bannagher	A place in Northern Ireland, but name often used in local saying to portray something unbeatable
A-waiting on	Not expected to live.
Old codger	Elderly man
Whatever's for ye, won't go by ye	Fate is in control.
Flown the coop	Escaped or ran away.
Coast is clear	Safe to engage in particular activity.
Taking a hand out of you	Making a fool of you.
Garbage	Nonsense.
Bunkum	Nonsense.

Weans	Children.
Gipein	Acting foolishly.
Titivatin	Fussing over appearance.
No goat's toe	Something special.
Shenanigans	Silly behaviour.
Ric Rac	Decorative trimming on clothes.
Hardy weather	Very cold.
Scunnered	Fed-up with something or feeling sick.
Poking	Interfering.
Prattlin'	Unnecessary talking.
Farl	Scone.
Fadge	Scone made from potato and flour.
Keeping an eye out	Being observant.
Twerp	Name for someone who isn't particularly liked.
All the turf in the bog wouldn't warm me to her	Couldn't be persuaded to like a particular person.
Weather hardy enough	Cold enough.
Gift of the gab	Obsessive talker.
Swing the pan	Make a meal by frying the ingredients.
Dandering	Walking slowly.
Like a cleg to a blanket	Attach firmly.
Gift o' the gab	Obsessive talker.
Langled goat	Securely tied.
Blethering	Talking about nothing in particular.
Heth	For sure.

Stick to your ribs	A substantial meal.
Comeuppence	Payback for something not approved of.
Gosoon	Silly young fellow.
Brylcream	A gel men used to use to keep their hair tidy.
Making a cod of	Making a fool of.
Put you over	Something to make you sleep.
Twelfth day	A date the Protestant community celebrate every July.
Plouterin'	Walking around without purpose.
Conacre	Leasing neighbour's land for tilling or grazing.
Cretonne	Fabric suitable for curtains.
Wee gleed	Small amount.
March hedge	Hedge separating two pieces of land.
Treadle	Pedal- powered sewing machine.
Free State	Another term for the South of Ireland.
Once- over	Check out.
Letting the cat out of the bag	Disclosing a secret.